LOOK FOR THE LATEST NOVEL FROM
JENNIFER KAUFMAN AND KAREN MACK

A VERSION
OF THE TRUTH

Coming Soon
from Delacorte Press

#1 *Los Angeles Times* Bestseller!

a novel

"The fusion of bibliomania and romantic comedy is appealingly offbeat."
—Janet Maslin, *New York Times*

literacy and longing in L

jennifer kaufman and karen mack

"The most delightful read of the year." —Liz Smith, *New York Post*

"With glamorous Los Angeles as a backdrop and a likeable heroine who is passionate about great literature, *Literacy and Longing in L.A.* is a must-read for any woman embarking on a summer book binge." —*Pages*

"Clever." —*Week*

"Buying—and reading—[this book] will cheer you up too, with its funny, pointed insights about life in L.A., its lovely celebration of books."
—*New Orleans Times-Picayune*

"I'm absolutely crazy about [this] book . . . lighthearted, quick-witted, absolutely astonishing learning!"
—Carolyn See, author of *Making a Literary Life*

"A poignant and witty tale of life, love, and letters in Los Angles . . . [a] brilliant debut novel."
—Karen Quinn, author of *The Ivy Chronicles*

"A wonderful story that completely won me over—insecure, bookish Dora will appeal to anyone who has ever found solace or inspiration in reading. . . . At times breezy, sexy, profound."
—Denise Hamilton, author of *Prisoner of Memory*

"A delightfully stylish romp through life and love in southern California in which our heroine offers irrefutable proof that literacy and L.A. are not mutually exclusive."
—Judith Ryan Hendricks, author of *The Baker's Apprentice*

"Jennifer Kaufman and Karen Mack have a lot of nerve! How dare they come up with the brilliant idea to write a novel about a woman who tells her life story through her obsession with books! And how dare they execute it so beautifully?!"
—Sara Nelson, author of *So Many Books, So Little Time*

LITERACY
AND
LONGING
IN L.A.

Jennifer Kaufman
and
Karen Mack

DELTA TRADE PAPERBACKS

LITERACY AND LONGING IN L.A.
A Delta Book

PUBLISHING HISTORY
Delacorte Press hardcover edition published June 2006
Delta trade paperback edition / June 2007

Published by Bantam Dell
A Division of Random House, Inc.
New York, New York

Cover photo © Ghislain & Marie David de Lossy / Getty Images
Cover design by Christine Van Bree

Book design by Glen Edelstein

Library of Congress Catalog Card Number: 2005058263

Delta is a registered trademark of Random House, Inc., and the colophon is a trademark of Random House, Inc.

ISBN 978-0-385-34018-2

Printed in the United States of America
Published simultaneously in Canada

www.bantamdell.com

BVG 10 9 8 7 6 5 4 3 2 1

We would like to thank
our families who inspire us

and

Molly Friedrich, Frances Jalet-Miller,
and Danielle Perez,
who believed in us.

A Happy Birthday

This evening, I sat by an open window
and read till the light was gone and the book
was no more than a part of the darkness.
I could easily have switched on a lamp,
but I wanted to ride this day down into night,
to sit alone and smooth the unreadable page
with the pale gray ghost of my hand.
                            —TED KOOSER, POET LAUREATE OF
                                THE UNITED STATES

LITERACY AND LONGING IN L.A.

Preface

> "I have always imagined that Paradise
> will be a kind of library."
> ~ Jorge Luis Borges (1899–1986) ~

When I was seven, my mother drove the family car off a thirty-foot bridge. My sister and I were in the backseat and after the dive, the sky-blue Cadillac Seville flipped over into the craggy ravine and landed on its roof. There wasn't much water in the river below and the upside-down car sank slowly in the muck, its headlights streaming through the fog. I don't remember being scared exactly, just too dumbfounded to speak. Then my mother said in a perfectly calm voice, "Do you think you girls can push open the doors?" It was as if she was asking us to turn down the television or put the dishes back on the shelves. She was very matter-of-fact. The radio was still playing as we tumbled over each other, somersaulting out into the shadowy gloom, and I remember thinking that this was just like the Tunnel of Love at Willow Grove's amusement park that had recently been bulldozed and turned into a suburban shopping mall.

"Okay, let's pull ourselves together here," my mother announced over the incongruous sounds of background music. The dark water was gurgling away, our voices echoed when we talked, and I imagined us huddled together in a little wooden rowboat, magically floating down an ersatz river on some weird joyride gone slightly amiss.

"Smile," my mother said abruptly to my sister, Virginia, when she saw her sucking on her lip. Virginia chipped one of her two front teeth in the accident but, other than that, we were both unharmed.

"Wider. I can't see."

"Do I have to? I don't feel like smiling," Virginia said, and stomped her foot in the gunk.

"She doesn't mean smile, like 'BE HAPPY,' stupid," I scoffed. "She means open your mouth so she can see if you're bleeding. Geez!"

"Well, I'm not," she retorted, but I could see she was now in tears, rubbing her nose and eyes with her mud-stained sweatshirt.

"Does it hurt?" I asked sheepishly.

"No, it doesn't hurt, Dora. I just don't like it here. It's creepy and I want to go home." She was scared, my mother was dazed, and I, as usual, was completely detached—a knack I have since perfected in order to deal with life's crushing disappointments or precarious entanglements.

"We're okay," I told her. (I was always telling her

that.) "Anyway, Mom's the one who should be upset. Dad is going to kill her."

"No, he's not," my sister replied. "Maybe we don't even have to tell him."

"Are you kidding? Look at the car! This is the second one she's ruined this year."

Meanwhile, my mother was standing behind our belly-up, bashed-in, virtually unrecognizable vehicle. "Oh my lord," she suddenly exclaimed. "Your father's new clubs are in the trunk. Now, did he tell me to take them out this morning? . . . I can't remember. . . ."

When the police finally arrived with a tow truck and an ambulance, my sister and I clambered up from the muddy riverbed and bundled into a squad car while my mother stood outside wrapping her long mohair coat around her. Her tone was shaky as she ran her hands through her matted, blood-soaked hair and I suddenly realized she had hit her head. The idea that we had been involved in a near-fatal accident never entered my mind.

At the time of the crash, we were in east central Pennsylvania, ninety miles northwest of Philadelphia. It was an area known as the coal country of Schuylkill County, where rolling green pastures were blighted by deep brown scars, heaps of piled-up slag, and decaying railroad tracks. Even the billboards were battered with peeling, unintelligible messages from a bygone era. We were headed for Pottsville to visit the dilapidated childhood home of John O'Hara and I remember feeling relieved that we probably wouldn't be touring this author's home anytime soon. I've since learned that O'Hara called

Pottsville a "god-awful town" and couldn't wait to get out.

My mother told the police that she was looking down at the map from the Philadelphia Historical Society, and when she looked up we were plunging into the dark, swirling waters of the Schuylkill River. I guess they believed her, because the cop pointed out that we were a few hours from the spot in Chadds Ford where Andrew Wyeth's father, N. C. Wyeth, drove his car onto a railroad track with his four-year-old grandson in the backseat. The car was smashed to smithereens by an on-coming train and no one ever knew whether it was suicide or just a freak accident. Why he insisted on telling this story in front of us, I will never understand. But it sure cheered my mother right up, with her penchant for literary legends, and she subsequently peppered him with questions.

Later that night, my father joined us at a nearby motel and her mood darkened as she argued with him about her drinking. "The girls are fine. I was just distracted." We knew her distraction was in a neat little silver flask. She gave more of the usual denials, and my father responded with patronizing disdain and exasperation. He left home for the first time shortly afterwards.

Life after that deteriorated into a series of dramatic comings and goings, yelling and screaming, doors slamming in the night, and then silence. The mornings after always felt like a hangover, my sister and I staring numbly at each other, avoiding the unmentionable.

My mother stuck it out, however, always the martyr. She was part of that upper-middle-class Northeastern generation of women who believed life offered them no decent alternative to marriage, motherhood, or home-making. In the coming tumultuous years, she and her circle of friends survived divorce, widowhood, disease, children who disappeared or disappointed them, and children like my sister and me, who chose careers and moved away.

In those early days, though, this was just one of many literary tours that filled my childhood. While other kids were spending July at the shore and August at summer camp or in the Poconos, we squandered all our free time visiting the family homes and haunts of famous writers. We trekked through their gardens (they always had gardens), had drinks at their local taverns, peeked into their bedrooms, and bought souvenirs and postcards from whoever was hawking them nearby. My mother always quoted extensively from their works while my sister and I huddled bleary-eyed in the backseat and played with smuggled Barbies.

Such lofty-minded trips generally culminated in long, uneventful weekends at secluded B&Bs that backed up onto cornfields or auto salvage lots. Most of the time, my sister and I were at such loose ends we'd resort to reading the dusty, yellow-paged Penguin Classics or *Reader's Digest* condensed books that filled the shelves in the main living room, occasionally ripping out the pages and making paper hats, boats, or spitballs. When we did venture out, we'd generally wind up walking through deserted towns, past vacant shops and abandoned gas stations.

My mother was always searching for something that would give her life weight, that would take her away from her life of desperation and domesticity. I spent years buried in books, trying to avoid a similar fate. Then, all at once, there was this flash of certainty and the fuzziness disappeared. Robert Frost said, "What you want, what you're hanging around in the world waiting for, is for something to occur to you." That's what happened. All of a sudden, something occurred to me.

Master of the Universe

"All the best stories in the world are but one story in reality,
the story of escape. It is the only thing which
interests us all and at all times, how to escape."
~ Arthur Christopher Benson (1862–1925) ~

Women do different things when they're depressed. Some smoke, others drink, some call their therapists, some eat. My mother used to go ballistic when she and my father had a fight, then she'd booze for days on end and vanish into her bedroom. My sister was more into the global chill mode; give 'em the silent treatment and, in the meantime, gorge on frozen Sara Lee banana cake. And I do what I have always done—go off on a book bender that can last for days.

I fall into this state for different reasons. Sometimes it's after an "I hate your fucking guts" fight. Other times it's symptomatic of my state of mind, ennui up to my ears, my life gone awry, and that feeling of dread whenever I'm asked what I'm doing. How can anyone sort all this out? All things considered, I'd rather read. It's the perfect escape.

I have a whole mantra for my book binges. First of all, I open a bottle of good red wine. Then I turn off my cell phone, turn on my answering machine, and gather all the books I've been meaning to read or reread and haven't. Finally, I fill up the tub with thirty-dollar bubble bath, fold a little towel at the end of the tub so it just fits in the crick of my neck, and turn on my music. I have an old powder-blue plastic Deco radio near the tub that I bought at a garage sale in Hollywood a few years ago. The oddest thing: the radio only receives one AM radio station, which plays jazz standards from the forties and fifties, and it suits me just fine.

Within my bathroom walls is a self-contained field of dreams and I am in total control, the master of my own elegantly devised universe. The outside world disappears and here, there is only peace and a profound sense of well-being.

Most of the people in my life take a dim view of this . . . what would you call it? Monomania? Eccentricity? My sister is perhaps the most diplomatic. We both know that I have a tendency to lose my tether to reality when I close myself off like this. But then she'll joke that I'm really just another boring bibliomaniac and what I really need is a little fresh air. She always was a whiz with words. She actually informed me that a book she read by Nicholas Basbanes (appropriately called *Among the Gently Mad*) states that the first documented use of the word *bibliomania* came in 1750 when the fourth earl of Chesterfield sent a letter to his illegitimate son warning him that this consuming diversion with books should be avoided like "the bubonic plague." Ho hum.

I peel off my clothes and throw them on the floor. As I'm walking to the tub, I glance at the floor-to-ceiling mirror that covers the south wall of my bathroom. Oh god. Wait a minute. You know how you look in the mirror and you look the same and you look the same and all of a sudden you look ten years older? It's fitting that at age thirty-five I should notice this. My waist is thicker, my breasts saggier, the beginnings of—shit, is that cellulite on the backs of my thighs? Why is it that you think this age thing won't happen to you? Oh, and look at the backs of my elbows! They look like old-lady wrinkled elbows with a sharp, bony protrusion.

I've never been able to figure out my looks. I've been told I'm striking. But what does that mean? It's something people say when they can't give you the usual compliments, like "you're beautiful." It could be my height that puts them off. I'm almost five foot ten, which has only recently become fashionable. I also have enormous feet. Size 10 on a good day.

When I was young, I hated my tall, too-thin, sticklike figure, which my mother described as willowy. She'd argue that my looks were special and would be appreciated when I got older. Just give yourself time, she'd say. You'll see. You'll outshine all those other girls with hourglass figures. I felt like Frankie in *The Member of the Wedding*: "a big freak . . . legs too long . . . shoulders too narrow . . . belonging to no club and a member of nothing in the world."

It wasn't just my appearance. I always felt like an oddball, the exception in a world where I imagined other families were normal and happy. Virginia and I endured the secrets and shame of an absent father and an alcoholic mother, and the few friends I had, I kept at a distance, always relieved when they didn't come over. The fact of the matter was that I was embarrassed that my mother couldn't cope, and in some ways, she passed that on to me.

I shut my eyes as I get into the tub. I have purposely made the water scalding hot and when I dip my foot in, my toes turn red and start to sting. Too hot. I add a little cold, letting the water run through my fingers as I listen to a tinny version of Coltrane blasting out "Love Supreme." Paul Desmond once said that listening to late-night jazz is like having a very dry martini. I think he's right.

I stick my foot back in and then ease my body into the water. Still too hot. I twist the spigot with my toes, adding more cold. There. Perfect. I pick up *The Transit of Venus,* an obscure novel by Shirley Hazzard, whose newest book, *The Great Fire,* has become a favorite among book clubs. The premise is fascinating. It's about two beautiful orphaned sisters whose lives are as predestined as the rotation of the planets. I try to concentrate. The prose is dense and complex; I have to keep rereading paragraphs. I start to daydream and lose my place. This isn't working for me. Basically, I'm still depressed.

Maybe it's just the time of year. It's Christmas, I'm alone, and my social prospects are nonexistent. This is the season to be somewhere else, and for the majority of my friends, that means packing up the kids and maybe a few of their best friends and migrating to second homes in Maui, Aspen, Cabo, Sun Valley, and the second tier, Palm Springs and Las Vegas.

Being in West L.A. in December is like being banished to an isolated retreat or even a rehab center where parties and other forms of merriment are verboten. Not that I'm complaining. If you come from the east, the weather here in December is glorious. Right up until the El Niño rains in late January and February, the world is temperate, mild, and forgiving. Natural disasters like fires, floods, landslides, and earthquakes don't happen in West L.A.

This year I have no plans to go anywhere and I am occasionally nagged by that insidious feeling of "missing out." When I was with Palmer, we used to go to the Four Seasons on Maui every year. We'd get the corner suite and even bribe a beachboy to reserve our lounges every day to avoid getting up at five a.m. like everyone else. (In truth, most of our friends just had their nannies do it.) Now I hear Palmer is going to St. Barts. He thinks it's "younger, hipper, and more fun," unlike being with me. I used to sit by the pool in the shade and read all day.

The phone rings. It's my sister, Virginia. She sounds worried. "I know you're there, Dora. Why haven't you returned my calls? If you don't pick up I'm coming over . . ." I pick up.

"I'm okay," I say.

"You don't sound okay. Are you doing another one of your book-hermit things?" Nobody knows me like Virginia.

"I've been a little upset."

"A little, like twenty-four hours little or a little, like three days little?"

"Like three days little."

"Doesn't sound little to me. Do you want me to come over?"

I look around. My place is a shambles. "No. Really. I'm fine. I was just going out."

I convince her that I'm simply marvelous and she buys it. She just doesn't get it. She has a husband and a baby. Who can blame her?

I pick up the Hazzard book and try again. This is so depressing. I have just finished an early chapter about Ted Tice, Paul Ivory, and Caro, and I can already tell they are all eventually doomed to lives of unspeakable loss and tragedy. For one thing, Paul is gay, or at the very least bisexual, and for another—oh forget it.

I get out of the tub, grab a robe, and go back to the bookshelf, leaving wet footprints in my wake. It's not really intentional, but generally speaking I gravitate toward a certain theme for these lost weekends and, at the moment, I am set on choosing books about relationships that don't work out. Since most of the world's greatest classics deal with this subject, I have lots of options. Also, for some strange reason, my books are loosely organized into categories so it's easy to make a selection based on my mood. Let's see, do I want to steep myself in obsessive love . . . something like *Wuthering Heights,* where Heathcliff never did get it on with Cathy . . . unrequited love, dysfunctional love, adulterous love . . . Oh, here's Dorothy Parker . . . the brilliant cynic with deadpan wit alternating with fits of spiteful alcoholic rage (hmmmm) and Austen, the optimist. Her love affairs always work out. Not interested. Over here are the dysfunctional family books, including my mother's dog-eared copy of *The Optimist's Daughter,* and on the shelf below, the functional family books, mostly fantasies, sci-fi, or adventure classics that I have treasured since my childhood. I finally gather up the following: *Sentimental Education* by Flaubert (I lent Virginia my copy of *Madame Bovary,* which should be right beside it, and she never returned it. You see? That's why I don't lend books. It fucks up my whole library.), *Anna Karenina, The End of the Affair* (miracles and horrid disfigurements), *Wuthering Heights* (all right, I feel like wallowing), and *A Farewell to Arms*. God, what a dreary bunch of bathmates. Perfect for my grim, listless state of mind. That'll do for now. Oh well, I'll throw in Parker too. What the hell, a little comic relief.

I pad back into the bathroom with an armful of books and sink back into the tub. I add more hot water. Okay. I'm ready for my period of forlorn contemplation and occasional outbursts of exhilaration prompted by a particularly brilliant passage. What an insufferable lunatic I have become.

Over the next few days I read and I read. Days blur into nights. I snack on anything in my cupboard that doesn't require cooking. The Domino's guy and I have become close friends. He thinks I have agoraphobia. My red wine runs out and I start on the dessert wine. But I don't start before five. Even in my pathetic condition, I do have my standards.

• • •

My god, it's Wednesday afternoon already. I've got to get out of here. Where's my robe? Geez, this place is a mess. Should I clean up first? No. It'll kill the rest of the day. Maybe I'll buy a book. My mother would be appalled to learn that none of my friends go to the library anymore. If you want a book, you just go to the bookstore that's closest to your house and buy it. Hardcover, trade paperback, mass market, it doesn't make any difference. People who pay twenty dollars for parking don't quibble over the price of a book.

I live four blocks from McKenzie's, a small local bookstore on San Vicente, one of those dinosaurs that doesn't exist anymore except in affluent neighborhoods. It's a place where the salespeople actually read and can tell you where you can locate books by Evelyn Waugh or Michael Frayn. They'll also give you a list of other books by the same author, quote some of their favorite passages, and then add some completely random piece of information, such as the fact that Mark Twain's brilliant *The Adventures of Huckleberry Finn* went through seventeen hundred revisions, and the most recent draft was unearthed in a Hollywood attic some years ago.

There isn't a reason in the world for me to hit that damn bookstore again this week. I have four brand-new books by my bedside and two more on the kitchen counter. Then there are the three Booker Prize winners that are still in the bag in the trunk of my car and one new nonfiction literary history of Henry James in my purse, which I plan to start when I go to the hairdresser's next week.

I collect new books the way my girlfriends buy designer handbags. Sometimes, I just like to know I have them and actually reading them is beside the point. Not that I don't eventually end up reading them one by one. I do. But the mere act of buying them makes me happy—the world is more promising, more fulfilling. It's hard to explain, but I feel, somehow, more optimistic. The whole act just cheers me up.

I pull into the parking lot, turn off the motor, and rummage through my purse for lip gloss and concealer. I flip down the mirror and take a good look at my bare, unmade-up face. Terrible, just terrible. Even worse than I thought. That's it for me. No more book binges.

My hair is nice, though. It used to be "dirty blonde," but Franck, my brilliant Belgian hairdresser, has fixed all that. I now have that natural, sun-kissed California look that no one can get without a lot of money and a cauldron of chemicals.

I smear on some Nars cherry lip gloss, decide to bag the rest of the makeup, and head in. McKenzie's is like no other bookstore. It is a complex of three white, cottage-like buildings situated around a small tree-lined plaza with benches for customers to sit and read, nurse a cappuccino, or just hang out. There is a small café that sells newspapers and magazines, and a big sign over the cash register reads "No Cell Phones." Other buildings house history, psychology, fiction, and nonfiction. I always start off in the fiction building, where there are long tables laden with the latest hardbacks. And occasionally, when I have time, I'll wander briefly through the other buildings. Each one has the same basic feel of being in someone's messy library or living room, an ambiance that appeals to someone who is obviously a bookworm or an intellectual and who compulsively owns and collects countless numbers of books. Even though there is some semblance of order, books are always stacked high in every corner, on the brick floor, on window ledges, even on the cash register table, where one has to literally shove them on the floor before making a purchase.

I always feel a little put out in the beginning at the mess and disarray, but then the subliminal message takes over, that this is the place for the true book lover, a person who, naturally, is oblivious to order in the outside world. The fantasy is carried out right down to the employees and the rap they give you when you buy a book. "Are you a member of KUSC?" they ask kindly. That's one of two classical cultural radio stations in L.A.

and if you know what's good for you, you say yes and get a 10 percent discount.

The people who work here are an essential part of the whole mystique. The women all have the same "I don't care what I look like" attitude, the kind of thing you'd see in photo essays about the seventies when Ivy League radical coeds had wild flyaway hair and wore faded bell-bottoms and no makeup. The girls at McKenzie's look this way, with their pale faces, unmanicured hands, those round-toed black canvas Mary Janes, long skirts, and bagged-out sweaters with fuzzy textures. They do, however, wear bras and obviously love a good literary conversation. They also know their authors in an impressive but smug sort of way.

It doesn't seem as if any of them are all that busy except the lean, scrawny guy in an apron who runs the café in the back. At the moment he's making a latte as he carries on an animated conversation with a customer about an obscure poet who he says has Neruda-esque leanings. His name is Ken and he has spiky red hair, a face covered with an explosion of freckles, and a sparse iodine-red goatee. If he were a woman, the red-hair thing would probably work, but on Ken, it's somehow geeky and unfortunate, as if he were an alien from the red planet. He has odd pinkish, translucent skin with haunting puffy, watery blue eyes, and his eyelashes and eyebrows are so pale they seem invisible. As I glance in his direction, he zones out into a calm, fogged-over gaze like a narcoleptic.

And then there is Fred. He is looking me over, inspecting me. And in truth, that's why I am here. One of the girls told me he has a degree in comparative literature and he did his thesis on heterogeneous space in post-modern literature. What does that mean?

Virginia would probably say he looks like a bum, but there is something engaging about him in a disheveled kind of way. He has the stance of an aging ex-football player who's put on a few pounds, yet he still possesses the thick strong neck and prominent Adam's apple of a former athlete. When you look straight at him, his face is nice. But from the side, you can tell his nose has been broken a couple of times and his chin is sharp and jutting. I watch him stride around the shop with a certain air of unconscious grandeur, even though he's too tall and bearish to be navigating the narrow straits of the place.

Right now, he's helping a woman and her friend choose the next selection for their book club. He gives them an evasive half smile and looks away, sweeping back his shaggy bangs in a distracted kind of way. Why is it women always seem to fall for men who divert their attention elsewhere and focus anywhere but on their face? They dig the absentmindedness and inattentiveness when, in fact, the pose is often calculated to make an impression. Nevertheless, Fred is appealing in an untrustworthy, Southern gentleman sort of way. He has a slight drawl, although I could be imagining that. But he does seem like the kind of guy who could sit on his veranda with his big black retriever, smoking a stogy and watching the sun set over his cotton fields. The look, however, is strictly L.A.—jeans, a faded gray Gap

T-shirt under a stretched-out, old V-necked sweater, and red-rimmed eyes as if he's been up all night doing god knows what.

The overall effect is disconcerting. The energy in the air around him amps up the molecular composition of the place, compelling housewives, students, and literary losers to seek his counsel. The man knows his effect on people and uses it.

I see the women close in on him. The prettier of the two is dressed in what has become the young, affluent Brentwood housewife uniform—Juicy sweats. The designer outfit consists of tight, body-hugging velour pants that sit ultra-low on the hips and matching sweatshirts that are purposely unzipped just down to the cleavage. A friend of mine read in the Jacksonville paper that the city council was about to pass a "butt crack" law, which would label this kind of attire "lewd exhibitionism." But this is L.A., and no one seems to be complaining. It's kind of the opposite of what sweats are all about—relaxed, comfortable, with no hint of forced sex appeal. Remember putting on sweats when you felt fat or bloated? Well, forget it. The figure has to be absolutely perfect, and if it isn't, there's no way to camouflage anything. So now, schlepping around in any old comfortable pair of sweats to run an errand is passé.

All this runs through my mind as I watch them talk to Fred about a few options. They finally request twenty copies of *Tuesdays with Morrie,* and I see someone breeze past them sneering under her breath, "That figures."

Her name is Sara, a childlike Goth girl who looks like

she's in her early twenties. She has shoe-polish black hair, chewed-off fingernails, multiple piercings in her ears and left nostril, and cracked, peeling, kewpie-doll lips that glisten with a fine film of strawberry-tinged ChapStick. Her face has the plush, rounded innocence of a child and yet there is an air of intimidating self-sufficiency about her. Today she's wearing an incredibly short miniskirt over her petite but shapely legs that are so white you know she could care less that L.A. is a beach town. The rest of her ensemble includes scuffed white leatherette sixties go-go boots with a kitten heel, a midriff-revealing crepe blouse, and a heavy, metal dragon on a long, frayed shoelace around her neck. There is an innocence about her that belies her appearance and her breathy little girl voice is punctuated with expletives like "asshole" and "fuck you." Such a demeanor is particularly jarring in a setting like McKenzie's, but her coworkers clearly regard her with respect, and I've heard she knows every female writer who has written anything of note in the last two hundred years.

I can't tell if this fetching social misfit has rebellion on her mind or she just doesn't want to reveal how adorable she is beneath all that black smudged kohl and bare skin. This girl definitely has a past, but she giggles like a kid with a wad of Bazooka in her mouth, and it is hard not to follow her around with my eyes. If she asked my opinion, I'd tell her to comb her hair, but that would probably be it. Her hair is the only thing that bothers me, oddly enough. I guess it's "the look," but it's all messy and tangled in teased, rat's-nest clumps and soft, mushy, wadded fluff. It seems as if she has purposely gelled it to have the appearance of "I just slept in a Greyhound bus station and was attacked by a band of homeless men who clawed at my clothes and completely ruined my hair." You couldn't get a comb through it if you tried, and then it would be an extremely painful process.

Maybe that's the point that girls like Sara are tacitly addressing. Hair is beside the point—a time-consuming, unfulfilling way to go off on another fucking tangent, rather than getting on with your life, which leads me right back to where I am at the moment, roaming around the bookstore on a dead afternoon wondering how to approach Fred.

He is now busy with a frazzled-looking businessman who asks in a tense voice where the CliffsNotes section is located. Fred points toward the rear of the store and then asks him, "Which book?"

"*The Scarlet Letter*," the man replies. "My kid's hysterical. He just wrote a five-page paper and then somehow deleted it and it's due tomorrow."

Sara gives the guy a commiserating look. "Tell your son that Thomas Carlyle gave his only copy of *The French Revolution* to his friend to read and the guy's maid thought it was garbage and lit the fire with it. Carlyle had a few rotten nights, but then he wrote the thing all over again."

Fred looks at her in amusement. "Sara, I'm sure that's going to make the kid feel much better."

Then he turns to me and smiles. "Oh, hey, how are you? What can I help you with today?"

The first thing that pops into my head is that he recognizes me. The second thing is that the man who barbecued Carlyle's manuscript was the writer and critic John Stuart Mill, and he ended up giving the book a rave review. However, instead of belaboring the point, I consider telling him I've just finished a 675-page historical thriller on seventeenth-century Oxford, England, by Iain Pears called *An Instance of the Fingerpost* and that I have been totally unsuccessful in getting anyone else in my life to read it. The book is a kind of Dickensian whodunit set in Restoration England that begins with an unexplained death in a small college town and builds up into a revelation that has to do with grand events in England and the world. It is intellectual, original, and chock-full of smoke and mirrors, but, unfortunately, has quotes by Cicero and Francis Bacon in the beginning, which definitely put off several of my less esoteric friends. It also has a cast of twenty-seven characters in the back that went on for several pages and includes names like Charles II, Christopher Wren, and John Locke. Even the name of the novel seems to be a deterrent, although I once explained to my sister that the title was a delicious part of the whole mystery.

"Delicious?" she sniffed. She actually was somewhat interested until I told her that the narrator seems clear-minded and sympathetic at first, until three hundred or so pages later when you learn that he's fucking bonkers and is writing from the seventeenth-century English version of the booby hatch. She gave me a pained look and responded, "Who has time to read books like that?" implying, of course, that I do.

Fred is waiting for my response and I hesitate. I don't usually have the desire, as so many pious, voracious readers do, to show off how inherently superior my literary tastes are, but I weigh whether I will make an exception in this case. Then I change my mind. I quickly ask if he knows of a sequel to the Pears book. He tells me that one just came out and it's quite good.

"Not as good as the earlier book but an easier read. I'll go get it."

He returns empty-handed and says, "We must be all out." I decide to order it (a reason to give him my name and phone number), and as I'm heading out the door, feeling pretty good about our encounter, he calls my name. "Hey, Dora," he teases. I turn back expectantly and he says, "Do you want to pay for those or what?"

I realize that I'm clutching a bunch of books that I meant to purchase along with the Iain Pears. Shit. Shit. Shit. I'm an idiot. I blurt out, "I bet you think I'm one of those screwed-up kleptomaniac housewives who steals T-shirts to get her husband's attention." I give him a big lip-glossy smile. He looks at me like I'm insane. Nice, Dora.

The Stakeout

> "It is with books as with men; a very
> small number play a great part."
> ~ Voltaire (1694–1778) ~

Normally in my neighborhood it's gridlock at this hour. There are five exclusive private schools within a four-block radius and Sunset Boulevard is jammed with Range Rovers, BMWs, Mercedeses, and Hummers, many sporting vanity license plates that say things like "US2BHIS." In between, people in exercise clothes and leather Pumas hang out in the local Starbucks, power walk, bike along San Vicente Boulevard's tree-lined bike path, or shop in specialized boutiques that sell hundred-dollar tie-dyed T-shirts. Palmer used to marvel at the large numbers of people who spend their days with no visible means of support. "We could be in Florida," he said, "except nobody's old."

I'm heading home when I get a second wind and decide to take a slight detour. It's one of those spur-of-the-moment things that you can't seem to explain. Especially after what can only be described as a seriously awkward moment. No. *Inept* would be a better word. I think about what I said to Fred and then what I should have said. Then I go over it again in a different scenario. It turns over and over in my mind like an annoying melody that I can't get out of my head. First I say this, then he says that. Oh, this is so ludicrous I have to stop. It's a comment on my state of mind that I'm even analyzing this at all.

So, instead, here I am, sitting in my car like an undercover agent, while I wait for Palmer, my second husband, to emerge from the gated house that he and I shared for five years. This was our oasis, at least for a while. The house is one of those hybrid architectural buildings reminiscent of Old Hollywood. Part Italian villa, part Spanish hacienda. When we first moved in, I had it painted a faded terra-cotta, which is just now starting to look authentic. The driveway is lush with impatiens and lined with the requisite palm trees. I park on the narrow windy road in front of our house, my car wedged between a crisp navy van advertising Bel Air Plumbing and a battered wooden gardener's truck. In Bel Air, you're either a guest and you're parked inside the gates, or you're service personnel and you're outside the gates, an L.A. version of *Upstairs, Downstairs.*

Then there's that in-between category: personal trainers, yoga instructors, dog walkers, and masseuses. These people are often privy to the codes of their clients' alarm systems and a few end up living gratis in the guesthouse. I remember right before I moved out last year, my neighbor's masseuse, a rather sensitive young man named Roy, was held up at gunpoint by the now-infamous Bel Air Burglar as he entered their gate. Their dog, an imported German shepherd, sat immobile on his bed as the robbery was taking place. The dog was trained in Frankfurt and only understood commands like *sitzen* and *attacke*!

I reach behind me and grab one of the six books I had thrown into the car. One thing I'm glad about: I'm never bored and I never mind waiting—anywhere. Unless, of course, I've forgotten my book, in which case I just run off and buy another one. I read at the DMV, in movie lines, in bank teller lines, or when the shuttle from L.A. to San Francisco is four hours late. Layovers in unfamiliar airports are a treat, as are jury notices that arrive at my home and give me license to sit around and read all day, knowing that I'm doing my civic duty. On my last jury duty, I was rejected from two trials, one because I told the judge in voir dire that I thought the defendant, a skinhead with tattoos, looked guilty, and the other because the attorneys got a load of the hostile jury pool and settled the case. That day, I actually got to finish Jonathan Franzen's *The Corrections*.

What to read now? Maybe Alice Munro's *Lives of Girls and Women*. A quote on the back talks about the dark side of womanhood. Maybe something lighter. How about Kate Braverman's *Lithium for Medea*? Oh god, forget it. This is even more depressing. A woman who has a terrible relationship with her mother as well as every man in her life.

I burrow through the trunk of my fifteen-year-old cobalt-blue Mercedes 280, a graduation gift from my father. It is still a lovely old coach with faulty wiring and a broken windshield wiper that I've been meaning to fix for the last five years. Every time it rains, which isn't very often, I vow to take the thing in and then immediately lose interest when the sun comes out.

It's a sad commentary that I've been with my car longer than any man in my life. I'm not one of those people who affectionately bestows a name upon their car, but I can understand the inclination to do so.

The gates to the long sloping driveway slowly begin to open and I dive behind my car as a grim-looking plumber carrying his toolbox emerges. We were always having trouble with the water system, which belched greenish-looking water no matter how many experts we called in. I used to joke that our house was West L.A.'s version of the Love Canal. I do have some sense of pleasure that this problem has not been resolved and that my replacement will have to deal with the endless stream of aeroscopic engineers, construction supervisors, and plumbers.

Palmer is now living with an elegant, beautifully put-together woman named Kimberly, who he thinks will be the next domestic diva. She first came to Palmer for legal advice regarding a line of cookware she wanted to sell on the Home Shopping Network. Already the host of a cheery little show on the Food Network, she had just signed a multimedia deal that included her own magazine. She uses phrases on the air such as "Ladies, we can make our families happy without working our tushies off," and includes tricks like turning old bed linens into junky tablecloths.

Last year, the top job at Sony Pictures opened up, and in a surprise move, the Sony brass named Palmer to replace the retiring studio head. His latest string of movies has been financially successful, and now he has a house on the Vineyard, another in Cabo, and I see his name on the letterhead of a dozen charities.

I've spent the last year trying to figure out how I feel about all this. I thought back to the times when I'd toss and turn all night worrying about something, and in the morning, when I'd wake up bleary-eyed and conflicted, he'd get that look on his face and effortlessly work it all out. There was this calm brilliance about him that had nothing to do with money. I think I loved him. I certainly admired him. But not for his success. That just seemed to get in the way.

One day, shortly before the breakup, I found him arranging his neckties according to color and pattern. He used to collect Hermès ties with their endless whimsical micro patterns—sailboats, penguins, golf clubs, whales, baseball bats, hot air balloons, beach umbrellas, trotters, fox hunters, Labradors, and so on, ad nauseam. I scanned the array of expensive patterned silks that covered the entire king-size bed—a sea of ties. "You must have five hundred of these, and look at them," I said with disdain, "they all look alike. Wait! You're missing the one with the dollar bills all over it."

He picked up a tie and threw it at me. "How come you're always such a downer, Dora?" That's me, Dora the Downer.

For a while, Palmer and I tried the marriage counselor route. I remember the therapist took a look at us and said, "Couples shouldn't divorce unless one of you clearly doesn't like the other." It was good advice and I went with it for a while, but eventually he found solace in his work and his new girlfriend. A friend of mine says that I have deficient wiring because I've never been dumped. What she doesn't realize is this: I always manage to extricate myself first, before things get too dramatic. It's easier that way. But now I'm thinking maybe I should have tried harder. Oh god, it's all so confusing. I do wish him well, although it wouldn't make me unhappy if his next movie is skewered by the critics and flops at the box office. No. I don't mean that.

Emily Post and Grand Larceny

"I never travel without my diary. One should always
have something sensational to read in the train."
~ Oscar Wilde (1854–1900), *The Importance of Being Earnest* ~

My first husband, Jack, was a different story. He was
the classic catch in a high-school sort of way—
handsome, popular, athletic, and he liked to party. That's
where I met him, by the way, at a party. For the first time
in my life, he made me feel "in." He was also the first
man to tell me that I was sexy, beautiful, and desirable—
how could I not love him forever?

I wish I had a better reason for finding him so appealing. But I don't. I married him because he was a hunk.
That's it. No one understood it. But the thing is, men do
this all the time and no one says boo about it. Why do
women have to come up with all sorts of explanations for

doing the same thing? I didn't try to impress him with my book stuff because I knew he didn't care. To tell you the truth, it was actually liberating . . . and very romantic.

But as Shakespeare wisely pointed out in *The Tempest*, romantic love is so much more complicated than that. Even though Jack set me on fire in bed, alas, it couldn't compensate for the fact that he had no intellectual curiosity whatsoever . . . he read car magazines, played video games, watched NASCAR on TV, and smoked pot. When you take out the sex factor, we had nothing in common. One day it just hit me. In all my years of making stupid decisions, this was the capper.

I had just graduated from Columbia and he was studying for his real estate license, the only classes he'd attended since high school. When we decided to get married, I was twenty-one years old and even as I was marching down the aisle, resplendent in Madeira lace, trying to ignore my disappointed relatives, mainly my mother, I knew I was making a mistake.

I landed my job at the *Los Angeles Times* two weeks after my wedding. That's when I met Darlene. I was the hot new reporter (there's always a hot new reporter) and my world was filled with infinite possibilities. Darlene, however, was buried in Classifieds, selling twenty words to anyone with a charge card and something to offer.

She was ten years older than me and married to a cop. The hierarchy at the *Times* was a caste system with Editorial on top and Classifieds somewhere near subzero. People treated Darlene with the same affection they reserved for their maid. They were nice but they weren't sharing their drinks or their secrets with her. It didn't help that she looked like a female serial killer—long straight blonde hair that she bleached herself, black roots, epic tits, too much sun, and too much booze. Of course, I found her tremendously amusing and we threw back more than a few on several occasions after work. I particularly enjoyed these evenings because it prolonged the inevitable trip home and put off the nearly nightly confrontations with Jack. He was feeling insecure about the marriage, not surprisingly. I also thought he was back seeing his old girlfriend, a wretched creature he'd lived with for a few years before dumping her for me.

One night Darlene and I were at Cassidy's, a once-lively spot wedged between two strip malls, which had spiraled downward until now the only time the place was full was on St. Patrick's Day, when they gave away frothy mugs of green beer on tap. I had once seen the bartender, an aging thug with a long blond ponytail and a receding hairline, topping off the barrels using the hose in the back alley. His wife, a hefty Armenian girl with short hair and a mustache, waited tables and served as the bouncer when things got rowdy.

It was, however, a cop hangout and Darlene's husband, Mel, would sometimes meet us and shoot the breeze for a couple of hours. Mel, an LAPD cop, was a meaty guy with a stubbled face and a cracked, hoarse, smoker's laugh. Every now and then he'd give me a semi-reliable tip, which once turned into a pretty big story on the front page of the Metro section.

That night, I was not in the best of moods when my cell phone rang and it was Jack. He sounded uncharacteristically upbeat.

"Hey, I have to show this condo tonight. The woman can't get there until seven and then she wants to see what the view looks like at night."

I responded in mock sympathy, "Gee, that's too bad. I guess you're stuck late, then, huh?"

"Till ten at least."

"Oh, okay. Don't wake me when you come in, because I'm dead tired." I must have looked relieved, because Darlene gave me a quizzical look.

"You know what," I said, "he's full of shit. This is the third time this week. But the worst part is, I don't care."

Darlene was sympathetic but firm. "Get rid of him. You made a mistake. Bite the bullet. Move on."

"But we just got married and I'm embarrassed. Plus, our living room is littered with all these gifts, and I need to at least write the thank-you notes before I leave him." It's strange when anachronisms like Emily Post pop up in your life.

"God, are you nuts. Who cares about the gifts? Return them. No, wait! Give them to me. Just kidding." Darlene never worried about what other people thought. I, on the other hand, felt guilty. No, it was worse than that. I felt like an awful person for not loving him.

When I got home that night there was an angry message on the answering machine from Jack's ex-girlfriend, berating him for being late and telling him that she "couldn't take it anymore." Assuming "it" was the affair they'd been having and never one for confrontations, I called Darlene and we devised a plan.

Jack came home late and I pretended I was asleep. The next morning, after he left for work, I called Darlene, who had been waiting for the "all clear" sign from around the corner. She pulled up in a banged-up purple van with black flames emblazoned on the side, which she'd gotten from Rent-A-Wreck, a place down the block that looked like a salvage yard. This was Darlene's idea of being unobtrusive.

My place was on the second floor of what was jokingly called garden apartments. I guess the two dying azalea bushes were the garden part. The white stucco building had seen better days but not much better, and the open hallways left no room for privacy. Darlene parked the van right in front and came bounding up the steps with unbridled enthusiasm. For some warped reason, this whole thing really charged her up. "Dora, you can't believe this killer van. And if I get it back to them by noon, they'll give me a '68 Mustang for the rest of the day."

"Darlene, we need to focus here." And then I saw Mrs. Richter peeking through her curtains. My nosy German landlord and his wife lived down the hall, and to them, the whole world was a soap opera, which in my case happened to be the truth. She stuck her head out and said hello, which was a "tell me what's going on" kind of hello. I swear those people installed motion detectors. I nonchalantly answered, "Oh, hi," as I ducked back into my apartment. I heard her Tevas flapping down the hall.

"What's going on?"

Since it didn't seem fair that Mrs. Richter should know about the split before Jack, I decided to lie. "Spring cleaning," I said. Not bad for the middle of January. I could tell the old bat didn't believe me, but she didn't come out again.

Darlene was waiting inside, surveying the place. I was about to object as she lifted the Jack Daniel's bottle and poured herself a large tumblerful, but what the hell, I joined her.

"You shouldn't leave all this stuff. You're crazy."

"I don't want it," I replied. On this I was clear.

Darlene sat down. "Well, at least take the couch. Do you know how much these things cost?" She was referring to a distressed brown leather monster I'd always hated. For someone as deliciously handsome as Jack was, he really had no taste. All the furnishings were different colors of mud with green or gold flecks. If I were to categorize it, I would call it stupid stud furniture, but perhaps that would be too harsh.

"Do you honestly believe the two of us can carry this three-hundred-pound couch down the stairs?"

She was adamant. "Let me just think a minute. What if we drove down to Westwood Boulevard, picked up a couple of those construction guys who hang out on the corner waiting for work, and offer them maybe twenty dollars each? That would work."

"You don't understand, Darlene. I don't want the couch," I repeated.

She shook her head in disbelief. It was a tribute to her grip on reality that she thought I was the one who was nuts. "Dora, no one leaves stuff like this."

She and I spent the next twenty minutes arguing about what I should take, while I was getting more and more nervous that Jack would unexpectedly appear. In the end, she convinced me to take at least a few of the more practical wedding gifts from my side of the family, and, indeed, I was grateful to have some pots, pans, plates, and silverware for my next place.

Acting as if we were committing grand larceny, we carried out bulging black Hefty bags filled with my clothes and box after box of my books, which I had meticulously saved since I was twelve, including textbooks with water-stained covers. I must learn to travel lighter.

For a long time after that, I felt guilty and liberated at the same time. I wouldn't have to quiz him for his real estate license and pretend how difficult it was. I wouldn't have to tune out the damn TV, or ignore the aftertaste of marijuana mixed with tobacco on his breath. Or feel like a sap every time we went to a party and I couldn't think of a thing to say to him or his friends.

He insisted that no one would ever love me as much as he did, and at the time, I believed him. His girlfriend gave me the excuse to leave, but I knew he was still in love with me. Afterwards, when the inevitable pain of the breakup hit us, we met for coffee and we both had a good cry. He was sympathetic and resigned in the beginning but then came the zinger. "I helped you become the beautiful, self-confident woman you are and you stomped all over me and left me in the dust."

The Roust

"I divide all readers into two classes:
Those who read to remember
and those who read to forget."
~ William Lyon Phelps (1865–1943) ~

I jump behind a bush as a silver Porsche 911 Turbo convertible races out of the driveway, driven by one of Palmer's best friends, Hootie. Must be a new car. Like this slug would ever need to get from 0 to 60 in four seconds. His golf clubs are sticking out of the back of his car like plumes on a rooster and he's probably headed to Bel Air Country Club for his afternoon rounds. The scion of an old Southern family, he currently spends his days golfing and his nights watching videos of himself golfing. At one time handsome, almost patrician, he is now a lush with a puffy face and a bulbous nose covered with spider veins who tells unfunny jokes with boorish sexual references.

Oddly enough, Palmer is nothing like his friends. He went to Yale, and for some reason gravitated toward those guys with three last names who graduated from St. Paul's or Exeter with a C-minus average and spent their entire undergraduate careers getting shit-faced in the same clubs where their fathers and grandfathers once held court. Talk about the original affirmative action.

Not that Palmer was like that. He grew up in working-class New Jersey, went to Yale on a full scholarship, and was the first in his family to graduate from college. He is smart and ambitious, the kind of person who could hold down three jobs and still end up with a 4.0. His family owned a ma-and-pa grocery store, and Little Joey, as the Palmers called him to differentiate him from his father, Big Joey, spent every waking hour helping out in the store. He still notices the prices of food items and pays particular attention to the cost of a quart of milk, feeling that it's a bellwether for fluctuations in the economy.

Given all of Palmer's obvious attributes, it always amazed me how impressed he was with old money. Even these clowns, the kind of people who juxtapose fancy cars with bad skin, bad breath, and slightly agape flies, were elevated in his eyes because of their once-fashionable social standing. He's still grateful for the fact that they anointed him "Palmer" the first week of school as they ushered him into their snobby group, and he continues to find them interesting in spite of their pretentious and slightly depraved lifestyles. When I suggested that these people were just losers taking up space, he shot back that I was the real snob here, not them.

Palmer loved everything that I hated, including fancy parties, corporate intrigue, business networking, and the whole Hollywood scene. I especially hated going to his Young Presidents Organization (YPO) weekend extravaganzas. This was an organization for mostly second-generation presidents of companies who liked to get together in places like Vail or Tucson to talk about interest rates and balancing their portfolios. They had boring seminars during the day and endless cocktail parties at night in dark reception rooms located in the basement level of the hotels. The wives were expected to come along, look beautiful, and spend their time participating in stupid activities like Asian flower arranging, shopping sprees at local malls, or guided tours by ancient docents of obscure museums.

I went along the first time to a weekend in Monterey, but after three excruciating days of socializing with women I never would have talked to ordinarily, I told him to forget about bringing me along the next time. He went alone after that, but always came home silent, resentful, and full of accusatory pronouncements like "I was the only one who didn't bring his wife" or "You missed a great speech by Buzz Aldrin about orbiting hotels on Mars."

But it wasn't all Palmer's fault. He was out in the world and I stayed home and read. Not that I let myself indulge all the time, but I'd have to admit that the book-binge thing sometimes got out of control. After all, I had plenty of time to kill. He had evolved into a workaholic and I was lost in the blissful, dreamlike otherworldness of books. Compared to reality, it was much more enticing.

In retrospect, I made a mistake not going back to work. After my father died, I thought I'd take a short sabbatical. But how did it turn into five years? I just couldn't seem to pull myself together. And Palmer was happy to have me all to himself. I should have remembered how miserable and bored my mother was just being the corporate wife. But now I'm not even the corporate wife. I'm just one of those thirtysomething women who roam around Los Angeles, speeding down the freeway with nowhere to go.

I am jolted out of my reverie by Steve, the neighborhood Bel Air patrolman. He taps on the window and peers in at me. "Hey, Dora. What's up?" He's friendly but clearly wants to know what the hell I'm doing here. I suddenly get queasy at the prospect of him maybe calling Palmer. Do they have a restraining order against me? Not possible. I've never showed signs of aggression or threatening behavior that would warrant such measures. Granted, it *is* weird that I'm hanging out in front of Palmer's gate.

Even I don't know why I'm here. I give Steve one of my most of-course-this-is-perfectly-normal looks and say, "Just came to pick up a few things." Sure, that's why I've been hiding in the bushes. "Guess no one's home. I'll try later." He doesn't believe it for a second. How humiliating. And I remember how I used to complain to him about all the tourists who cruised our streets and, god forbid, if anyone parked by my gate to try to get a glimpse of the actress next door. I'd call Steve all agitated and make him come right over and roust the guy to move on.

I start my car and try to get out of the parking spot I had wedged myself into. Not easy. I never was very good at parallel parking. I think if you don't grow up in L.A., you never quite get the hang of it. Finally, I angle it out. If a car could have its tail between its legs, that's my once proud vehicle as I slowly head home.

The Wasteland

"I read much of the night and go south in the winter."
~ T. S. Eliot (1888–1965) *The Waste Land, "The Burial of the Dead"* ~

I pull into my apartment building and one of four uni-formed valets takes my car. The ads for this place de-scribe it as L.A.'s only month-to-month, ultra-luxury high-rise oceanfront residence. They say it's comparable to the finest five-star hotel, but I say it's assisted living for the socially impaired. It's certainly one of the first places West L.A. people think of when they get divorced and can't figure out where to go for that sticky in-between time. I moved in a year ago, furnished it from Ikea (ex-cept for my antique iron bed), and haven't had the energy or motivation to look for more suitable quarters. It was supposed to be temporary, like a brief vacation, but somehow inertia set in, not to mention getting seduced by the embarrassing number of amenities. Everything I hate to do is taken care of, including picking up my laundry, parking my car, carrying up the groceries, and reconnecting me to the Internet when my computer freezes up. There's even a concierge that makes dinner reservations and arranges travel. So here I am in a place that grates on me every time I pull into the palatial circular driveway and walk through the marble entry. Oh well, maybe just a few more months.

Victor the Doorman greets me, "Hey Dora, how ya doin'? Your sister's upstairs."

My first thought is "Oh Christ, I don't have the energy for this right now." My sister, Virginia, drops by whenever her baby, Camille, is driving her crazy, which seems to be every other minute lately. Virginia is three years older than me and it took years of fertility treatments to have this baby. Right now there are sleep issues (like I don't have any) and lately she's been throwing the baby in the car, driving around, and ending up at my place.

As I walk through the door, the enormous amount of paraphernalia that my sister carries around with her is strewn all over the living room and the phone is ringing. My sister ignores it while trying to comfort her screaming, overtired child. She looks even more disheveled than usual and there is a large greasy spot in the middle of her stretched-out T-shirt. Virginia and I look so different that people always react with suspicion when we tell them we're sisters. She is five foot two with olive skin and dark, inquisitive eyes. When she smiles, you can still see that one of her front teeth is slightly chipped, the result of the accident on the bridge years ago. You'd think she would've at least had the tooth capped, but she's always made a point of saying looks aren't important.

She's let her hair go gray and when I tell her that she looks ten years older because of it, she argues that her girlfriends think her hair is a beautiful shade of silver. One should never rely on girlfriends for things like this. They tend to try to make you feel good. You should always rely on sisters, who tell you the awful truth no matter how bad it makes you feel. Then there is the issue of her weight. I wouldn't say that she's fat, but she's a size 12, which in this part of town is considered politically incorrect, right up there with smoking, drinking, and eating desserts. It doesn't help that sizes in the Beverly Hills stores start at 0 and usually end at 8. I must say that when I travel, it amazes me how much heavier everyone is. What seems normal in L.A. is anorexic anywhere else.

My sister avoids the shopping problem by sticking to oversized sweats decorated with animal decals, glitter, or rhinestones. I don't comment on her wardrobe anymore. I've learned it's easier to just shut up about it.

The baby's shrieks are reaching fever pitch and the phone is still ringing. I pick her up and walk to the balcony so we can both look at the ocean. Camille releases a series of weak little staccato sighs and curls into me. I can feel her whole body relax.

In the midst of all this chaos, Virginia answers the phone. It's my mother. Perfect timing. Why can't we be like normal families and never talk to each other?

"Hi, Mom. Wait a minute. I'll give you Dora." I can hear my mother's strong, stern voice still talking as Virginia gives me the phone and takes Camille. Mother is obviously annoyed. "Who's this? Dora? Where's Virginia? Am I disturbing you?"

"No, Mom. It's okay," I lie. "What's up?"

"Well, the answer is 'roast pig.' It's the subject of one of Charles Lamb's most famous essays. Does it fit?"

For a moment I can't figure out what she is talking about, but then I remember I was struggling with that crossword clue for two nights and finally couldn't stand it anymore. I usually call Virginia when I feel like cheating because she used to do the *New York Times* Sunday crossword puzzle in about an hour and then cheerfully tell me how easy it was. But lately, with Camille, she's so frazzled it's a waste. So I called my mom, who doesn't have Virginia's graduate degree in the classics, but is the most avid reader of your basic moldy classics that I know and sometimes has an answer.

"Gee, Mom, that's great. I knew you'd get it, you're . . ." The baby is now howling so loud in the background that I can't hear myself talk. "I'll call you later, okay?"

"You know, your sister doesn't know how to deal with that child. When you kids were babies—"

"Mom, I gotta go, okay? I'll call you later."

Virginia places Camille in her Portacrib in my bedroom and shuts the door. I look at her in disbelief. "What are you doing?"

"Well, she hasn't slept a wink today and she is so strung out that I can't stand it. Dr. Friedman says I just have to bite the bullet and let her cry it out or she'll never get on a schedule and Andy and I will be walking zombies for the rest of our lives."

"Not that I'm an expert, but Dr. Friedman isn't here listening to the screaming, and maybe if you just held her and rocked her she'd nod off. I can't stand it when she wails." We look at each other and rush into the bedroom.

It always ends like this when Virginia comes over. I give her my opinion, which then gives her permission to do what she wants, which is to comfort the baby. It all seems so simple. But then I'm not there at two in the morning. Virginia rocks Camille, who eventually conks out, and we immediately hit the white wine and cheese. It's at this point that Virginia says something sweet about her husband, Andy, a Ph.D. in psychology and an expert on aging (how depressing), who treats his wife with undying respect (she's the one with the trust fund). It's one of those marriages where there's only the two of them, and, of course, now Camille. She gave up her job teaching Latin at a preppy boarding school to move out here with him and they've been happily married most of my adult life, something that neither my mother nor I could ever achieve.

Sometimes when we're sitting together like this, the baby asleep, the afternoon clouds closing in, I flash on our tumultuous lives as kids. Mother was always recovering from her two-martini cocktail hour, which started at three in the afternoon and ended several hours after dinner, which she often missed, and Father popped in and out of our lives in a series of long separations.

I still have dreams about him that give Ginny and me a good laugh. He's been abducted by evil aliens like Meg's father in *A Wrinkle in Time*, kidnapped by terrorists, taken against his will, forced to leave us, but unlike Odysseus, he never braved the Fates to come home.

Growing up, my father was intimidating and demanding, but those qualities were tempered by an irresistible charisma. At dinner parties, he dominated the conversation and charmed all the women—he was always the star. My mother tolerated his celestial aura but would frequently describe him by repeating Alice Roosevelt Longworth's quote about her father, Teddy: "He wanted to be the corpse at every funeral, the bride at every wedding, and the baby at every christening."

My father was all that my mother wasn't—maybe that was the attraction. And he loved to have a good time. She disapproved of the circus, the zoo, amusement parks, and even Christmas. And he relished those things. So she'd stay home while we'd all climb in his Seville and come home hours later, the car trashed with cotton candy sticks, Cracker Jacks, shriveled balloons, and the remains of whatever fast food we'd eaten.

But these idyllic days were rare. When he lived with us, he was either at the office or traveling to some exotic land, chasing down the latest woven chenille or ornate Aubusson, which he produced on hundreds of looms around the world. The owner of a textile mill, he was a self-made tycoon—absent six days a week and asleep on the couch on the seventh, lulled by the constant drone of the Phillies games. His fortunes rose and fell with the price of goods, but he managed to leave us each a modest trust fund, which Virginia tells me, at the rate I'm going, I've got maybe five years of left.

In those days, dinner was usually something the housekeeper would put in the oven at three in the afternoon and we'd take out whenever my father came home from work. During the meal, he would cover up my mother's absences with games of twenty questions and "What in the World?" My brilliant sister would always excel in the current events category. She gobbled up every newspaper she could get her hands on, and before I could stumble onto the answer, she'd grin and throw it out in a stage whisper. But when it came to literature, I was the master. One night, I remember him asking us to quote something from a classic family saga. He was expecting something from *The Swiss Family Robinson* or *Little Women,* but the first thing that popped into my head was Lady Bracknell's response to hearing that Jack had lost both his parents. "To lose one parent, Mr. Worthing, may be regarded as a misfortune; to lose both looks like carelessness."* It was a competition of sorts, but we both basked in his sense of pride and his undivided attention.

Long after the dishes were cleared, Mother would come floating downstairs, giving me a lovely smile and rummaging through the shelves for a can of Campbell's soup or kidney beans. There were periods, however, when she was glorious. She had a long, patrician nose and dark, wavy, lustrous hair swept back with diamond-

---

* Oscar Wilde, *The Importance of Being Earnest.*

studded tortoiseshell combs and hairpins. When we were in grade school she would announce her own schedule of holidays and we would take turns skipping school. We'd go downtown to the Philadelphia Museum of Art or to a concert with Eugene Ormandy and the Philadelphia Orchestra and then to the Crystal Tea Room at Wanamaker's department store, where we'd get cucumber sandwiches with the crusts cut off and rice pudding. We were her little pets for the day, and she'd buy us ribbons, hair clips, or a new pair of shoes.

On weekends, we went to the library, where I'd roam around bored and restless while my mother would sink into a cubicle and hunker down for what seemed like hours. She was a masterful reader and, next to gin, it was the most important thing in her life. It was of paramount importance to her that I read too and often she'd say to me, "No matter what happens to you, Dora, you can always pick up a book," in the way I imagined other mothers would comfort their daughters with words of endearment. Or at the very least, advise them to get off the couch and do something.

Incidentally, it's no accident that my mother named me Dora. I don't tell many people, but Dora is short for Eudora Welty, one of my mother's idols. It all sounds so, well, bookish, but at the time, my mother identified with Welty's voracious literary appetites and used to proudly tell me that she and Welty had the same literary background, from Chaucer and Virgil to Yeats, Matthew Arnold, and Virginia Woolf (guess who was named after her). I think she also admired Welty's intensely private persona and secretly envied the fact that she was an independent, eccentric woman who gloried in books and her camellia garden and was quite content to live alone.

Some biographers claim that Welty's mother was so obsessed with books that she once rushed into a burning house not to save the children, but to save a set of valuable Dickens volumes. I don't think my mother would go to that extreme, but she certainly admired the single-mindedness of it all. Anyway, Welty was said to be genteel and straightforward and that's the way my mother usually comes across.

After my father left for good, my mother stopped doing much of anything and the locked-bedroom-door incidents grew longer. We were never quite sure if she was reading, recovering, sleeping, or drinking. During this period, Virginia became the caretaker: shopping, cooking, tidying up; while I mimicked my mother's retreat to the only safe harbor I knew, my books.

We've become even closer since she moved to L.A. I look at her sitting on my white wicker rocker. The sun is just about to plop into the ocean, my favorite time. She smiles at me.

"Thanks for the rescue. It's so peaceful here, I hate to leave. Plus, as soon as I walk in the door, Andy is on me to help type his Alzheimer's speech. He's such a pain."

This is my favorite subject and I'm rolling. "Why doesn't he just hire someone? He can afford it. Why do husbands take their smart wives and turn them into secretaries?"

Virginia laughs. "Tolstoy's wife copied *War and Peace* in longhand three times."

"No offense, Virginia, but Andy isn't Tolstoy."

"Oh well, Dora. What can I say? Do you want to come over for dinner? Andy's probably home wondering which bridge I drove off of." (We give each other a knowing look—and laugh.)

"I can't," I lie. "Meeting some friends."

"Oh, who?"

"Just some old friends from work."

"I know a nice guy. Friend of Andy's."

As if that would be an asset. "No thanks."

"You know, Dora, L.A. isn't like New York. You have to make an effort here. You can't just walk into a bar on East Fifty-seventh Street and start talking to your neighbors. It's not that kind of town."

"And what? You want me to join a dating service? Go on the Internet? I'd rather shoot myself. Anyway, I'm not looking" (except at the bookstore, but no need to mention that here). "I'm fine." Even to me, I sound defensive.

"You're turning into a hermit. Even Andy says so."

"Fuck Andy. Go home. You're late."

Virginia's mouth curls up in a mock petulant scowl as she leans over to kiss me good-bye. "Okay, Dora, but you really should meet his friend. He's nice and he reads."

"Big deal. No. I love you. Good-bye."

Virginia gathers all her stuff, gently picks up Camille, who is now sleeping soundly, and she's gone.

I wish people would stop trying to fix me up. It never

works out and things are always strained. From the moment we say "hello" and I start listening to his life story, I'm waiting for a chance to escape. I think back to my conversation with Fred at the bookstore. He's a flirt, no doubt about it. Not really my type. If I saw him on the street, chances are I'd walk right past him. Still, I'm definitely attracted to him. I bet right now he's fucking some Brentwood housewife in her faux English Tudor mansion while her husband, the dermatologist, is at Men's Week at the Golden Door. What's the matter with me? We had a three-minute conversation. He's probably one of those moody, dysfunctional guys who's critical of everything and doesn't even like the sound of the surf.

I turn on my goofy garage-sale radio and grab my latest tome. I always feel best about myself when I'm engrossed in a good book. Then I don't worry that I'm in limbo, living in a place that's not really my home, spending my days floating around from one thing to the next. Tomorrow is a big day. I'm interviewing for a writing position at my old newspaper. I'm going to try not to think about it.

So now it's three a.m. and tonight, like so many others, I'm wide awake. I look out the window. The world is dark and deserted. All the normal, well-adjusted people are asleep. Insomnia. Why do I feel that I'm the only one that suffers from this affliction? I give up. Turning on the light and opening my book once again is generally the only alternative to this misery. Although Dorothy Parker would definitely disagree. In her philosophy, the whole institution of reading was responsible for her sleepless nights. She joked that all the best minds had been "anti-reading" for years.* She even said, "I wish I'd never learned to read . . . then I wouldn't have been mucking about with a lot of French authors at this hour . . ."*

That leaves the question, what to do if you don't want to read to get yourself to sleep? Sheep are out. Dorothy Parker hated sheep. "I can tell the minute there's one in the room. They needn't think I'm going to lie here in the dark and count their unpleasant little faces for them."*

I can make lists of things I need to do. No, that would only stress me out. I could get up and make a glass of warm milk. I could organize my closet. Or my desk. I could call the 1-800 number for the Bank of America and check my balance. No, that's another stomach-churning exercise.

People don't realize how serious a problem this is. There was a case last year in the Valley where a man with insomnia would go into his garage in the middle of the night and use his power saw. His woodworking was the only thing that gave him solace. And the neighbors were suing. This doesn't help me.

I grab a book on my bedside table that my sister gave me a few weeks ago. *How Proust Can Change Your Life* by Alain de Botton. It says here it's a "self-help manual for the intelligent person." I could use some help right now.

---

* "The Little Hours," *The Portable Dorothy Parker,* Penguin Books.

Interview with Miss Piggy

"The best effect of any book is that it
excites the reader to self activity."

~ Thomas Carlyle (1795–1881) ~

Getting dressed is a lot trickier than I imagined. What an ordeal. All these things I used to take for granted, like putting on an outfit and rushing out the door without worrying what I looked like, are so much more difficult now. Plus, it's been a long time since I wore "work clothes," whatever that means. I have already put on and taken off a couple of Gucci suits, thinking they were too trendy, one Banana Republic outfit, thinking it was too suburban, and a sweater and shortish pleated skirt that gave me that "trying to look too young" look. By the end of it all, I'm sweating, harassed, late, and thoroughly discouraged. I finally settle on a simple black suit I purchased three years ago at Bloomingdale's for the funeral of my brother-in-law's mother, who died of dementia and everyone said it was a blessing. Okay, I'm ready. I hate the way I look. Ordinary.

I get in the car and head downtown. Here's the thing: I do not drive on the freeway. That's not something I admit to anyone except my closest friends, because in this city it's like having a debilitating disease or being bipolar. When I first moved here, the intricate network of concrete and steel was daunting, to say the least. Anybody's vision of automotive hell, right down to the banshee-screaming sirens and thunderous din that assault your consciousness as you brave the elements, strapped to your seat. Like a fighter pilot. Driving in this town is certainly not for the fainthearted. When you factor in road rage and all those zoned-out bizarros and angry people who are just on the edge of insanity, it's even more frightening. Nevertheless, I always managed to motor up and down the ramps like any other normal commuter on the 101 or the 10 and to dutifully yield to the zooming traffic that was muscling down on top of me.

Then one night, I lost my nerve. I was driving to USC on assignment to interview a seventeen-year-old freshman who had just sold a screenplay for a million dollars when my car stalled in the fast lane of the Santa Monica freeway. It was black-dark, impossible to see anything but a blaze of out-of-focus exploding nebulas that enveloped my car. Semis blasted their horns as they swerved to avoid hitting me. And I remember praying that I would wake up from this nightmare and the burning, white-coal core of panic would subside. I was shivering and drenched in sweat as I kept turning on the ignition only to hear weak clicks and then silence. Just as a truck pulled up behind me and stopped (maybe a good Samaritan, maybe Ted Bundy's brother), I turned the key and the car miraculously started. I had enough power to creep along at five miles an hour across four lanes of traffic to the nearest off-ramp. I coasted down to a gas station in the middle of Watts, where an unflappable Korean attendant called a cab and waited with me until it arrived.

Remember that old saying, "When you fall off a horse you should get right back on"? Well, I didn't. I kept avoiding the freeway and now, every time I even consider it, my palms sweat and my vision blurs, and I feel like I'm going to hyperventilate so I go home and have a glass of wine. I heard about a therapist who specializes in freeway disorders but I was afraid of all the other stuff she might dig up, so I never went to see her. So now, in a city where there is no public transportation, I am relegated to only those areas of L.A. served by Sepulveda and Olympic. I pull into the *Times* building after an hour and a half—a trip that should have taken thirty minutes.

It's a little disorienting going back to a place where I once worked. My instinct is to pull into the same parking space, but instead I take a parking ticket that needs to be validated and pull into the visitor's lot. Trying to act like I belong, I ask the burly security guy where Al is, the kindly, bespectacled guard I used to bring lattes to from the corner café, which isn't there anymore. He informs me curtly that Al retired four years ago. "Check your purse, ma'am?"

The newsroom is the same, thank god, with rows of reporter cubicles outfitted with computers and bulletin boards overflowing with cartoons, irreverent slogans, daily assignments, and bizarre photos of attack dogs, creepy over-the-hill actresses, and bloody crime scenes. The same thirtysomething, greasy-haired reporters hunch over their telephones and laptops, blotting out everything around them and pounding away at one story or another. No one looks up when people pass by. No one registers any reaction. That's the way I used to be, completely absorbed in whatever assignment I was working on, jaws clenched in concentration. I wonder if I can even do that anymore. I approach the assistant Metro editor's office and knock. God, is she ever young. She can't be more than twenty-five and she seems vaguely distracted. Her only redeeming feature is that she's fat. She greets me the way you would greet a bad blind date, trying to be polite but keeping it as short as possible. I give her my résumé. She barely glances at it.

Her office is a pretty good size but the air is close and stuffy, the window firmly shut. There's a half-eaten piece of pastry smeared on a napkin by the phone, a couple of empty, dirty coffee cups with lipstick stains on the rims, and picked-through copies of the *New York Times* and the *Wall Street Journal* strewn in a messy pile on the floor. Well, she's an editor.

I'm always amazed when people describe this job as

glamorous. It's not. It's a job in an office. You eat, you talk on the phone, you read, you make decisions. You rarely meet anybody except for other editors and reporters. And you don't even get to go to fun events. There are rewards, naturally. But they are mostly internal and abstract. Like in any art, I suppose. And the pace is relentless—a constant struggle to stay hot and new and on top of everything all the time. The whole process can drive you nuts if you let it. I guess that's why this woman's here. She seems all business and boy, is she a grump.

She looks at me skeptically and scowls. "So, you worked here. When? Seven years ago?" The scourge of irrelevance clings to me like flakes of dandruff.

"Well, almost." Might as well be twenty. She's waiting for more. What to say? Do I tell her the truth? That the *Times* was my dream job. That I'd just had an enormous run of luck—a few breaking stories had attracted attention, one of which culminated in the resignation of some key figures in the mayor's office. That the senior editor had called me in and given me a plum beat. That I felt privileged, part of the inner circle. And that when my father became ill, I left abruptly and then failed to return.

My mother proved incapable of caring for him. Just changing a dressing or giving him his medication on time was more than she could handle. She'd disappear for hours at a time and when she returned, drifting in, a cloud of cashmere, her cheeks flushed with the cold and the booze, she'd attempt a conversation, a few inquiries into his health. Then she'd fall asleep on the living room sofa, the lights blazing, her reading glasses halfway down her nose and a book perched precariously on her lap.

My sister was newly married and Andy had just accepted a position at UCLA. My father would've never asked Virginia to leave her husband to care for him. But I was single, my job was expendable, and he didn't protest when I told him I was moving home to help. Regardless, I wanted to be with him. Palmer was very understanding. We hadn't been dating that long.

I drove my father to his office every day until he was too sick to continue. Then I cared for him until the end. He never asked me about my job or if I missed it, and I never brought it up.

After he died, months later, when my sister and I were cleaning out his old mahogany desk, I found a blue file folder labeled "Dora." It was filled with every article I'd ever written, neatly cut out with the date printed in blue ink on top. As far as I knew, he didn't even have a subscription to the *Times*. He must have bought it at the newsstand near his office, which sold out-of-state papers and magazines.

When I close my eyes, I can still see him in his prime, roaring into the living room, fresh from the office, wearing his dark pin-striped suit despite the September heat, regaling us with his adventures in the fabric trade, making the intricacies of his business sound as intriguing as national security. And then I see him frail, giving me a soft smile as I helped him into his office building. I feel tears welling up inside of me and I want him back, robust, handsome, looking at me expectantly, waiting for my answers.

"So, the reasons you left?" I look at this girl who is impatiently fidgeting with the papers on her desk, spraying her glasses with a pocket-size bottle of Optimetrix lens cleaner and swiping them with a miniature chamois. Her cell phone rings and she holds up her finger like "this will just be a minute" and then proceeds to have a five-minute conversation while I am sitting immobile staring at her. She hangs up. "Sorry, what were you saying?"

"I had some opportunities in Philadelphia, so I moved back for a year," I answer. Now she's meticulously cleaning her keyboard with a small paintbrush. How rude. Wouldn't it be great if some disgruntled employee burst through the door with a gun and blew her head off? *Pow!* What a satisfying vision. The only one who would be disappointed would be her twin sister, the hunchback.

And when she asks what I've been doing since then, a fine film of perspiration collects on my upper lip. What *have* I been doing for the past five years, that's a good question. I had rehearsed what I thought was a reasonable answer, but it now sounds lame and unprofessional, nothing that a twenty-five-year-old hotshot would understand. Telling her I got married was my first mistake, the nagging banality of becoming just another housewife in a ho-hum marriage. It went downhill from there. It was all blah, blah, blah, I did volunteer work, yadda, yadda, yadda, I set up my husband's office, blah, blah, blah. Just as I'm about to roll into what made me such a good reporter, she looks at her watch and says, "Well, I'll get back to you soon."

I want to bolt but I compose myself, acting as though it's been a thoroughly pleasant meeting, and make my way to the elevator. What would make her want to hire me? Anything? Okay, let's be fair about this. I screwed up. I should have told her right away about my journalistic awards. I should have offered to freelance, I should have taken it upon myself to tell her about some of my more interesting angles on a run-of-the-mill news story. My forte was finding an unusual slant and running with it. The editors I worked with liked that. She might have liked that too, if I had bothered to tell her. Which I didn't. I got nervous and went on too long about stupid stuff, which she clearly had no interest in. This just confirms my theory that things usually wind up worse than you expect them to be.

I decide to see if my old friend Brooke is still working in Style. She was an assistant editor when I left and even though we haven't kept in touch, I know she'll be happy to see me.

The Style section has an entirely different feel than downstairs. Still the cubicles and concentrated energy, but there are metal racks of designer samples blocking the aisles, boxes of shoes and bags stacked along the hallways, artsy fashion black-and-white blowups covering the walls. I find Brooke on the phone arguing with an editor. She's beginning to get that overworked, harried look that creeps up on you if you don't watch it. She slams down the receiver. "What a jerk!" she mutters, then sees me and smiles.

"Hey! What are you doing here, girl? God, you look so elegant. How are you? Let's go outside for a smoke."

We walk around to the back of the building and Brooke lights up. I'd forgotten about the smoking. It's been years since I've been around people that smoked. In West L.A. you're considered a pariah if you smoke. People look at you like you're killing them and there's this immediate hostile reaction that's akin to road rage. But like most people under thirty, Brooke is oblivious to all this, and I sit there inhaling her smoke while I tell her my story.

"I'm trying to maybe go back to work because I'm separated and I'm kind of at odds, but not really."

"God, Dora, I'm sorry to hear that, but why would you want to come back here?" she says with obvious reference to that phone call. "Honestly, I know it sounds strange but I think I get more and more antisocial every year. I'm even beginning to dread interviewing people about their problems," she confessed, adding that she spends her weekends meditating with a yogi and staying away from crowds.

"I just realized one day that I could care less what sources have to tell me for these stories and when they call me back to elaborate or give me more quotes I find it so annoying. Pretty grim, hey, for someone in the news business."

I feel better talking to her. The old misery-loves-company axiom, but I still know that, in my heart, I would trade places with her in a minute.

She can tell I'm discouraged. "Listen, Dora, if you really want to come back, I'll talk to Eddie, who still has a lot of clout around here, and I know he always liked you. In fact, why didn't you go to see him?"

I tell her that his office had sent me to that editor in Metro who couldn't wait to get rid of me.

"You mean Miss Piggy? Everyone hates her. She's so rude. Don't worry about it. Maybe it's the air in her office. It's suffocating. Do you still have a copy of your résumé? I'll make some calls, okay?"

As I walk out, I remember how I used to feel a combination of pity and disdain when older writers tried to make a comeback. Being in your thirties is not that old, but in the news business it might as well be. And now here I am trying to do something with my life and ending up exactly where I thought I would end up, which is why I dreaded doing this in the first place.

Stray Dogs and Other Companions

"Classic. A book which people praise and don't read."
~ Mark Twain (1835–1910) ~

I drive back to Brentwood in a brooding funk. For the first few miles or so, I work myself into a hyped-up, articulate rant in which my imaginary retorts to Miss Piggy are so blunt and uncomplimentary that I end up getting into terrible trouble. Daggers start flying across her office and, well, you get the picture. Some things are better left unsaid. Then again, some things aren't. Why IS it that I always think of the perfect thing to say when it's too late? Like with Fred. There I go again. I've got to stop massaging to death that pathetic scenario in the bookstore.

I cruise down the street just beyond Chinatown and

turn on the radio. It's daylight but the streets have a deserted, menacing quality about them that prompts me to lock my doors. If I could navigate the freeways, this wouldn't be an issue. When I was a reporter, I'd drive around the neighborhood with a brazen, no-problem attitude, filing stories in an urban sprawl where whites, Latinos, blacks, Middle Easterners, and Asians all live in separate neighborhoods. The melting pot doesn't exist in this town—people stay in their cars, shielded by metal and tinted glass.

I decide to call Darlene. I don't feel like going home and dwelling on my failures. Or, for that matter, having to give Virginia an upbeat, bullshit report.

Darlene is happy to hear from me, the way she always is, and my mood starts to brighten.

"Hey, you," she croons. "Where are you?"

"I'm in our old stomping grounds, near the *Times*."

"Oh god. Don't remind me. How did the interview go?"

"Terrific. You want to have lunch?"

"I'd love to. I knew you'd do great. You're so amazing. Good for you."

"Great."

Darlene doesn't fit in with my other friends, nor would she want to. They think she's low-rent and bonkers and she thinks they're shallow and spoiled. They're both right. My time with her is a welcome respite from the insular life in West Los Angeles. She is the only one of my friends who doesn't have any credit cards and still doesn't own a cell phone. Also, Darlene rarely buys books. She goes to the Malibu library to check out her trashy sci-fi fantasies and romances, which she's always trying to get me to read.

We normally spend most of our time discussing her newest failed romance or her latest harebrained scheme to make money. This afternoon, it's a do-it-yourself pre-fab "Charming Swiss Chalet" kit, which she's ordered sight unseen from a catalog and which she's going to build in Big Bear, a mountain resort ninety miles from L.A.—the white trash version of Arrowhead. Darlene has vacationed in Big Bear for as long as I can remember, and the first and last time I accompanied her there we stayed in her friend's ramshackle, dingy A-frame house by the lake. It was dark and dank, furnished in early kitsch mountain resort with seventies fake wood panel-ing, a thick, mustard-yellow multicolored shag rug that smelled faintly of mildew, and enough water damage to lead me to believe this was not a good place to be in a rainstorm. The walls were covered with homey sayings in needlepoint, like "There's no place like fucking home" and "Hello, where's the beer?" and there was a cramped, cluttered kitchen with ancient windows that spewed shards of paint flakes when you tried to open them.

The house was located in the kind of bedraggled mountain neighborhood where there were no sidewalks and people's lawns were cluttered with rusted swing sets, mattresses with springs poking through, Big Wheels, firewood, tires, and other junk that usually is hidden away in garages. Her next-door neighbor had an enor-mous RV parked on the lawn that was painted an alarm-ing shade of teal and had blotches of seascapes and seals camouflaging a fading paint job. Our morning walks along weed-lined streets ended up on the main drag where we'd get breakfast at a diner connected to a Gas-and-Shop and watch the kids in the back make gray slushy snowballs. The area had its share of beer-bellied bikers and scuzzy, scratch-assed locals who were still lit at nine a.m. when we'd order our eggs and juice. There is something depressing about a place where life just doesn't shape up.

I meet her on the beach outside her apartment build-ing, which is advertised as ocean view, but can only be called ocean view if you stand in a corner and look over her neighbor's garage. Her unit is a one bedroom that faces the street, and whenever I duck in there to use the bathroom, it's always cluttered with catalogs and para-phernalia from her latest project. Right now the apart-ment contains sample light fixtures and synthetic rug swatches, not to mention undecipherable blueprints that apparently came with the chalet-building kit.

Last year, Darlene supposedly made a bundle selling porno vampire-themed movie posters over the Internet. She mentioned it a few times, but I always changed the subject. Too weird. In addition, there's her dog, Brawley, an overweight Rottweiler, who always rushes me for at-tention or a walk. Darlene only walks him at dawn or at dusk because the dog regularly pees on people instead of the usual lampposts or hydrants.

A few years ago, Darlene underwent a life crisis. Her husband, Mel, got hit by the proverbial lightning bolt one day at the precinct when he first spotted Detective

Maria Gonzales, a member of the Bicycle Co-ordination Unit (BCU) of the Venice Beach Patrol. She was raven-haired, perky, and ambitious, with killer calves. She had an AA degree from Antelope Valley College in Lancaster, north of L.A., and was in line for a promotion to the central bureau. She had her eye on Mel from the moment she met him as he was racing down the stairs to assist her with a homeless drunk perp who was feeling her up as she was taking him down. She was sweet and bubbly to Mel and a bitch to everyone else.

Mel and Darlene were about to celebrate their tenth wedding anniversary when he announced he'd fallen for someone else. "I felt as if my body was taking a punch," she told me. She begged him to stay, told him she'd change. All to no avail. There was a period of emotional wrangling, but he was out of there by Christmas.

Darlene went into a funk, which lasted six months. Classifieds gave her too much empty time to think, so she quit her job at the *Times* and through a friend of a friend got into the Teamsters, where she is now a driver for the studios. During this period, she met me for a drink a couple of times a week and cried in her beer. The Teamster job is great for her. She went from "Please come back" to "Drop dead." The pay is terrific and she gets to drive the stars around. But both of us know that, deep down, she'd return it all to have Mel back again.

On her last job, she drove a famous male action star, and Darlene was flattered instead of insulted when he greeted her every morning with "nice tits." She's one of the few people who knows My Big Freeway Secret.

Sometimes when I'm desperate and she's not working, she'll offer to be my driver. She's given me several freeway lessons, which have all ended disastrously. The last one we just said "Fuck it," and ended up in some bar off the 405 swilling beer and laughing uproariously.

That's the thing about Darlene. She thinks the best of everyone. In fact, I've never heard her say a bad word about anyone. She's still best friends with Mel and I hear that Detective Gonzales is long gone—maybe at some point she and Mel will get back together. At the moment, she likes cute, young guys she meets at Hollywood clubs who are totally inappropriate for her. I'm hoping it's a passing phase, because inevitably she gets jilted, not to mention the danger factor. Currently, she's still mooning over her latest disaster.

"He was so gorgeous and awesome Saturday night. He loved my outfit—you know, that yellow miniskirt. But he hasn't called since he left Sunday morning. I just can't believe he hasn't called me."

"You pick him up in a bar. You bring him home. He hasn't called? You're lucky you're alive."

"Oh, Dora. You don't understand. He really liked me."

I always try to be kind when we get to this point in the conversation, and there is just no good way to say it. She's almost forty. They're twenty-five. They like her in the nightclub lights and they come to their senses in the morning. But why bother trying to tell her this. "Darlene, maybe he has a girlfriend and thought better of it the next day. Why can't you just give someone your own age a chance?"

"You know I don't like older men, Dora. I don't find them attractive. They're so uncool. I'd rather just have moments with someone I'm into than a long, drawn-out relationship with someone who leaves me cold. Anyway, I don't need a man to support me. I'm just fine the way I am."

"That's not the point. It's nice to have someone to come home to."

"I could say the same thing to you, Dora."

"Okay. Forget it."

We decide to drive back into town, stopping by McKenzie's first because Darlene wants to get another one of her dumb fantasies that the library doesn't carry.

I debate whether to tell her anything about Fred. She'd be too enthusiastic, too encouraging, the exact opposite of everyone else in my life. So I say nothing. Really, there is nothing to say anyway.

As soon as we walk into the place, Darlene starts bitching about how expensive all the books are and that anyone knows you can go to Costco and get the same books a lot cheaper. I immediately look around to see if Fred is nearby and if anyone has overheard. Fred is, in fact, across the room helping a flirtatious woman with a book club selection.

Frankly, I'm not a huge fan of this whole phenomenon of book clubs, although the concept is appealing—deep and incisive conversations on the merits of a certain turn of a phrase or an unexpected plot twist. But nobody I know reads the same books I do. They read self-helps and thrillers and bios of movie stars. There's no end to the crap that's around. This same crap is made into movies and pretty soon they won't even read the crap anymore. So joining one of my friends' book clubs is out.

I have this fantasy book club in my mind where other people feel as passionately as I do about reading. As if it were a really good kiss. The sheer pleasure and intimacy of having a relationship with a novelist and all the characters is transcendent—even sensual. Certain passages keep resonating in my head long after I've closed the book, and I often can't wait to get back to the story, as if it were a secret lover.

When I tell Virginia this, she thinks it's all too extreme. She reads, she tells me, to find out what happens. And she doesn't get half as caught up with the language and the stories behind the stories.

But for me, reading is so much more. Books teach you how other people think, and what they're feeling, and how they change from ordinary beings to extraordinary ones. Often they are so appealing and intelligent, you'd rather spend time reading about them than doing anything else.

And unlike life, if you don't like what you're reading, you can slam the book shut and then . . . peace. That friendly, cajoling voice is cut off until you decide to open the book again. Which is why I may not be the best candidate for book clubs. I like to read on my own terms, in my own time. And the same goes for in-depth discussions. I'm just too opinionated and outspoken. I'd alienate everyone in the room. No one would like me. They'd kick me out.

My least favorite time to discuss books is on vacation.

Why is it when you are lazing by a pool, in the middle of a tropical paradise, and enjoying your solitude with a great book, someone inevitably has the urge to break into your reverie with "Is that any good? What's it about?" My inclination is to stalk off, but I give them an uninviting smile and tell them I just started it even if I'm halfway through.

It all reminds me of the time Palmer and I were lounging by the pool in Cabo and spied a couple on the other side reading, sort of, while they lunched and snoozed. When they left to go talk to another couple, Palmer casually walked over to the empty chairs and moved the man's bookmark about fifty pages or so backward.

"Ha ha," I whispered, "very funny." But when they got back, the man settled happily in his chair and resumed reading as if it were right where he left off. Palmer kept nudging me and winking. I miss those things about him.

When Palmer and I first started dating we used to joke about the unspoken hierarchy of readers and the private way in which they tackle a book. At the top of the heap are the purists—people who read to soak up the elegantly constructed literary style and savor the brilliant metaphors, inventive characters, breathtaking imagery, and sparkling dialogue. The story is beside the point. I had a lit prof once who preached that one should always read the end of a novel first so the plot won't be a distraction.

Not far behind are the academics—readers who never quite got over how they read a book in their freshman English class, underlining or highlighting, turning down pages, looking up words they're not familiar with, and scribbling pithy comments in the margins.

The book worshipers come next. They keep their books covered (and not because they're romance novels), use bookmarks, and absolutely never let the book touch the floor. They look at the book as a sentient being, a living, breathing object of desire that needs to be treated with absolute respect. They read every word, even the footnotes.

Then there are the readers who just want a good old-fashioned story and make no bones about it. They skip over long descriptive passages, skim though digressions, and zero in on who, what, and where to the nth degree. A subcategory of this is people who read books for sex, violence, or any other particular proclivity, and speed-read passages that don't interest them.

Or how about the multitask readers, those who read while cooking, cleaning, talking on the phone, or driving. Which is stupid—not that I haven't done it.

The bottom-feeders come next and include the status readers, a group of wannabes who don't really want to read the book at all but want to be seen with it, like arm candy, the proverbial young blonde on the arm of a tycoon. They skim the book for plot and carry it around like a designer bag. Even worse are the people who listen to audio books, the new version of condensed books, or read novelizations of current movies. These people consider themselves readers, but they're not. What's most annoying is when they join in a conversation and act as though they've actually read it. I group the narcoleptic readers in this nonreader category. People who use books as Ambien and have had the same book sitting on their bedside table for the last six months. Also the bathroom readers—you know, the ones with the magazine racks near their toilets that hold old *New Yorkers*, *Chicken Soup for the Soul* books, and dog-eared collections of dirty jokes. I have never personally engaged in this activity because my mother insists that it gives you hemorrhoids. And who would want THAT?

Then there are the readers who like to hang out in bookstore cafés nursing tepid cappuccinos, hogging the table for hours while they leisurely read unpurchased books, leaving them in piles on the table for the salespeople to put away.

And let's not forget the hopeless unfinishers—people who like choosing books, buying books, starting books, but the one thing they can't seem to do is finish books. They continually deceive themselves, thinking this is the one book they are going to read all the way through, and I do think they are well-intentioned, but like diets and New Year's resolutions, the will to persevere usually fades. I must confess that sometimes I fall into this category.

The most frustrating category of all includes people who read a book and just don't get it. I know, I'm a snob. I admit it. But once they tell you their analysis, there is really nothing you can do except change the subject. A few years ago, one of my good friends read *Atonement* and told me how much she loved it. When I casually mentioned that most of the action in the book took place in the mind of Briony, she was at first surprised, and then bereft at her lack of comprehension. I hate when I do that.

Palmer used to tell me that I was my own worst enemy, grouping people in clichéd categories and never giving anyone a chance. He argued that the only people I could tolerate were "stray dogs," like Darlene, who are so far outside the mainstream as to be unclassifiable and thus interesting only to me. He'd sometimes add with an arched eyebrow, "Is there any place in your world, Dora, for the nonweird?"

I look around. Fred is still dealing with the book-club lady when Darlene breezes past them and says, "How do you find anything in this place?" Sara appears and asks Darlene if she needs help.

Darlene is now looking for a vampire romance and Sara suggests Pam Keesey's collection of lesbian vampire stories. Sara goes on to explain that the women in these stories are sexy, potent symbols of feminist power but the X-rated dialogue and erotic rhetoric narrows their appeal to the general public. Darlene gives me a look that says it all and tells Sara, "Maybe just a Nora Roberts." As Sara turns to find her the books, Darlene does that sophisticated gesture of finger in a circle around her brain to suggest this girl's fucking nuts.

Meanwhile, I wander aimlessly down another aisle, wondering how to approach Fred, and start to read the off-the-wall reviews attached to McKenzie's Staff Picks of the Week books. The one attached to Jorge Luis Borges's short stories reads, "A romantic mama's boy collection of enigmatic parables." There's also an assortment of books by Graham Greene, who is this month's featured author. The note on *The End of the Affair* is a winner: "Here's a blatant, chauvinistic take on a tortured love affair by a famous philandering, superstitious atheist."

"I didn't write that," Fred says from somewhere behind me in a dusky voice.

"That's good," I laugh, "because it doesn't exactly make me want to read it. Anyway, I've already seen the movie so I know how it all comes out." (Great, now talk about the movie when I've actually read the book three times. That'll impress him.)

"Any other suggestions?" I ask casually. "How about something pithy I can read at two in the morning?"

He looks at me with a sly grin. "Give me a few minutes to think about it."

"Sure," I counter, but he's already walked off.

I see him conferring with the other employees and I strain to hear what they are saying. The last few times I stopped in here I noticed I was eavesdropping on his conversations. He always has something interesting, even provocative, to say and the banter back and forth makes my day. Occasionally the whole bunch of them will exchange hyperintellectual in-jokes and it's at that point that I think to myself, "Geez, do people actually talk like that?" They'll collapse into gales of laughter and I feel like someone seated at the wrong table at a dinner party.

The other day they were talking about the French novelist Georges Perec, who wrote a postmodern mystery filled with literary puzzles and wordplay. The idea is to figure out why the main character, Anton Vowl, has disappeared along with the letter *e*. The *e*-less book is called *La Disparition* and there is no "here" or "there," no "sleep," no "sex," no "love," no "life." I guess you could substitute words like fornication and copulation, but somehow it's just not the same. If this wasn't insanely esoteric enough, they then gushed over Perec's most well-known classic (right!), *Life: A User's Manual*. At first I thought it was one of those self-help, rehab books. But no. It's a book that takes the blueprints of a Paris apartment building, cuts it into a grid that represents a hundred different rooms, and elaborates on one room per chapter, portraying the events that take place there. The game goes on because this, in turn, corresponds to a hypothetical chessboard. Alas, Perec only gets to the ninety-ninth floor/square/chapter because, as one of the kids joyfully points out, this is an unsuccessful quest for perfection. And, like the knight's tour, it is naturally doomed for failure.

It's at this point I'm thinking, "Gee, why don't they all just read Cervantes' *Don Quixote* (with an *e*) if they want a simple but brilliant tale about a delusional knight on a hapless quest?" I'm also thinking that kids in the chess club should never mix with English lit students.

They went on to discuss the relative merits of Henry Miller's *Tropic of Cancer* and *Tropic of Capricorn,* and the trilogy about his life, *The Rosy Crucifixion.* Fred said he liked the trilogy best because it's all about Miller's debaucherous, bohemian, absolutely beat-ass lifestyle, but one of the girls sneered that Miller was just another dirty writer who used women for personal indulgence and literary material. The only thing I remember about Henry Miller was flipping through the chapters looking for sex. Isn't that what everyone did?

There's a fine line between interesting literary discussions and pompous bullshit. It's one of those areas where you're either fascinated with what someone has to say or you feel that if they don't shut the hell up that instant you're going to blow their brains out.

It's fitting that when I'm busy thinking about all this, a man dressed in a white silk T-shirt, Armani jeans, and three-thousand-dollar crocodile loafers (which he wears like bedroom slippers, crushing the backs) approaches Fred and pronounces triumphantly that he has finally polished off the Brits and is "doing" the Russians.

"And just which Russians have you been doing?" Fred answers as he looks in my direction. I know that he's really talking to me, and as the customer starts rattling off a syllabus of long Russian names ending in "sky" and "kov," Fred takes my arm and leads me to another aisle.

"Excuse me, I'll be back in a minute," he tells him. "Jesus, this guy is such a pain," Fred whispers. The man peers around the corner, looking impatient and a bit suspicious.

"Is there anything else I can find for you?" Fred asks me, hoping to keep the guy at bay.

I'm beginning to enjoy the game. "My sunglasses, the black cashmere sweater I left in the restaurant the other night, and the key to the trunk of my car, which I haven't been able to open in three months."

Fred's eyes start to sparkle. The Russian is still hovering. Fred leans into me and says, "How about *Anna Karenina*? There's a new translation over here. Terrific story. The plot's a grabber from the first page. Beautiful insatiable drama queen, marries a loser, hooks up with another loser, falls into ruin, confesses all, flees to Italy with her lover. Who can blame them? I don't want to give away too much." He hands me the novel and winks.

I wink back. "Thanks. I've read it. Great story, though. Sex, lies, infidelity. Sounds like my neighborhood." Fred gives me a good long look as the czarist finally snaps and lumbers over. I hand him back the Tolstoy and just as he is about to say more, Darlene comes up behind me and declares, "I'm starved. Let's go." She's obviously been listening to our conversation and in her dingbat mode suggests, "Gee, Dora, maybe you two can have a drink sometime and talk about it."

Fred flashes one of those amused half-smiles as he looks Darlene over. I know what he's thinking. Not your typical Brentwood housewife. Darlene happens to be wearing a pair of jeans with enormous embroidered bells and a tight T-shirt that says "Angel." Her long blonde hair is even more in need of a dye job than usual. I'm mortified and quickly gather my things to leave. Darlene jabs me with her elbow, and nods in Fred's direction.

"Killer smile," she says in a too-loud voice.

I push her out the door.

"Well, that was fun," Darlene says as we walk to the parking lot. "I think he likes you."

Ivanhoe

> "I think reading a novel is almost next
> best to having something to do."
>
> ~ Margaret Oliphant, Scottish novelist (1827–1897) ~

When an invitation says "festive attire" I am always stumped. What is festive, anyway? Is it about color or mood? My mood is "I don't want to go," so I figure I'll focus on color. I swipe at the clothes lined up in my closet. Grim, grim, grim. I seem to have fallen into the Barneys all black, slightly black, or off-black lately. Nothing festive about that. So I throw on my little black Dolce and add a pilled pink cashmere sweater. That's the festive part.

This is the L.A. Public Library's main fundraiser, not as chic as its New York sister, but just as grandiloquent. My old college roommate, Pamela, is running the show and I'm at her table. The event is held in the elaborate rotunda of the downtown Central Library, a grand old edifice with stately domed ceilings, Italian marble floors, and two-thousand-pound chandeliers, built eighty years ago when libraries were as honored as places of worship and downtown L.A. was still considered center city.

The rotunda is turned into a ballroom befitting a movie set. Elaborate tables are scattered around, covered with twelve layers of linens, enough silver for the duke of Windsor, and an amazing array of crystal. Violinists stroll through the crowd, playing music so patently corny that it reminds me of music last heard at Dome of the Sea, a tacky restaurant in Las Vegas that features strolling Venetian violinists. I scan the crowd, trying to find Pamela. It seems that at this event "festive" means Chanel jackets, Chanel suits, and Chanel handbags. The library has turned into a trunk show. She'll fit right in.

"Finally, you're here." I knew Pamela would point out that I was late.

Pamela is my age but is married to a retired real estate magnate in his seventies. She always wears a nubby tweed Chanel something and I'm always nagging her to put on some weight.

Then there's her six-year-old daughter, Madison. Pamela is obsessed with her. I continually have to endure every brilliant pearl that falls from her daughter's lips, every nuance, every sneeze. So many women fall into this trap and end up boring everyone to death with details that parents should keep to themselves. It's almost as if parenthood sucks up every available brain cell, and like the canary, whose brain cells regenerate every year, all previous data is erased forever and all you hear is this year's song. I read about a scientist in Upstate New York who keeps thousands of canaries in an aviary behind his house and slaughters hundreds of them semiannually to study their brains. Not that I am recommending that or anything, but people do tend to get single-minded after they have children. And it only gets worse. You go from sleeping problems to potty training to preschool, prep school, adolescent angst, tattoos and piercings. Then they start boring you with their child's first fabulous internship or job and how brilliant little Johnny is and how everyone loves him at the office. It's all so predictable and tiresome. Even if you like the person, and I do like Pamela, there is only so much of this you can take before you want to throttle them. I usually tell my sister when I've heard enough about Camille, but I don't want to hurt Pamela's feelings.

"Dora, are you listening to me?" I guess I zoned out. She is pointing to our table. The hook for this event is that every guest gets to sit with an author, who is usually promoting their latest book. The authors love it. Free trip to L.A. And the patrons love it because they get to have a semi-intimate conversation with semi-important authors. I notice that another friend of ours and her husband are seated in Siberia behind a pillar. Their author, a musicologist from Columbia University, is seated at the other end of the long narrow table. I can see even from this vantage that my friend is clenching her jaw and her husband is staring out into space. Pamela will hear about this tomorrow. The A-list authors such as David Halberstam, Scott Berg, and Frank McCourt are seated up front. I walk over to my table. Since Pamela is on the dinner committee, I thought I'd get someone interesting. Unfortunately, my author is a San Francisco gynecologist who sometimes hosts the "Your Health" segment of the nightly news. Pamela has also put the requisite single guy at our table to "balance it out."

This man is a fairly well-known television agent with bulging eyes and a thinning crown of hair. He also has one of those barrel-waisted bodies with thin, spindly legs, a birdlike affliction that affects so many sedentary, high-powered urban men and makes them look like Armani-clad pregnant chickens. He is also a good twenty years older than I am. Of course. I knew it. I knew they'd stick me next to someone like this. I can just hear Pamela now: *Oh, Dora, you have so much in common. You both like books. You both like the theater.* Meanwhile, he asked for Perrier. He doesn't drink. What a bore. When the salad arrives, he asks for it with the dressing on the side. I hate when people do that. Oh no. Here it comes. The South Beach Diet. Save me. I'm glad I didn't waste my new Prada jacket on this dud of an event. Now the agent is launching into an endless discussion concerning the SAG retirement plan, which interests the gyno, and the two of them then get into a serious discussion about the state of off-network shows, particularly those concerning bodily functions. I sip my wine. It's not great but it's getting better.

Just as the beef tenderloin with risotto cakes is being

served, I notice Palmer and his girlfriend seated at one of the A-tables on the other side of the podium. How could I have missed him? But I forget, he usually strolls into an event just as everyone is being seated. He catches my eye and waves. Oh Christ, he's pushing out his chair. Dammit, I'm not in the mood to deal with this now. Palmer leans over Kimberly's shoulder, sweeps back a frosted blonde tress, and whispers in her ear. I see her squeeze his hand in an annoying, knowing sort of way and then I am sure of it. He's coming over here to fulfill a social obligation or, maybe, pay his respects as if I were his dowager aunt. I watch him walk across the room. There is this wealthy, sunny sparkle to his demeanor that I remember admiring when I first met him. He's wearing an expensive, imported, impeccably tailored tuxedo with a trendy white pleated shirt, the kind that the young male turks of Hollywood wear to the Oscars and that require no bow tie. I'm certain that she picked it out for him. His sandy, gray-flecked hair is longer than I remember, and he has onyx-and-diamond studs and matching cuff links. He looks tall and victorious, moving with the graceful stride of a man who no longer has to worry about success or status. He stares straight at me with a kind of quiet resolve while the rest of the room stares at him.

"Dora, you look terrific."

"So do you, Palmer," I say, and I mean it.

He has a bemused smile, taking in the various people at my table and making the obvious assessment. He raises his eyebrows. "Can I get any of you a drink? I'm on my way to the bar."

"I'm fine," I say, and then realize he's making an offer. "But I'll come with you if you'd like."

He takes my elbow and more or less escorts me out of the rotunda and into the vestibule, where there is a small bar set up. It's an odd feeling, me standing there with him, both of us all dressed up, calm and decorous, and making pleasant conversation that is completely unrelated to what I imagine either of us is thinking.

I flash on the night we met, an event much like this. I was busy interviewing someone when Palmer sent me a glass of champagne from across the room. The waiter pointed him out to me and we smiled. We ended up going to a late-night bar, discovered our favorite book was *Huck Finn,* and, well, I don't feel like going down memory lane right now.

One thing is clear. The quick, overbearing petulance is gone. So is the bitterness and disappointment. Palmer is back to his old enigmatic, charming, sexy self. And I realize that he couldn't have done it with me. It occurs to me that maybe, somehow, he's heard about my little clandestine visits to his house. But no, that's crazy, he couldn't possibly know. Could he?

"So, how've you been, Palmer?" I say, testing the waters, avoiding any physical contact.

"Fine. I've been thinking about you," he says with an endearing smile. He leans in close, planting his hand against the wall as if he is an officer detaining me for a sobriety check. I register a twinge of surprise and then start rambling on about some silly topic, anything to get past the moment. He stands there silently and then lightly touches my hair. "So, Dora, do you ever think of me?"

"Of course I do, Palmer," I say, consciously squelching the urge to make some nasty remark about the girlfriend. To be honest, I'm actually relieved. No, this is not a shakedown. But I don't want to get into what we really think about each other at the moment, not now, maybe never.

"Thank you," he says, suddenly serious. "I just wanted to tell you that I still care about you. I don't want us to be total strangers. Okay?"

"Okay," I say, unconvinced. Does he really want that or is he just being polite? Why is it that with some men, once the relationship is over, it's over, and with others, it leaves a trail of remorse, indecision, and endless fantasies of what could have been that plague you for years? It doesn't even have much to do with sex. I had a lover in college who set me on fire every time he touched me, but when his conversations started boring me, I cut it off with a single message on his answering machine. Palmer is different. All that promise and earnestness and undisputed intelligence. I should have been content. I should have been patient. I should have overlooked the fact that after we were married he was a lover who cared deeply about having me but seemed to care more about having a new car, a good address, a service for twelve, and a membership in a country club. I suddenly feel guilty and uncomfortable and cornered like a rat. In a trap.

"Call me sometime. At the office," he says abruptly.

"Okay, Palmer." I smile tightly. Like I'd really call him at home.

"By the way, how did you get down here?" he said. He *would* ask me that. He's also one of the few people who knows My Big Freeway Secret.

"I managed." (My version of "I called a car service.")

"That's my girl."

We finish our drinks and return to the ballroom like any complacent married couple taking a breather. He squeezes my shoulder as I turn my back on him and head to the table. The high-pitched din of the room jolts my nervous system like a car backfiring on the highway and I focus on half-eaten desserts, an array of cut-glass wine goblets, and women rummaging through their favor bags; the anticlimactic winding down of a long-anticipated event.

As I walk back to the table, I spy a woman I used to work with at the *Times*. She's married to a lawyer, has two angelic kids, and is now producing a hot new series on Fox. She sees me and says, "Hey, a blast from the past. How are you?"

How am I? I feel like a complete loser. "Just great. How are you?"

"Working like a maniac. Leaving for New York tomorrow."

"Really busy, huh?"

"Yeah. And they all shoot away from L.A. Lots of traveling right now. What are you up to?"

Spying on my husband, getting dumped on by a

twenty-five-year-old editor, OD'ing on books. "Oh, same old, same old."

"Well, you look great. Really. Take care." She gives me a sideways kiss and leaves. I pull my shoulders up into a rigid block and watch her walk off.

I reach our table, take a long swig of somebody's untouched wine, and make a big deal of looking at my watch. "Oh, I'm so sorry. I have a babysitter problem. I have to run." Pamela shoots me a look, and with a guilty wave, I make my escape.

Walking down the magnificent hallway, I pass a series of life-sized paintings illustrating Sir Walter Scott's story of *Ivanhoe,* depicting the days of romance and chivalry. Everything depresses me now.

● ● ●

I feel a rush of relief as I enter my apartment. I look at the clock; still relatively early considering I went all the way downtown and back. I rip off my clothes and throw on my favorite sweats, old faded Gap men's with a drawstring waist and a baggy bottom. I pad into the kitchen, open the fridge, and grab a half-filled bottle of something—what is this? Sherry? Where did I get it? Must have been a Christmas gift. This is something you give to old people. Uh-oh. I hate when I start feeling over the hill. How old was Kimberly, anyway? She had that youthful glow that makes me crazy. I wonder what they're doing right now. Oh, it IS only nine thirty, they're probably still there. Although Palmer does like to cut out early. When we were dating, we actually devised our own rules for ducking out—that "never before the cake thing" ... gone. I need something stronger. I pour myself a shot of vodka. I was so tense with Palmer I don't remember drinking anything at all.

What was up with him, anyway? I don't know what to think of our conversation. I pick up Flaubert. *Madame Bovary* is in vogue these days, but at the moment, I am plowing through *Sentimental Education* because I heard a critic on NPR say that the book exposes all the hollowness and fragility of youthful ideals and is an insidious devaluation of the power of love. Naturally I ran right out and got it. I get a rush these days from the inevitable pitfalls of the human condition. Here we go. A young man's passion for an older woman that goes on and on and on until the penultimate reunion at the end with the white-haired Madame Arnoux. Oh god. I can't take it. I'm beat.

Palmer did look exceptionally attractive tonight. He looked like he was having fun. He always looked like he was having fun. That was part of my initial attraction to him. That, and the fact that he made me feel like I was the only one. When did he stop making me feel that way? Maybe when his career blasted into the stratosphere. Suddenly, it was a whole new world, cluttered with social obligations, speaking engagements, weekend business trips, and long absences.

It all worked for Palmer, the new house, the decorators, the social secretary, the lingering effect he had on people, especially women, when he entered a room. I was happy for him. I just couldn't figure out where I fit in. The more Palmer was away (and he was away a lot) the more I felt left behind. A therapist once asked me if it was the same way I felt when my father left home and my mother dissolved into dust. I don't know. I just couldn't snap out of it. The whole thing left Palmer baffled.

To make matters worse, Palmer started in with the "wouldn't it be great to start a family" thing. That frightened me. Another absentee father? I don't think so.

In the beginning, Palmer said he respected my feelings and he could wait. Just how long was never specified, although I somehow knew it had nothing to do with my biological clock. As far as I could tell, I didn't have one. Why I didn't was a different matter, which Palmer eventually felt compelled to bring up whenever we'd have an argument about something else. The resulting interval of tense noncommunication would go on for at least two or three days, and the more he brought it up, the angrier I got.

When I look back, I'm sorry I didn't realize how ambivalent and conflicted I was about having children and even sorrier I didn't share those fears with Palmer. What I had observed from my childhood only confirmed my disheartening belief that happiness is unattainable within a traditional family.

I put off the inevitable for months before Palmer finally took the lead and announced that he was leaving. By this time, we both wanted out. "The terrible thing is," he said, "I would stay, if you gave me just the slightest bit of encouragement or hope. I suppose I could go on like this forever." But, of course, he couldn't. And then he met Kimberly. There had been no other emotional outburst on either side. In the end, I was the one to move out. I didn't feel right keeping anything that Palmer and I had acquired together. I knew what it meant to him and it meant nothing to me.

Now it's two a.m. When I was married to Palmer, this was the hour when he would stir and then I would stir, then he'd turn over and I'd turn over, and we'd settle into a comforting embrace where our bodies fit together like pieces of a puzzle. That I do miss.

The Beauty Thing

"Was this the face that launched a thousand ships?"
~ Christopher Marlowe (1564–1593), *Dr. Faustus* ~

In West L.A., as one closes in on forty, and by that I mean thirty, one feels compelled to start having "consultations" and a few little "procedures" (they're never called surgeries) in order to avoid the big one, which women always end up doing anyway. My appointment has been scheduled for several weeks, ever since I scrutinized the monotonous perfection of a gamine young actress on some talk show, swearing she never had anything done, and knowing the doctor who did it.

I am ushered into Dr. H.'s consultation room by a slim, overly solicitous Asian man in his early twenties. The room is stark white with an oversized leather dentist's chair in the middle and nothing else except a little stool placed directly in front of it. I sit in the large chair and wait. This is the only doctor's office that has brand-new magazines, usually *Vogue* and *Bazaar,* along with *Variety* and *Entertainment Weekly.* Dr. H. breezes in about fifteen minutes later with a white coat over his khakis, a white dress shirt, and one of those miner's lights wrapped around his forehead. He's handsome, soft-spoken, about fifty, and acts as if he has all the time in the world to just stare at my face. Women uniformly rave about what a nice man he is.

I start the conversation a bit tentatively, trying very hard not to stare directly into his face, but he IS sitting smack in front of me and there really isn't anyplace else to look. "I'm here because I hate my neck and I'm in my thirties. I'm not getting any younger, lord knows, so I wanted to know what you think about the possibility of maybe, well, you know, doing some sort of a lift. I've had, oh gosh, what's the name of that filler?"

"Collagen?" he says.

"No, it's like that, but . . ."

"Restylane?"

"No, not that, although I did try that and it was painful and didn't even last. . . ."

"Fascia? Perlane? Radiance? CosmoPlast?"

"That's it. CosmoPlast. But it's so expensive, and lately, even that doesn't do the trick. You know what I mean."

He takes a small pair of silver tweezers out of his pocket and hands me a mirror so I can see my face. He lifts some skin I didn't know I had from my upper eyelid. "We could get rid of this excess skin and then you'd look younger and fresher." Meaning, of course, that I look old and tired now. "This is the perfect age to start a program." He smiles. "I can't make you look twenty again, but we wouldn't want that anyway, would we?"

I hate it when doctors talk to you in that patronizing tone. Where do they learn this crap, from some half-baked bedside-manner medical finishing school?

I smile back at him and say, "Sounds great! I have a few more questions."

"Take all the time you need," he says. Wait! Are his hands shaking? I think his hands are shaking. Yes. They definitely are. He sees me furtively staring at them.

I want to say, Do you think you can make me beautiful, happy, meaningful, committed, and confident so that those episodes of self-doubt that now string together to form my days will be replaced by renewed aspirations and heart-stopping conviction? But instead I say, "Are your hands shaking?"

He smiles benevolently. "A little too much coffee." I guess.

Then there's always the obligatory consultation after the consultation. That's the one where you sit in a pleasant little office to talk over the cost with the doctor's assistant/girlfriend/ex-wife/sister, whatever. She has a perfect face and flawless complexion. The poster girl for the office. Why not? She gets every procedure for free. She acts like your big sister and smiles a lot. She explains a breakdown of costs and aftercare facilities, and then pulls out three big books of before and after pictures. All the women in the "before" pictures look like jowly old hound dogs as opposed to the "after" pictures, where they look serene, youthful, and tight.

"What date were you thinking of?" she asks, assuming this is a fait accompli.

I look at my empty calendar and say, "I've got a hectic few months, but March would be good." I've always thought March was a crap month. Nothing like the Ides of March for a face-lift.

"Well, our first opening is in April, but I'll put you on the wait-list for a cancellation." She hands me a folder full of legal documents that look suspiciously like a last will and testament. It is a business, after all.

You know, now that I think about it, this shaky hand thing bothers me a little. Maybe I'll call the next guy on my list. The one that Pamela says is so great.

What to do next? I'm feeling a little down and haggy. Too early to go home. I don't want another cappuccino. Maybe I'll walk over to Rodeo and check out the cruise line at Barneys. Cruise line, what an anachronism . . . conjures up images of Vuitton trunks and black tie dinners on yachts, when in reality it's just Disney at Sea.

The streets are crowded with tourists in pastels laden with digital cameras and shopping bags. I amble by the expertly dressed windows of Valentino, Dolce & Gabbana, Armani, and Prada. I had a dream once, as a child, that I was shopping with my mother on Madison Avenue at Christmastime. All of a sudden, the window displays started opening up onto the sidewalk and mannequins beckoned me like sirens to take whatever I wanted. Most children would have been terrified, but in my dream, I was overjoyed.

I told Palmer about this once and he said it was a deep-seated, latent shopaholic complex, and then he gave me a wicked smile.

I walk into Barneys and my salesgirl, Ellen, spots me across the room. She's in her early thirties, blonde, fifteen pounds overweight, and quite attractive. She lives in an apartment south of Wilshire with her mother, who is a school administrator. She greets me with a big smile.

"Did you get my message? I'm holding those shoes you looked at a few weeks ago. They're going on sale Thursday, 40 percent off."

"Gee, I'm not sure." I can't even remember them.

She presses on. "They are such gorgeous shoes. I just couldn't sell them to someone with cankles."

"Cankles?"

"You know, those cows whose ankles are the same size as their calves. Cankles."

It wasn't like Ellen to be this unkind. She'd better get out now before she turns into one of those resentful women who work in high-end stores from Rodeo to Madison and have nothing but disdain for their wealthy customers.

She brings out the shoes. Tall strappy plum sandals with jewels glistening across the metallic leather. $495 on sale for $300. A bargain.

"Do you want to take them home on approval?"

I feel cornered, so I tell her okay and take the sandals

I didn't like enough to buy retail, but maybe I'll like them better now.

What I usually end up doing on days like this is going on endless errands so that by five p.m. I'm totally exhausted, even though I've accomplished nothing. Little things become so important. I remember there is a jacket in my car that I meant to return before all the sales started, but I don't have the sales slip, which means I have to go home first and then start all over. By the time I finally get home, the thought of going back into town is out of the question, so the merchandise will probably sit in my trunk where it's already been for a couple of months. I probably lost the sales slip anyway, so maybe I'll just keep it.

I check my messages as soon as I get back to my place. Nothing from the *Times*. Another message from my sister, who wants to come over with the baby. And then the phone rings.

"This is McKenzie's calling. We found the book you wanted."

It's Fred. "Oh, hi. Thanks a lot. How late are you open?"

"Until eight. I'll put it in the North room under your name."

"Okay. Thanks. I'll try to get there before you close."

"Sure. Great." He doesn't care.

Stop Me If You've Heard
This One Before

"There are two motives for reading a book;
one that you enjoy it, the other that you can
boast about it."

~ Bertrand Russell (1872–1970), *The Conquest of Happiness* ~

Almost eight p.m. I'm having a tough time getting myself together. Maybe I should forget the whole thing and pick up the book in the morning. I actually do feel kind of junky, my throat feels thick; and it hurts a little when I swallow. I pop two Tylenol and flop into bed. At times like this, I usually call the doctor. It's a strange thing. Just calling and having him recommend something makes me feel better, even before I pick up the prescription. Sometimes I'll go through the motions of driving to the pharmacy and picking up the drug, but then, I often don't even bother to take it. Just having it is enough. I've talked to my friends about this, and they say this is the reason doctors tell you to "take two aspirin and call me in the morning." Medical professionals know all about this phenomenon which I call Auditory Relief Syndrome (ARS). It's the soothing power of the doctor's voice. He makes you feel better simply by talking to you.

Maybe some tea. I pad to the kitchen and pour some Evian into the teapot. Which tea would be best for this situation? Chai Light, Tropical Green, Chamomile, Earl Grey? This one sounds good. "Lemon Booster, for those pre-cold aches and pains." I need to relax. I'm just exhausted. That's the problem. The tea sucks, so I go back to the kitchen, brew some strong coffee, and pour it into a glass with some ice. I take a sip, then add some vodka. Much better.

I pull my hair back into a ponytail and select a jean skirt and a baggy sweater (which is old, but not in a good way). Why bother with makeup? It's just the bookstore. I glance in the mirror, satisfied. Basically, I look like shit. Who am I fooling? This is one of those times when I float into something rather than actually making a decision. I'll get a notion in my head that doesn't really make any sense. Next I get ambivalent and then I just want to get it over with. The decision is beside the point.

I get into my car and head for McKenzie's. It is now eight fifteen and the place looks pretty deserted. Maybe I should forget it. The store is locked, so I knock on the door. Fred appears from around the corner and opens up. He's obviously combed his hair and slicked it back somehow, maybe with water. "Come on in," he says. I try to step around him to get in the door and accidentally kick over a pile of books. They go flying across the room and Fred mock winces. "Whoops," he says. He picks up one of the books and tosses it like a basketball into the corner.

"The Iain Pears, right?" He heads into the back room to get the book and adds, "Where's your friend?" I have to think for a minute and then I realize he means Darlene. "She's working tonight. She's a Teamster." I can tell he's intrigued. He comes back with the book and lays it on the counter.

"Does she drive a semi or what?"

"She actually drives the stars around in limousines, although she had to qualify in big rigs."

"I like that in a woman." He grins.

Now is the time for me to say something provocative. So much easier to talk about someone else. "Before she was a driver she was an animal trainer and she used to keep a humongous iguana and a trained rat in her apartment." I can tell he's liking this.

"Are all your friends this unconventional?" Like he's not.

"Actually, Darlene's not all that weird when you get to know her." A total lie, but it sounds good. He hands me the book and I start combing through my purse for a credit card.

"Well, what do you consider weird?"

I am beginning to feel a little pressure to come up with something clever, but my mind is a total blank. "How about some of the people you work with?" Shit.

That was a mistake. Criticizing his coworkers. They're probably his best friends.

"But they're supposed to be weird," he says good-naturedly.

I should leave. "Well, thanks for the book," I say casually.

"You're welcome. How about a drink?"

Whoa! Where did that come from? It's not as if I didn't want this to happen, but still, I'm not all that sure that now is the time to start something. Don't be ridiculous. It's a drink, not a marriage proposal . . . ha ha ha. Oh shit, why not. What else do I have to do—did I put on mascara? Did I even brush my teeth?

"Okay. Sure. I'd love to." There. That sounded reasonably normal.

Fred locks up and suggests we cross the street to the neighborhood Starbucks. By the time we emerge into the courtyard, it is dark and the streetlights bordering San Vicente Boulevard are ablaze with a soft, billowy light. Fred slings his backpack over one shoulder and then extends his hand. "You know, I don't think we've been formally introduced. I'm Fred."

I take his hand and feel his strong, firm grip. "I'm Dora, glad to meet you."

We jaywalk across the boulevard into the center park-like divider which is lined with two-hundred-year-old endangered flowering pepper trees that have now been declared historic landmarks. In the daytime, people use this greenbelt for picnic lunches, jogging, and tai chi lessons. Right now, however, it's quiet and serene, except, of course, for the cars whizzing by on both sides.

This Starbucks, unlike most, has expensive espresso machines for sale and leather armchairs arranged around little wooden cocktail tables. Fred tosses his backpack onto one of the chairs and gets in line. "What would you like?"

I was already up to my ears in caffeine and vodka and the last thing I wanted was another coffee. I'm thinking why don't we just go to a bar and have a drink, but this is sort of a first date, I guess. You never do anything you really want and you never say anything you really think, so I tell him I want a latte. I wonder what *he'd* really like to drink. He orders a bottle of water. Great. Not exactly a signal we were going to sit around and shoot the breeze.

We sit down and he glances at the seven-hundred-page tome on my lap.

"Are you really going to read this?"

"Yes," I lie. (Actually, I'm halfway through it already. When McKenzie's didn't have it, I picked it up at Borders. There is only so much I'm willing to tell him at this point. What to say?)

"So, what are you reading now?" That's original.

"At the moment I'm reading some postmodern, edgy first novels by a couple of guys who teach creative writing at NYU. I love the style. It's so sparse and abstract."

I am speechless. I just don't have anything to say about that. A voice from behind says, "Oh, don't listen to him. . . . He's such a pretentious bore. Anyway, the word *postmodern* is so tiresome and passé. He should be ashamed." I look up and see Sara from the bookstore, who plops down on the chair next to me. Her hair is even more disheveled than before, if that's possible. Think extreme bed head, ten days in a student hostel, and a discount Eurorail pass and you start to get the idea of the wreck that was plopped on her head. She winks and pinches his cheek. I'm a little embarrassed about my earlier comment.

"So, who's this?" she says, eyeing me.

"Her name is Dora and she's straight. I think," Fred replies.

"Too bad. Has anyone ever told you that you resemble Nicole Kidman?" Sara says.

Not recently. "Actually I think I look more like Virginia Woolf."

Sara, like most nineteen-year-old hyperintellectual know-it-alls, says, "I thought that movie was pretty flawed, actually. But the public isn't ready for the real Virginia Woolf of *To the Lighthouse* and the Bloomsbury crowd, where Victorian lesbians wrote passionate letters to each other and ran around the countryside wearing those ridiculous hats and offing themselves right and left."

Fred interrupts. "This is Sara's thing. Unappreciated dead gay writers."

Without even looking at him, Sara retorts, "Okay, Fred likes more contemporary topics. Let's talk about Ann Bannon, the queen of lesbian pulp, who's ten times more interesting than your sophomoric, self-important, patriarchal literati who think they've discovered the new wave of writing. Or then again, for you classicists, how about Willa Cather, or should I say William Cather, who changed her name at Sarah Lawrence, cut her hair, wore men's suits, and took on a male persona for *My Antonia*."

Fred, not at all offended, says, "I must have missed that."

"Well, they don't teach that in high school," Sara retorts.

I look at the two of them and think, this is great. Maybe I won't have to open my mouth at all. Not so fast. Sara leans in and searchingly asks me, "So, what kind of books do you like?"

"Yikes." I start manically thinking aloud. "There are so many different categories, it's impossible to just name a few, don't you think?"

"Try," Sara presses.

"Okay, okay, I'm thinking. I like stories about lovers, seduction, sex, marriage, violence, murder, dreams, and death, and also stories that focus on the family with all its dysfunction and grief. I love writers who make their women characters independent, smart, and courageous but also passionate and romantic. I love plots about bitter old men and women who turn all soft and mushy for the love of a child. I love writers who focus on women who reach middle age and then ask, 'Now what?' or lonely disappointed women who live in suburbia and can't get out, or authors who write about the pain of growing up, searching for identity. But most of all I love books about spontaneous love affairs that go wrong or veer off into uncharted territory. It's the sudden twists of fate that I like and the unexpected outcomes. Doesn't everyone?"

"Jesus, Dora." Fred is taken aback. He's quiet for a minute and then starts to say something.

I'm on a roll. I keep blathering on. "How about authors like Carson McCullers, Anne Tyler, William Styron, Mary Gordon, Faulkner, Fitzgerald, Mary McCarthy, Alice Munro?" I look up and realize that they are both staring at me. How embarrassing. I've fallen into that god-awful abyss that voracious readers often fall into, a pious, smug, self-congratulatory, virtuous display of "what a thoughtful, superior, and sensitive well-read person I am." They've probably heard this a zillion times. They work in a bookstore. I'm such a bore.

"My personal favorite," says Fred, "is Dorothy Parker, who wrote lines like, 'His voice was as intimate as the rustle of sheets and he kissed easily.' "

My god. Just kill me now.

Happy Talk

"People say that life is the thing, but I prefer reading."
~ Logan Pearsall Smith, American essayist (1865–1946), *Afterthoughts* ~

How long does it take for a man to call a woman he's interested in, presuming of course he IS interested, which I think he is. One thing I refuse to do is sit by the phone and wait, although I did give him my cell phone. Let's see, he gets in around ten, probably distracted and busy until lunch. He could call then, but men usually wait until about five, the twilight zone, when the promise of something is in the air.

I look at the clock, seven a.m. The phone rings.

"God, Dora, I've been trying to reach you all night. It's me, Brooke."

"Brooke?" I hear a loud roar behind her.

"Did I wake you? Dora? Can you hear me? I'm on this shit assignment covering some security breach at the airport. . . . Wait a second . . . I'll walk inside."

"Hey, Brooke," I say, half asleep.

"Listen, Dora. Focus. Are you there? I had a late meeting with Eddie in Metro and I told him about the interview and he wants you to e-mail him your résumé, and include a portfolio with some of your better articles."

"That's great. You're so nice. It may take me a while to get it all together, though." Shit. Where did I put all that stuff?

"Well, don't let it sit too long, okay? Do it today. Gotta run. I'll call you later."

"Thanks, Brooke. I really appreciate it."

I rack my brain trying to remember where I put the box with all my old articles. The last time I remember seeing it, I think it was in Palmer's garage. But then, I moved most of that stuff to a storage facility on Jefferson by the airport. Or maybe it's in the basement here. I don't know where the hell it is. Why can't I ever get organized? My sister has every piece of paper she's ever owned in plastic file boxes with airtight lids organized in alphabetical order.

I spend the better part of the morning going through the basement storage and Containers R Us by the airport. After four fruitless hours, as much as I didn't want to, I decide I better call Palmer. I call him at the studio. His second assistant answers.

"Mr. Palmer's office."

"Hi, Stacy. This is Dora. Can I talk to Palmer?" A

pause. I'm clearly getting the "pain in the ass ex-wife" treatment.

"Well . . . I'll see if he's in." Like she doesn't know.

Palmer picks up immediately. "Hey, Dora. I'm on the other line. Let me just get off."

"That's okay. I can call back."

I hear him say to the other person, "I'll get back to you." And then to snotty Stacy, "Close the door, will you?

"So. To what do I owe this pleasure?"

"Palmer, I have a little problem."

"Okay . . ." he says tentatively.

I tell him what's going on and that I need to get into his garage.

"Is there someone who can let me in?"

"Why don't I just meet you there around noon?" he offers.

"Oh, that's okay. You don't really need to."

"I know I don't need to. Be gracious, Dora."

"You're right. I'll see you at noon. But I can't stay."

He laughs. "That's not gracious. How about lunch afterwards?"

"I'm a mess. I've been digging through boxes of garbage all morning and I have to get everything organized by the end of the day, and you know that's not my forte."

"Oh. It's not?" he teases. "Come on. Let me take you to lunch. I don't care if you're a mess. You always look great."

I fall for it every time. He CAN be charming. "Thanks. That's nice. Okay. See you later."

A few hours later, I ring the bell, drive through the gate,

and go directly to the garage. No hiding in the bushes for me. No siree. This time I'm an invited guest but I'm still not going inside. I wonder where the girlfriend is.

The garage door automatically opens from a remote somewhere. I am faced with a tower of my old boxes of books. I'm amazed at the sheer numbers, books from my childhood, from my old school, from all my old apartments. I guess I'll have to take this stuff home. If I don't watch out, I could end up in *People* magazine—one of those old ladies with cats who meets an untimely death from all the crap they collected. I can see the headlines now, "Literary Pack Rat Dies in Fiery Inferno." I can't believe Palmer hasn't asked me to get rid of it all.

I start to go through the boxes. Books from my European period, my Victorian period, my Russian lit period, my Faulkner period, my Fitzgerald period, and my "I can't stand my life" period. And there it is, my productive period, all my stuff from the *Times*.

"Do you want the girls from the office to help you get it together?" Palmer asks from behind me. I'm sure Stacy would be thrilled.

"No, thanks. I can do it."

"I made a reservation at the Bel Air Hotel."

"Palmer, look at me." I'm wearing old sweats and a long-sleeved gray T-shirt my sister gave me right after the separation that says "tranquility" down the arm. I won't even talk about the nervous sweat.

"You look like you belong. We'll eat outside. Only the tourists dress up."

We pull up to the Bel Air Hotel, a pink Spanish oasis

surrounded by twelve acres of lush gardens with towering palms and cascading willows. As I walk past water-
falls, arched bridges, and tranquil ponds, I come to the
big attraction. A family of snow-white swans that serve
as a backdrop for the hundreds of weddings that take
place here every year. I've seen wedding pictures with
the bride standing regally next to Athena, the prized
mother swan, and her five gray cygnets, appropriately
named after the daughters of Atlas.

We approach the terrace, an idyllic loggia with a
eucalyptus-burning fireplace. The tables are covered
with luxurious Italian linens, and the whole room exudes
a kind of low-key elegance. Carla, the hostess, a former
Scandinavian actress, greets Palmer with a peck on the
cheek and shows him to his usual table. I smile meekly as
we walk to the corner banquette.

We slide into the circular booth and I try not to take
the tablecloth with me. I glance over at Palmer. I sometimes forget how good-looking he is. It's not only the
noble profile. It's his hands. When I first met him, I told
him his hands reminded me of a Rodin sculpture, those
large, strong hands with long graceful fingers. I could
never date a man with stumpy, gnomey little hands. I am
hit by a whiff of his aftershave and a wave of nostalgia
slams into me. I have to stop this. It's no wonder the
French say lunch is the sexiest meal.

The waiter gives us the menu. I briefly consider white
asparagus soup (it's in season now) and a grilled veg-
etable salad. And then I see it. A twenty-dollar burger—
eight ounces of succulent black Angus beef, crispy fries,

and your choice of cheese, bacon, or mushrooms. It's calling to me. Women in L.A. don't order cheeseburgers. They order things like the spa Cobb. I look at Palmer and say, "You go first."

He says, "I'll have the spa Cobb."

Oh well. It's been close to the worst six months of my life. I'm going for it. "I'll take the burger with bacon. And cheese."

Palmer doesn't say a word, although I think I see a slight smile dancing at the edges of his mouth. "Would you like a glass of wine with that?" Would I like to belt down a drink? At this awkward juncture? It sure would ease up the conversation. Maybe he should have a drink. No, I can't. If I have any chance of putting together that portfolio this afternoon, I'd better not. "No, thanks."

"So. You're going back to work," he states rather than asks.

"I hope so. It was a mistake for me to quit." Oops. I hope he doesn't take this personally. He does.

"Who asked you to quit?" There's a slight edge to his voice.

"Well, you know. My dad and that whole thing . . ."

"I know, but I always thought you were too good a writer not to work. Plus, I think it's when you're the happiest. Am I right?"

"I think the only time I'm really happy is when I'm reading. 'Books make sense of life'*—somebody said that. Anyway, that's how I feel."

---

* Julian Barnes, *Flaubert's Parrot*.

"Really? No other happy moments?" His tone has suddenly turned intimate and intense. "Didn't I ever make you happy?"

I am disarmed. I don't know what I expected but it wasn't this. I think back to the times when Palmer and I would get in bed and talk half the night about nothing, or when I'd wake up to blaring TV news, running water, banging drawers, and the bitter-roasted smell of steaming coffee by my bedside. It was good, really good, when we'd get all dressed up to go to yet another event and then decide, right before we got there, to bag it and go out to dinner, just the two of us. Or when he'd get that look when I'd enter the room and his hand would brush my arm, signaling our own special code. And then there was that couples thing in the evening, sitting outside on the loggia when we didn't talk at all. It's nice when silence is comforting like that.

"Yes, Palmer. You did make me happy."

He is quiet for a moment. "Thank you for saying that."

There is an awkward silence as we both stare at nothing across the room. He studies my face for a moment and starts to smile.

Then my cell phone rings. I answer it.

"Hey!" Oh god, it's him. Why did I answer it? I wasn't thinking.

"I had a great time last night," Fred says.

I have to get off the phone right now. I look at Palmer as I respond in my most businesslike tone. "Can I call you back?"

"I guess this is a bad time. I'll call you back later," Fred says.

I hang up. I can tell Palmer knows it's another guy. Men have a sixth sense about this. The conversation makes an abrupt turn back to polite small talk. He asks about Virginia (they always did like each other). I ask about his mother (yuck).

Then he says, "I never meant to hurt you, Dora."

"I know you didn't." I should say more here. I should tell him that I never meant to hurt him. That I'm sorry I was so unhappy at the end. That I don't know if I'll ever be completely happy. But I don't.

He asks for the check. "If you need anything else, let me know." A polite kiss on the cheek. "Keep me posted on the job, okay?"

I get into my car and try to figure out that lunch. He still cares about me. That's clear. I still find him attractive. Neither one of us has recovered from the split. Wait. What am I thinking? Of course he's recovered from the split. He's living with gorgeous, together Kimberly. I think about calling Fred back. I'm not really in the mood. Lunch was confusing.

The phone rings. "Is this late enough?" It's Fred. He's cute. Funny. Easy. I laugh. He laughs. He wants to see me . . . tonight. A real date at a jazz joint with, hopefully, some kind of alcoholic beverages. Sounds fun.

Well, as Edith Wharton once said, "If only we'd stop trying to be happy, we could have a pretty good time."

Of Cabbages and Kings

> "Dancing is a wonderful training for girls:
> it's the first way you learn to guess what a
> man is going to do before he does it."
>
> ~ Christopher Morley, American novelist (1890–1957), *Kitty Foyle* ~

G lendale. Who goes to Glendale? It's the Valley. How did he ever find this place, in the middle of fucking nowhere? I feel like I've been driving for a week. It's my own fault. I didn't want to tell him about my freeway phobia, not yet anyway. And I didn't want him to pick me up because then I would've been stuck if things didn't go well. So now I've been driving for an hour and I'm at least twenty minutes late.

I tried not to be judgmental when Fred told me the club was in the Valley. But really, I don't know anyone who comes out here except to go to Costco. Oh, thank god, there's a valet parking guy. I pull up and he says, "What's the password?"

I throw back, "Rosebud."

He doesn't laugh. As it turns out, he really does want a password. I try to explain. "I guess my date forgot to tell me. His name is Fred . . . Fred . . ." Shit, I don't know his last name.

As I slip him a five-dollar bill, I ask him sweetly, "Can you park it close by?"

"No problem, ma'am."

I enter Paddy's Crab Shack and Jazz Club. Dancing and oysters on the half shell. The place looks like an old-fashioned, New Orleans–style seafood bar with beamed ceilings, cozy leather booths, dark wood paneling, and sawdust on the floor. The only way you could tag it as L.A. are the signed photos from old movie stars that line the walls. The ornate art deco bar is in the back and is flanked by a small, wooden dance floor. The jazz crowd mills around near the makeshift stage and I notice they are nothing like their hip N.Y. equivalents. From my vantage point, they're mostly graying nondescript guys who look like academics or maybe insurance adjusters, a few of whom are accompanied by their very bored-looking wives.

I find Fred sitting in a back booth nursing a bottle of Becks. There is a giant platter of half-eaten oysters on ice on the table.

"So I give up, what's the password?"

He looks up at me and smiles. "O Oysters, come and walk with us. The Walrus did beseech."

"Very cute. So what is it really?"

"It's sax." He winks.

I can't remember much of the evening. We started out with beer, and then switched to shots of tequila. The jazz trio didn't sound that great at the beginning, but by the end of the evening they were Duke Ellington performing one of his *Sacred Concerts*.

We never did get to his background or mine. I still don't know his last name. But I do know that he's writing a play, and that he's witty and smart, loves poetry, and has a photographic memory for everything from Lewis Carroll nonsense rhymes to obscure couplets by Alexander Pope.

Early on, I asked him if he ever heard of Ellen Bass's poem "Pray for Peace." At this point I was still sober enough to try to impress him. Blatantly showing off, I threw out, "There's a Buddhist flavor to one of her poems that's almost like an invocation of prayer. I love the image of bicycle wheels and the way Bass keeps repeating, 'Do less harm, less harm.' "

"Oh, 'Pray for Peace,' " he answered without hesitation. "I don't usually read poetry, but I liked that poem because it's good and it's easy to understand. Accessible like Robert Frost. Much of today's poetry is so damned obscure, it's frustrating to read. Deeply moving jabberwocky."

Uh-oh. This guy really knows what he's talking about. Now I'm going to have to think up an intelligent response. I gulp another shot of tequila. "You know, there's this pretentious theory"—(like I'm not being pretentious)—"that you should have to work a bit to understand a good poem. It's the element of obscurity that allows you to draw more personal meaning."

Fred smiles (the booze is kicking in for both of us, thank god), and recites, " 'You were lavish, daunting, a deluge of presence.' "*

At that, he offers me an oyster.

God, is he sexy!

"C. K. Williams. Won the Pulitzer in 2000. It's good, huh?" he says with a drawl. Or maybe a slur?

Who cares! I try to keep my head and stay on topic, but it's not easy.

In the middle of all this esoteric foreplay, something stunning happens. The jazz band takes a break and the canned music comes on. As Frank Sinatra croons "Fly Me to the Moon," Fred gazes drunkenly into my eyes and whispers romantically, "I'm tanked. Let's dance."

Now let's back up a little—I am a terrible dancer. I always feel self-conscious about it. I first discovered I had no talent in this area when my mother sent my sister and me to Mrs. Tavistock's Cotillion. I was seven years old and disco fever was sweeping the nation. Not, however, at the Meadowbrook Country Club, where forty captive second and third graders congregated twice a week to learn the fundamentals of ballroom dancing. I remember thinking that the only thing I could do well was the box step, and when would that ever come in handy?

But tonight I'm smooth, seductive, and sensuous.

---

*C. K. Williams, *The Singing*, "Scale:11."

Fred whisks me out onto the dance floor. Just once in my life, I want to feel whisked. And I do. I don't worry about the song or my nonexistent sense of rhythm. As Lord Byron wrote, "We chased the glowing hours with flying feet." At least it feels that way. We're also completely hammered.

Fred puts his palm in the arch of my back and the slow, slow, quick, quick routine rapidly morphs into fancy footwork with lots of twirls and arm expression, double turns, erotic holds, and sexy hip action. At one point, I kick off my shoes as he bends me over and whispers in my ear, " 'Ah, the female angel dancing alone in her stocking feet. She has been dancing forever, and now it is very late, even for musicians.' "*

"Who's that?" I murmur, still swaying away in his arms. He has his hand on my neck and I can feel his warm, moist breath on my face.

"That's Billy Collins—he's a jazzman, a Buddhist, a charmer, and a prince."†

"Like you," I sigh, buzzed to the brink, barely moving, unable to navigate any more than a simple bear hug. Bass's lines keep going through my head: "Do less harm. Do less harm." But I'm thinking, The harm's already done.

---

*Billy Collins, *Sailing Alone Around the Room*, "Questions About Angels."
†Donna Seaman, *Booklist*

The Morning After

"No girl was ever ruined by a book."
~ James J. Walker, mayor of New York (1881–1946) ~

My eyes are bloodshot and I have bruised blue circles beneath them. My matted hair is sticking up in clumps and my eyebrows look like someone combed them with a whisk. I am surrounded by the wreckage of my apartment, where heaps of discarded clothes lie where they were thrown in last night's frenzy of trying to find the right thing to wear. There is the lingering stench of perfume and cigarettes emanating from my body and my breath reeks of beer and fish. I hang on the doorjamb, as I let my sister in.

She gives me the once-over. "God, what happened to you? Are you sick? Because I can't catch a cold . . .

Camille gets it and then Andy and it costs me a whole month."

She is carrying a box filled with files, manila envelopes, labels, an assortment of writing instruments, and 24-lb. inkjet paper that is so bright it hurts my eyes.

"No, I'm not sick. What time is it?" I do vaguely remember asking her to come over and help me with my résumé.

"Dora, it's twelve noon." I hate it when people rub it in like that. Twelve noon.

"I have to pick up Camille in exactly two hours, so pull yourself together and let's do it," she says, as she opens the blinds and sliding doors in my living room and lets in a rush of blinding sunlight and sea air.

"Don't you want to hear about my date?"

"Oh. Sure." She's distracted, laying out all the supplies on my desk.

"Okay. He's interesting, I had a great time, and no, I didn't sleep with him." I was one drink away from fucking his brains out, but no need to mention that here.

"What does he do, anyway?" Virginia asks, predictably. Why is that the first thing everyone asks?

"He works at McKenzie's."

Virginia raises her eyebrows.

"He's a writer and he's brilliant, he's working on a play."

"And my babysitter is a screenwriter. And that waiter we like at Morton's is a director. It's that L.A. hyphenate thing—no one is really what they're doing. Everything is just temporary until their real career starts."

"You're a snob."

"Well, you are too. Just think about whether you'd even so much as have a cup of coffee with him if he were selling socks at Bloomingdale's. It's your whole book thing."

"Like you don't have one."

"Okay. Enough. We've been through this too many times." I hand her my rough draft.

"Jesus. This is a mess. It looks like you spent ten minutes on it."

"Well, I got a little sidetracked . . ." And I don't mean with Thomas Pynchon.

Virginia gives me an indulgent smile. "You're impossible, Dora."

She looks at her watch. Now she's all business. We spend the next two hours putting together a tight, professional-looking résumé and attaching some of my better articles. After ten years of helping Andy apply for different fellowships and grants, Virginia is a pro.

Now comes the issue of driving it downtown. Shit. Virginia looks at me pointedly on her way out and says, "Why don't you just call a messenger?"

It's four o'clock. The city is gridlocked. Sounds like a good idea to me. I walk her to the door. The résumé looks great. I'd hire me. "Thank you, Ratty. You saved me. If only I had your head. You're a wonder, a real wonder."

Virginia starts laughing. We used to compare ourselves to Rat and Mole. She, of course, was Rat, the clever, enterprising survivor. I, alas, was always Mole, holed up underground.

Years ago, when our mother first gave us *The Wind in*

the Willows, she said that one had to be worthy to read Kenneth Grahame's masterpiece and that it was a test of character. I did like the story, but at eight years old, I thought it was about animals and what was the big deal. It was only years later that I realized the book was right up there with *The Odyssey* and *Huck Finn* and included Homeric descriptions of nature and images of divine discontent and longing.

As she walks out the door, Virginia kisses me good-bye and says, "By the way, your stuff is really good, Dora. Don't give up. Call me if you need me." So now, here we are, twenty years later, Ratty helping the still awkward Mole safely ashore.

You Can Leave Your Hat On

"I'm re-reading it with a slow, deliberate carelessness."
~ T. E. Lawrence, aka Lawrence of Arabia (1888–1935) ~

I've often thought that a passionate affair happens once or twice in a lifetime. The kind of affair I'm thinking of is of the sex-all-night-long kind—sex in the car, on the kitchen counter, in the hallway, in an alley, whenever and whatever with none of the mundane thoughts of how he earns a living or where he lives or whether he calls his mother, or even if he gambles or plays around. All those considerations come afterwards, after you stop eating yogurt at two a.m. so you can muster the energy to have one more round before dawn, or after that giddy, dazed feeling of exhilaration gives way to routine, or maybe even after you reach thirty-five and realize the libido is expendable but a decent lifestyle is not.

All of this leads me to the night I went home with Fred. We had been to the requisite Thai restaurant where he dazzled me with his knowledge of *The Life and Adventures of Nicholas Nickleby;* we had driven to the beach and discussed Tennyson's poetical works and Tom Stoppard's newest play. We had just come from a tiresome coffee-klatsch with Ken and Sara, and I thought if I listened to any more competitive literary bantering I'd explode, so I was delighted and more than agreeable when Fred took my hand, led me out into the moonlight, and whispered, "Let's go to my place." He stroked my head and neck as if I were a child, and suddenly I was so aroused I almost stumbled off the curb. It's been a while since I felt like this. A long while.

Fred lives on the third floor of a nondescript, slightly run-down apartment building near UCLA. The building houses people on their way up and on their way down, a mix of grad students, young marrieds, and a Pakistani family whose cooking permeates the hallways with smells of curry, cumin, and stale incense. The elevator is out of order so Fred stands behind me, plants his broad hands on my back, and pushes me up the stairs. When we finally get to his apartment my heart is pounding, I'm out of breath, and my upper thighs are screaming with pain. We laugh, but I'm having second thoughts. Nothing like an arduous trek up three flights to drum home the fact that you are no spring chicken.

Things get worse as we step inside. It could be a grad

student's pad, complete with books piled all over, an un-kempt bedroom with a pile of laundry in the corner, a bi-cycle that takes up half the living room, and a plasma TV on the wall. There is no art, no frills. Then again, there's a Bose stereo system. It's a far cry from the gleaming steel and glass, critically hip Bel Air house I visited just a few weeks ago when Pamela thoughtfully fixed me up with a business associate of her husband's. We had dinner at her house, which consisted of four soup courses, a shrimp and mussel salad that I poked at with a mother-of-pearl cocktail fork, and a saucy little chardonnay with, as her husband put it, "just a hint of presumption." Mean-while, Pamela carried on this chirpy, albeit somewhat forced, conversation, well aware that the fix-up was a bust. Dessert was a fig confit finished off with a mint and peach brandy sauce.

When the fix-up first started talking, I tried to act in-terested, even though he looked suspiciously like an old fogey in hip clothing—starchy, custom-made Turnbull and Asser shirt with big collar, and a huge, elaborate black titanium sport watch with a shocking array of di-als and knobs, sort of like a Hummer for the wrist. This look was finished off with a brisk slap of Dior's Eau Sa-vage and when, at one point, he called Pamela's husband "darling," I wanted to bag it right there.

After dinner, we all piled into his Range Rover and drove up the ficus-tree-lined driveway to his swanky new house which was "just in the finishing stages," as he put it. He apparently had the same art consultant as Pamela and he showed us his latest acquisition from a group of

Cuban artists who did installations dealing with censored literature around the world. The piece consisted of fifty banner-like strips of paper lined up one above the other on a stark white wall in the living room. Each banner was printed with lines from famous novels that had been censored, including works by Dante, Ginsberg, Maurice Sendak, Neruda, and Orwell. "I call it my nifty fifty," said my date, to which none of us responded. I actually loved his scarlet Barcelona chairs and limestone slabbed kitchen with all its stunning, pristine, German techno-stainless hardware and self-closing, soundless cabinets, but I still couldn't bring myself to even shake his hand good-night. He was pretty much of a cretin.

I watch Fred's muscular back and neck as he moves some stuff from the sofa and then motions for me to sit down. There's always this moment just before you start an affair when you can either move forward or not. Sometimes it feels as if you are standing in a darkened subway station, edging closer and closer to the tracks, and you suddenly get this irrational impulse to fling yourself off the platform and into the path of a speeding train. There's a psychological term for this kind of fatal urge that, apparently, a lot of New Yorkers who ride the subway have experienced. But the point is, once you go to bed with someone, things change and you can't go back. When you're younger, you tend not to think about the consequences. You meet a guy, you're attracted, you make love, and he calls or he doesn't. Life goes on and you deal with it. But now I'm at an age where balance is important and one can't be too serious or too frivolous, and there's this slightly skewed, ever-present vertigo relating to how precarious it all can be.

Fred, on the other hand, acts like he's on autopilot. He goes to the stereo and turns on Randy Newman singing "You Can Leave Your Hat On." The song is a slow striptease:

> "Baby, take off your dress.
> Yes, Yes, Yes."

That's subtle. Then he strides to the makeshift bar, grabs a bottle of tequila, two shot glasses, and sits down on the couch beside me. He takes a swig and hands me the bottle. I stare for a moment at the empty glasses and dutifully take a gulp. A big one.

There's this jittery, inept feeling of dread as the alcohol burns through my upper scalp and behind my earlobes and sears all the way down to my gut. Then I feel a rush of warmth in my body as I silently watch him kick off one boot, then the other, slump down into the pillows, and stretch out his legs. I'm not comfortable. I decide I can still get out of this. I'm about to say something glib and then he surprises me.

He puts his arms around me and pulls me toward him in a forceful way. I thought I had more time. I thought we were going to discuss this. God, does it feel good. I'd forgotten about his drop-dead, Southern charm, take-no-prisoners sex appeal. His arms feel powerful and he keeps moving, pushing fabric aside, and tumbling pillows off the couch until he finally touches me. His hands stroke my head and slide down my neck and I can hear him breathing and smell the detergent on his skin as he gently brushes his lips over mine and then leans in and kisses me on the neck. I can't stand it. I'm awash with lust.

He pulls back and gives me an amused grin. "You like this, huh?" he says. "You changed your mind?"

So he's known all along. I laugh. "Just shut up," I say. I clearly want more. I start to unbutton my blouse.

"Not yet," he says. "What's the rush? Let's talk."

"God, Fred, are you serious?"

"Yes. Let's talk about why I like you."

"If you tell me I'm your soul mate, I'm leaving."

Fred doesn't respond, so I fall silent as he slips his hand under my blouse, gently presses in on my ribs, and starts to trace invisible circles around my breasts.

"I like your long, graceful neck and the way your ankles bend right here on your lovely legs and I like your teenage, firm little chest and the way you pant when I touch you. You have a magnificent mouth. It's soft and wet when I kiss you and your back has a curve that shows through your clothes when you walk."

His hands are moving down my legs now and he starts caressing the inside of my thighs. "I like the way you walk. Your shoulders are square and straight and I always know it's you, even from a distance, because no one I know moves the way you do."

I am far, far away now, his voice is all around me, and I hear myself moan. I let him take over. I'll let him do anything. It's like falling off a bridge. Here I go again.

House of Mirth

"Lily prided herself on her broad-minded recognition
of literature and always carried an Omar Khayyam in her
travelling-bag."

~ Edith Wharton (1862–1937), *The House of Mirth* ~

Pamela's birthday invitation arrived in a pink, pig-shaped envelope and said, "Come western and pig out." It was, apparently, some party planner's idea of different. Personally, I wouldn't send out a pig-shaped invitation for my birthday. Most of the people seem to be older, friends of Pamela's semi-retired husband, William, and the outfits incorporate every endangered species that ever existed—ostrich, crocodile, snakeskin. Luckily, no one's picketing.

One might question the wisdom of bringing Fred to an event like this. We've only been dating a few weeks. Dorothy Parker once said that she wanted printed on her tombstone "Wherever she went, including here, it was against her better judgment." I should have taken her advice and stayed home, but it is Pamela's birthday and I did want Fred to meet my friends.

It's raining as we drive up and down obscure side streets in West Hollywood looking for the address. We finally spot it—a warehouse, which has been redone to resemble a barn. In front of the building are life-size statues of heifers and horses standing on soggy bales of hay and a big hand-painted wooden sign over the entrance that says "Pamela's Double D Corral." The rain is coming down in sheets now as we pull up to the valet.

Pamela greets us at the door ebullient in leather chaps and a turquoise silk shirt.

"Hey! Look who the cat dragged in."

"Pamela, this is Fred. Sorry we're late."

William, who has whiskey on his breath and wears a tin sheriff's badge, hugs me and says, "We thought maybe Dora was driving."

He gives me a good-natured wink and a nudge. I shoot Pamela a look and try to divert the conversation elsewhere. I glance around at the scene. The sad truth about most parties is if you're not slightly inebriated, they're just not that much fun.

"Hi, Fred. We've heard so much about you," Pamela says. I hate when people say that. Then the person in question is always wondering what they've heard and what you've told them. And it has only been a few weeks.

Fred looks at me and says, "Well, all good I hope." Lame laughter.

"So, Dora, hear anything about the job yet?" Leave it to Pamela to bring up this cheery subject. "She used to be a crack reporter at the *Times*." She pushes my shoulder. "Did you tell him about all the awards you won?"

"Pamela, that was a while ago." Perfect. Let's just focus on my nonexistent career.

I see my old friend Heather by the bar motioning for us to come over. She's standing with her latest date, who, I've heard, is a successful young turk in the movie business.

She gives me a big hug. "Heather, you look gorgeous." Heather is one of those women who always looks good no matter what she's wearing. She's tall and has perfect peachy cream skin and exudes a kind of midwestern warmth and normalcy, although she is prone to overdosing on Ambien and sleepwalking through the neighborhood in her nightgown. In fact, one night, I heard there was a big misunderstanding with a cop who thought she had been abducted from somewhere else and dumped into her Brentwood neighborhood. Her husband had to straighten out the whole mess and that might have been the turning point in their relationship. She's been single for a couple years now.

She's wearing expensive Indian jewelry and a sterling silver conch belt. She seems to have an endless supply of cash from her ex-husband, who imports something from China, but nobody knows what.

As Fred and I start to order a drink, a twangy voice over the loudspeaker announces, "Howdy, folks, please find your tables, it's time to chow down."

We are seated at Pamela's table, which is a yee-haw oak-planked slab with benches. At each place setting there are bobble-head cowgirl dolls in Pamela's likeness and giant lethal bottles of 100-proof Patron tequila with shot glasses. There are also red bandanas, Wet-Naps, and plastic bibs, all of which give me a bad feeling about the food. That feeling is justified when, to the rollicking tune of "Friends in Low Places," choreographed cowboy waiters bring out huge platters of ribs dripping with viscous black barbecue sauce, behemoth bowls of baked beans with ladles, corn bread the size of bricks, and coleslaw swimming in a sea of mayonnaise.

Everyone is currently in an animated conversation about the weather. Two days of rain in L.A. and it becomes the center of conversation, like, say, a presidential election. Half of my friends just sit around the house and brood, waiting for the smother of black clouds to lift, like a bout of depression.

Pamela is grumbling about how dim and gloomy it is, too much rain and fog and she even canceled her dentist appointment, which is unusual for her because she loves him—he's this high-tech dentist with plasma TVs installed over each chair, first-run movies, and Bose earphones. He also caters to all the neurotic germ freaks in the city. Everything is covered with sterile plastic and there are motion sensors that open all the doors.

The pitch of the party is rising in direct proportion to the massive amounts of tequila that the guests are distractedly swigging. I notice that two women who I happen to know haven't talked for four years are now in a cozy conversation in the corner.

Meanwhile, William is yelling across the table to

Heather's date about the new Viacom acquisition and how his partners figured it out a few months ago and "made a few mil on that one." The other guy starts talking about all the consolidations, even in the agency business. William's radar perks up as he tries to figure out where the next big merger is and whether the latest public offerings are already too expensive. The conversation drifts to real estate, which is where it always drifts in Los Angeles. William talks shopping centers and anchor stores and adds that his partners are looking into some deals in Texas, Louisiana, and Tennessee.

Fred keeps excusing himself to escape outside to the Giddy-Up Saloon, where he belts down something else on the rocks and chats for an oh-so-long period of time with the bartender, who, by the end of the evening, is his newest best buddy.

He looks cute, though, more than cute. He made a point of not wearing anything that could even remotely be called western. In fact, he looks suspiciously preppy. It doesn't matter. When we first sit down, Pamela gives Fred a broad, open smile, and says, "I really love wandering through bookstores. It's such a feast." A feast? Fred does have that effect on women. He hands me a shot glass filled with tequila and says, "Bottoms up, baby."

Meanwhile, Heather, whose lot in life is to make everyone feel comfortable, looks up at Fred with her dolce vita face and asks, "So, what are the latest books . . . What do you recommend?"

He smiles at her. "What kinds of books do you like?"

"I don't like anything depressing. I like reading happy books."

I see the mocking and slightly flirtatious glint in Fred's eye. The minute you say something like this to a serious reader they think you're a complete lightweight. You might as well tell them you want to be a Laker Girl.

"Nothing depressing, eh? There are some new novels . . ." And he offers up some featherlight, frivolous fluff.

"You might like these," he says disingenuously.

Then he gives me a knowing, complicit nod. This is beginning to feel like something out of an Edith Wharton novel. Snobby men toying with women they think are beneath them. Heather doesn't get it. She thanks him and they continue talking, but I am annoyed.

Later on, during dinner, Pamela's husband, William (who we all put up with because he's so kind to Pamela), starts regaling everyone about their trip to Florence. They stayed at the Grand, of course, had a great *paglia e fieno* at this restaurant and scored an exquisite bottle of fourteen-dollar Chianti at that restaurant (forget about the fact that they're paying six hundred dollars a night for the room). He went on in a buoyant, booming voice about their tour guide who was a university art history professor and conspiratorially whispered the name of the fabulous shop where you can get leather purses made in the same factory as Prada for half the price.

Fred stifles a yawn, at which point Heather asks him in a sweet honey bunny sort of way, "Have you been there, Fred?"

"No, I don't much like traveling. I think it's a lot like golf or tennis. There are certain activities that people feel obligated to engage in when they reach a certain status in life. I'd rather just sit home and read *Death in Venice.*"

After a moment of awkward silence, I try to gloss things over and keep the conversation going. "Sort of like that book *The Accidental Tourist.* Remember, the guy who wrote travel books for people who didn't like to travel? He advised his readers on how to avoid human contact, where to find American food, and how to convince themselves they haven't really left home." I look around. No one's buying it. Everyone knows that's not what Fred meant.

Everyone except Heather. "Oh, was that a book? I thought it was an old movie. Didn't what's-her-name star in that? You know . . ."

"Maybe Annette Bening?" says another guest.

"No. No. It definitely wasn't Annette Bening. It was, you know, that girl from *Thelma and Louise.*"

Now the whole table's involved.

"Susan Sarandon?"

"No. The other one."

"I can just picture her. She's a big girl, dark hair. Really tall."

"Wasn't that guy from *Body Heat,* what's his name, William Hurt, in it?"

"Yes. Is he deaf?"

"No. He's not deaf. It was that role he played in *God's Children.*"

"It wasn't called *God's Children.* It was *Children of a Lesser God* and it was like thirty years ago."

Oh god. They need to stop. Where's Fred going? Back to the bar. At which point Pamela says triumphantly . . .

"Geena Davis! That's who it was. Effing Geena Davis!" (Pamela can't quite ever bring herself to curse. She also whispers the names of diseases.)

At this point, one of the band members grabs the mike and yells, "Cowboys and cowgals, now is the time to change pardners. I want all the cowpokes to take their napkins and glasses and move to the right three seats." Everyone is laughing as the men get up and move three seats clockwise.

William is now seated next to me and Pamela, the birthday girl, has a conspicuously empty seat to her right. I quickly say, "Oh, I think Fred went outside to make a phone call. I'll be right back."

Where the hell is he? I smile confidently as I whisk by the blur of guests and head for the bar. No Fred. Shit. I swing around and look out toward the parking lot. Maybe he left. Not that I can blame him. This party is truly over the top.

I finally spot him seated on a brick wall behind the kitchen entrance. He and the bartender are having a smoke. The storm seems to have eased a bit, but, there is a dark gray smear of fog out in the horizon and I can feel my hair frizzing up. When I finally reach him, he gives me a transparent smile and introduces his new buddy, Chad, a loose-limbed, dopey-looking guy with frosted-tipped hair who's studying to be an actor.

"Hi!" I say nonchalantly, attempting to at least keep up a veneer of "hey, we're all having fun here." "Everyone's changed seats for the cake and you're seated next to the hostess. Would you mind coming back in?"

"Yeah. In a minute." There is a chill in the air as I register his rebuff. A fine film of rain sifts down on my face and I absently untie my bandana and begin mopping my brow.

"Fred, they're all sitting there and it's kind of embarrassing." The bartender gives Fred a look that, I know, means "Jesus, is this chick uptight."

"Dora, I've tried but I have nothing to say to these people. Why don't we just sneak out the back, Jack?" he kids as he slides his arm around me and tries to give me an inebriated nuzzle. I am not in the mood. This is really not very nice.

"What's wrong with you, Dora? Lighten up."

"Okay. Never mind," I throw back. The bartender is now smirking.

"Catch you later," Fred says to the bartender, obviously changing his mind. He grudgingly squashes his cigarette butt into the wall and follows me back in about five steps behind, like a chastened schoolboy.

We get back to the table just as the lights are dimming. A cart pulled by a dwarf pony and bearing a fancy tiered cake is dramatically closing in on Pamela's seat.

"Oh, we all thought you guys had left," Heather blurts out in a treacly, well-meaning tone as a round of long-winded, drunken, teary toasts begins.

We sit down and Fred barely speaks. I should have let him sit outside. This is so bad. But he could try just a little. In the bookstore, he has an effortless grace with every stranger that walks in the door—a literary wonder with a dashing streak of charm and an uncanny ability to quote verbatim relevant passages. Now I watch him fidget with the bobble-head doll and then blankly stare into space. Is it only obvious to me or does everyone realize he doesn't want to be here?

Pamela is currently in a conversation with the woman across the table about preschools. Pamela tells the woman that Madison's school is very conscious of building self-esteem and has banned games that are hurtful to feelings. In fact, she proudly tells her, they don't play tag, instead they play Circle of Children, where no one is "out." It seems that even dodgeball is under a cloud. She goes on to elaborate that there are no red marks on tests because that too is stressful to children . . . lavender is much more calming.* Fred gives me a look.

Pamela, oblivious, leans into him and says, "So I hear you're a playwright?"

"Yes."

"What's your play about?"

"It's kind of complicated."

"Oh. How long have you been working on it?"

"A few years."

Pamela is struggling here to engage him.

"So, is it really true what they say about the death of the novel?"

He looks at her incredulously.

"What exactly do they say?" he replies, putting her on the spot.

---

* Christina Hoff Sommers and Sally Satel, M.D., *One Nation Under Therapy.*

"Well, you know, that people just want to watch TV and rent movies."

"Those people probably never read to begin with." An uncomfortable silence as she changes the subject.

"What's hot now? What are people reading?"

"The usual *New York Times* booklist stuff."

"Oh. Like . . . ?"

"Baldacci, Steel, Roberts, Clancy, things like that."

"Oh, I like Tom Clancy."

"Lots of people do."

Pamela stretches as she covertly loosens a notch on her belt and takes out her compact. She meticulously reapplies her lipstick and says, "Well, it was nice talking to you, Fred, but I guess I better mingle a little."

It's at this point that a couple at the next table, who had apparently been having a minor dispute, explode. She's yelling, "Fuck you!" He's shouting back, "Fuck you too!" She then races out into the rain in tears. He briefly apologizes to no one and runs after her.

Pamela mouths "uh-oh," pointedly ignores the outburst, and continues her hostessly duties. Fred looks at me and rolls his eyes.

Okay, so it's not the Algonquin Round Table here. He could at least have made an effort. Granted, it's a bad party. But not in a good way. Like in *Tender Is the Night* when Dick Diver said, "I want to give a really bad party . . . where there's a brawl and seductions and people going home with their feelings hurt and women passed out in the toilet."

There is no way to salvage this evening.

Where the Wild Things Are

"The fawn lifted its face to his.
It turned its head with a wide, wondering motion
and shook him through with the stare of its liquid eyes."
~ Marjorie Kinnan Rawlings (1896–1953), *The Yearling* ~

All things considered, last night was a disaster. We ducked out after the cake and when we got in the car, instead of just letting it rip—me telling him he was a jerk, him telling me that my friends were bourgeois and boring—we both avoided the confrontation. I've learned that this is usually a mistake, but by this time we had already morphed into sullen passengers exchanging pleasantries in an excruciatingly civil manner.

"Do you mind if I turn on the music?" Fred asks with a benign smile.

"Oh no, not at all," I answer evenly.

"I think we've heard enough country-western," he

says, which might have been funny had our moods been different.

Then he drops the bomb. "What's the best way to get you home?"

Now I'm mad. I was the one who was going to say "Take me home." But instead, I politely respond, "First get on the 10, and go north on the 405 and get off at Wilshire. Take Wilshire West to San Vicente and I'll give you the rest when we get there."

"Would it be better for me to take the 10 straight to Twenty-sixth Street, then go up to San Vicente?"

I don't know how much longer I can take this. "No, Twenty-sixth is usually pretty crowded, so the 405 would be best." If he asks me one more question regarding directions, I'm going to snap.

"Your friends are very nice." He doesn't mean it. Why is he saying this?

"Thank you." (You prick.) He drops me off saying he has to get up early, but we both know it's bullshit.

●   ●   ●

Darlene puts up with my rants all day. She called me this morning informing me that we couldn't go on our usual walk because there was a giant squid infestation and all the beaches were temporarily closed.

"Are you joking? What's a squid, anyway? Is that calamari?"

"Yeah, without the olive oil. How was last night?"

"Oh god, let's see. We go to this corny, expensive theme party in West Hollywood that was supposed to be a hoedown and which, I admit, was in poor taste, even for Pamela, and he proceeds to patronize all my friends and hang out with the bartender. When I asked him to please come back to the party and act like a grown-up, he went into a funk and was basically mute for the rest of the evening. He hates my friends."

"So what? I hate your friends." She laughed. "Just kidding. Not really."

"Well, it was uncomfortable as hell."

"Did you fuck him?"

"No, I didn't fuck him. He dumped me off at home. Couldn't wait to get rid of me. And personally, I couldn't wait to get rid of him."

"Why did you throw him into that kind of gonzo scene anyway?"

"It was the birthday party of one of my oldest friends," I huffed. "He could have been more cordial. I kept waiting for him to say something trenchant and provocative—lord knows, he had plenty of opportunity between Heather asking him about books and Pamela prodding him about his work, but instead he just sat there looking all judgmental and sanctimonious."

"He was insecure," Darlene insisted.

"No, he wasn't. He was disdainful and snobbish."

"Okay. Then he was both. He's still a hunk and a great fuck. What do you care? You know what your problem is, Dora? You turn all these stupid social things into major downers over nothing. You've been depressed since the separation and what are you doing now? Reading and going to doctors' appointments. I'm sorry. I know you're down. I don't want to hurt your feelings. Did I hurt your feelings?"

"No, Darlene. At this point I have no feelings."

"Okay. Let's talk about something positive. What's going on with the job?"

Oh, that's something positive. "I'm waiting to hear."

"I could call Sully, she's still in Classifieds. She might have heard something."

"Thanks . . . but no thanks," I say dejectedly.

"Chill, Dora. You'll get the job and the Bookprince will call you to apologize."

"No, he won't."

"He'll call you. They always call you."

"Not that I care, but they don't always call. I'm not twenty-five anymore. I'm divorced. Twice. Almost. I don't have a job. My money won't last much longer. And Dr. H. told me I could use a little lift right here." I point to my upper eyelid as if she could see what I was talking about.

"Well, fuck them all," Darlene said with a flourish. "Let's go do something."

We decide to meet for a late lunch and then take one of my favorite hikes, a two-mile trek through the Santa Monica Mountains, finishing at Inspiration Point, which offers a 360-degree view from downtown to the Pacific Ocean.

By the time we make it down the path, it's twilight. Darlene and I are wet and slick and sweaty like horses coming down from a long trail ride and the cold moist air turns our breath to steam. The moon, a thin shaving of tin, is already visible in the sky as we pull out of the parking lot and head toward Sunset.

Darlene spots him first—a hefty, black-tailed buck with ominous-looking antlers lying by the side of the road.

"Dora, stop! I think someone hit a deer."

I pull over and she leaps out to investigate. I see her bending over the body of the prostrate beast, peering into its dazed, gentle face. His fur is the color of a beagle, only matted and muddy, and there appears to be something black and sticky on his slightly pivoting, long, stiff ears.

"Is he dead?" I ask.

"I don't know. Do you have a mirror?"

"Yes. Why?"

Darlene is cupping the moist tip of the buck's snout in her fingers.

"I can't figure out if he's breathing or roadkill."

"Wait a minute." As I get out of the car with my compact, I see the buck suddenly spaz out in a series of convulsive movements in an attempt to get up. God, he has huge teeth. Do deer bite? Darlene jumps back.

"Well, I guess he's not dead," I say, a bit unnerved. "Maybe someone grazed him and he needs to, you know, just get his bearings," I add hopefully.

"Maybe, but I don't think we should leave him lying here. Do you think we can fit him in the trunk?"

"Darlene, he looks like he's over six feet and he must weigh close to two hundred pounds."

"How about the backseat then? Mel's about the same size."

Okay. Now I'm going crazy. I don't want to be here.

It's cold and dark and I'm stuck. I suddenly long for a hot bath and a book.

"You're kidding, right?"

"Of course I'm kidding. Pull your car behind the deer, put on your emergency lights, and I'll try to flag someone down with a van or something."

I move the car, get on my cell phone, and start calling different wildlife agencies, all of which are gone for the day and have elaborate answering machines that are totally useless. I remember there is an emergency animal hospital down on Sepulveda and I call them next. The man gives me a bland, routine dismissal.

"We don't handle wildlife here. There's Lyme disease up in the canyon. Also, it's illegal to administer any drugs—if we fix him up and set him free and then someone shoots him and eats him, they could get poisoned."

I try to figure out the logic of what I've just heard. He goes on to tell me there's a place in Torrance just off the 405 that might hold the deer until the Malibu Wildlife Agency opens in the morning. "Those people," he says, "will handle anything."

Meanwhile, I can just make out Darlene standing a few yards ahead, her white-streaked hair glowing in the streetlight as she motions to passing cars to stop. One man in a car slows down briefly, presumably to check her out, then speeds off.

"Sayonara, shithead!!" she bellows. "That's French for fuck you."

Finally, after a few more minutes, a black pickup pulls over on the bike lane. I see her long, sinuous body lean into the cab as she flings her mane at the driver. He doesn't have a chance.

"Okay," she shouts a few minutes later. "He says he'll take the deer."

"Okay what?" I answer, suddenly feeling protective and then worried that maybe he's thinking venison!

"He says he'll take it to a shelter—we just have to help him get it in the flatbed."

I try to act grateful and calm as the short, muscled-up man in a tight black T-shirt and jeans gets out of his truck, walks over to me, and flashes a wide, sharklike grin. Then he unbuckles his leather belt and pulls it like a whip out of his pants.

I glare at Darlene and my heart starts to pound.

"Relax, Dora. This is Bill. He's a real doll. Guess what! He thinks I look like Daryl Hannah. Anyways, he says he's going to tie the buck's hoofs together so he doesn't kick the shit out of us and then we'll all lift him into the truck," she says cheerfully. Sometimes Darlene has this weird kind of mother energy that is hugely comforting. In the moment.

Then Bill looks at us and says, "One of you has to ride in the back so the buck don't roll himself out."

I look at Darlene and we're both thinking the same thing. I can't drive on the goddamn freeway, so it's me and the stranger and the buck going on into the dark without her. I make one last attempt to worm out of this. "You know, the man at the shelter says deer in this area are infested with ticks that carry Lyme disease."

"Wash your hands when you get there, then," she shoots back.

So here's how it went down. The three of us held down the buck, tied his back legs, and heaved him into the truck as the dust flew off the animal in blinding, eye-stinging waves, like thick clouds of tear gas. Then I jumped in, covered us both up with a piece of greasy tarp, and held down the buck's head as good old Bill raced along the 405 in the emergency lane, his lights flashing, all the way to Torrance.

All the while, the animal struggled to right himself and I could sense he was gradually regaining his equilibrium and strength. He smelled earthy and woodsy like a wet pile of leaves and at one point he let out a windy, guttural sound like nothing I had ever heard. It wasn't a howl or a growl—more like the muffled, heartrending sob of a small child in distress.

As I lay beside him holding his warm, heavy head, I gazed down at the wild, guarded cast of his eyes. There was something so unnatural about it all—being that close to a creature that needs to get back to whatever wild place he came from as soon as possible. I felt a sense of urgency for him and for me.

The natural balance of the world was upset and both Darlene and I instinctively felt the call to set it right. I suddenly flash on Mole's rescue of Otter's young son on the Island of Pan and how he "felt a great Awe fall upon him, an awe that turned his muscles to water, bowed his head and rooted his feet to the ground. It was no panic terror—indeed he felt wonderfully at peace and happy . . ."*

When we finally reach the shelter, Bill jumps out, disappears inside, and argues with the techs for what seems like ages. Meanwhile, just as the buck has a renewed burst of energy and I am struggling to keep him down, my cell phone goes off. I automatically grab it from my purse with my free hand, thinking it's Darlene.

"Dora?"

Fred.

"Oh, hi."

"So, what's goin' on?"

"Oh. Nothing."

"You sound out of breath—are you okay?"

"I'm fine but, ah, Fred, I can't talk just now."

"Okay. I'll call you later."

I hang up. Great. My mother used to say a watched pot never boils. Somehow or other that also applies to getting calls from men. They wait until you are frantically trying to keep a giant buck from bolting out of the back of a pickup, and then they call.

---

*Kenneth Grahame, *The Wind in the Willows*, "The Piper at the Gates of Dawn."

Catch the Soap

"Tell him I've been too fucking busy—or vice versa."
~ Dorothy Parker (1893–1967) to Harold Ross (*The New Yorker*)
when asked why she had not delivered her manuscript on time. ~

The first thing I think of when I get home is ticks. Ticks on my scalp. Ticks under my nails. Ticks in hidden places where you don't even notice them until they are so swollen that whatever disease you have has metastasized and you are a goner. I need a drink. I open a brand-new bottle of something expensive that I'd been saving for the right occasion. This is it.

I turn on the water in the tub as hot as I can possibly stand it without searing my skin. I debate whether or not to call my doctor and tell him I've lain down with a buck. Maybe after the bath. I sink down into the water, submerging my head. Everything stings. I've got scratches all up and down my arm and a big black and blue mark on the side of my face where I accidentally banged my head on the side of the truck. I shampoo my sweaty hair at least five times. What I really need is white vinegar. I remember my mother used to put it in the humidifier to get rid of the bacteria. I jump out of the tub, buck naked, and head for the kitchen. I lean over the sink and douse myself with vinegar. Then the phone rings.

"Hey, it's Victor here. There's a gentleman who says you're expecting him, Fred Mud, can he come up?"

Shit. Fred Mud? Oh. Very funny. Who cares. What the hell. "Tell him to come up."

I answer the door in an old sleeveless T-shirt and sweats. My hair is dripping wet and I smell like a pickled something. He's obviously coming up to apologize. I guess we should sit and talk about it. Probably a good idea. I wish I didn't look like garbage.

Fred is standing in the doorway with a frosted bottle of Belvedere, the fancy one with the etched picture, and he has a puzzled grin. "Jesus, what happened to you?"

"Darlene and I rescued a deer. Come on in," I say quickly.

"Does it hurt?" He touches my face and I pull away. I'm still annoyed and tired and, when it comes to him, confused. Jesus, he looks great.

"Peace offering," he says, and gently strokes the back of my arm. I start to weaken as he croons, "Poor baby." Without a beat, he swoops me up, swings me around, and kisses me, slamming the door shut with his foot. He puts his hands under my shirt and slides them down into my sweats and presses my hips next to his. He whispers a lot of foolishness as he pushes me back into the room.

"God, Dora. You're beautiful."

A crazy urge suddenly comes over me. I pull off my T-shirt and sweats and throw myself at him. We are both heady with lust as we stumble and fall on the rug. He grins and hoists himself over me, crushing me with his body. He grabs my wet, vinegary hair, pulls my head back, and pins my arms behind my back. Then he starts doing something with his tongue. My whole body is trembling. The buttons from his shirt are digging into my chest and the stiff fabric of his pants feels good. I try to rip his shirt off and he laughs at my urgent struggle. It's shocking how much I want him.

"You won't respect me in the morning," he says with delight.

"You're right. You were naughty and you need to be punished. Do you mind if I get my handcuffs?" I say, still panting from the tussle.

He looks at me with strange, new interest. "Do you have handcuffs?"

"Maybe," I taunt him. "Follow me."

He's thrilled. There is something about a guy finding out you're a bad girl. Just the thought completely turns him on.

I lead Fred, like some Nubian slave, into my bedroom and motion for him to sit on the bed. His tongue isn't exactly hanging out of his mouth, but you get the picture. I open the drawer by the side of my bed, pull out my gleaming steel handcuffs, and dangle the keys provocatively in front of his face.

"You didn't believe me, did you?"

He's chortling like an adolescent. "Okay. Where did you get these?"

I wasn't going to tell him that I got them from Darlene as a separation gift . . . her ex, Mel the cop, had left them behind. I don't even want to think about what Darlene's done with them. "Just lay down," I say. But at that moment he spins around, tackles me, and handcuffs me to my handmade ivy-twined iron bed frame.

We are roaring with laughter as I kick my legs violently at his chest, twist my body back and forth, and wrap my legs around his waist and squeeze him like a vise. I pull him toward me and his body is heavy and strong and I'm gasping for breath. Lusting for him.

He knows. He props himself up on knees and unbuttons his shirt.

"How much do you want me?" he teases.

He puts his fingers in my mouth and then leans in and kisses me softly and slowly and our mouths get wet and warm and tingly and this guy really knows how to kiss. Great kissing can be almost like making love. If it's done right, it can magically obliterate all the extraneous limbs and sharp corners of your bodies. It's a rapturous feeling. Oh, my, my, my. This feels good . . . the sweet, hypnotic power of it all where you are outside yourself, suspended somewhere far away looking down on a scene where, for once, reality is better than fiction.

I remember when I was a teenager, there was a boy

named Chris who used to come over after school and sit in my bedroom and kiss me. We would start out slow, laughing and kidding around, but he knew and I knew that this was all leading somewhere we weren't ready to go. I learned it was all a question of acquiescence, letting your guard down and opening yourself up to a tangle of feelings and driving urges that sweep over you as a series of firewalls are released one by one.

Fred pulls off his pants and starts licking me under my arms, down my stomach, on the soles of my feet and other places that make me crazy.

There's always a moment when you can feel the yielding in your muscles and your bones and all you can think about is you want more. A selfish, ravenous sensation washes over you and if someone is good, and Fred is definitely good, you never want it to stop.

I had a discussion in college once with Pamela, before William, when she was a hell of a lot looser. The concept was that "doing it" with a guy you had a crush on was sort of like finding out his one BIG secret: Is he good in bed? By that we meant, is he gentle or rough? Does he take his time or get carried away? Is he robust and insistent or does he let you take the lead? Is it a religious experience or just hard-core? We decided that you never really discover a good lover's secret because they are different every time. It's all a question of patter—the strong, silent type never really did it for either of us in the sack. A good lover had to know how to talk, cajole, philosophize, wax poetic, gossip, confess, and flatter. And the dark other side, the raunchy, off-color rap that feverishly describes in whispers and murmurs every lurid move.

As we got older, though, we both realized that, alas, technique is never the whole story. How could it be that simple, after all? It's the ineffable qualities of a person, like temperament, sensibility, integrity, and idiosyncrasies, that truly capture a lover's imagination and send them to that coveted place of bliss. You can lick your chops over his physique, his bank account, his cool car, suave manners, whatever, but no matter how he acts in bed, that hideous word "connection" has to carry you through, it just does, or you inevitably end up blowing him off for no apparent good reason.

His face is next to mine as I strain my wrists against the cuffs and arch my back, pressing my breasts up against his bare chest. I have unlocked my legs from his waist now and obligingly let him lie down on top of me. He is rock hard and he lets me know it.

"Unlock the cuffs, Fred," I say with a moan. "I want you to fuck me. Right now."

"You can't have everything you want, Dora. That's no fun," he chides as he holds the keys up to my face and then flings them across the room.

He's stroking and moving. I feel as if sensation after sensation is piling up, swirling around me, carrying me off into a lost place.

As he goes down on me, he whispers, "Who would have thought my baby is a slut."

• • •

We doze off enveloped in a languorous embrace and wake up a few hours later, reeking of vinegar, vodka, and sex. I tell him I want a bath and he says, "Me too."

Aside from the view, the best feature of my apartment is the master bathroom. There is a big, old-fashioned claw-foot tub by the window, vintage white tile floor, and shiny stainless steel hardware with French *chaud* and *froid* on the handles.

Fred follows me into the bathroom, looks around at the disarray of books all over. He picks up a paperback version of Welty short stories and says to me, "You're the real thing, aren't you?" I am taken aback with the compliment.

"It's the perfect getaway. I can spend the whole week-end in here."

I pour loads of bubble bath in the tub, maybe a little too much; my entire body is hidden in giant drifts of white, snowy fluff. That's when I see the sparkle in Fred's eye.

He sits on the rim of the tub with a towel wrapped around his waist, picks up a bar of soap, and flips it like a lucky penny into the tub. It disappears below the surface for a moment and slowly floats down, grazing my leg.

"Dora! Catch the soap!" Then he jumps in.

We sit facing each other for one decorous moment, like a pregame salute. Let the wild rumpus begin. I dive for the soap, sliding against his thigh, while he grabs my wrist and lunges forward for the slippery prize. I push back against him in a kind of mat slam, my right hand

and foot jamming him in the stomach as I inadvertently slip back and dunk myself. His foot is now wedged between my thighs and he starts moving it seductively higher and higher.

"No fair," I say as I grab his foot and pull him under. I reach for the soap and see his hand underwater, grasping for it also; we both make contact at the same time and the soap suddenly shoots up in the air and sails across the bathroom tile floor, which is now flooded with water.

We both stare at the soap, which has skidded all the way to the carpet. We are out of breath and panting and covered in a film of slippery suds.

"Come here, baby," he breathes in my ear. "Let's do it this time without the cuffs."

What's in a Name

"Get stewed: Books are a load of crap."

~ Philip Larkin, British poet (1922–1985), *"A Study of Reading Habits"* ~

Have you ever eaten a messy, juicy chili cheese dog smothered with mustard and onions on a soft, steamed bun at two a.m., flush with the excitement of a new lover, slightly hungover and famished from all the sex? I could say that it's better than sex. It's not. But it sure caps off a night of sin.

We are sitting on swivel seats at the counter of what is advertised as the most famous hot dog stand in the country. The plaster walls are covered with signed pictures of dead actors and the smell of garlic and chili wafts out the door and down the street. The neighborhood has seen better days, far better. Some say F. Scott ate here during the dismal time he lived in Hollywood and turned out his three thousand pages of mostly worthless screenplays.

There is usually a line down the block waiting to get in, but right now, it's just me, Fred, and a couple of off-duty bouncers. I lean on the cracked white Formica counter, which glistens with a thin film of grease. Fred and I are surprisingly coherent considering we have downed a half bottle of Belvedere. Coherent and oddly empowered in the way lovers seem to get when they have totally satisfied one another.

"So Dora, my pet. Let's get personal. Tell me a secret."

A secret. And just as I was feeling so relaxed. "You tell me a secret."

"I asked you first."

Jesus. I could tell him my father left home when I was eight—no, too depressing. My mother was an alcoholic. I accidentally shoplifted a bra at Victoria's Secret. Since my separation my credit rating has gone into the toilet or, how about I put Botox in my forehead to keep it from furrowing when I read. Well, for sure, I'm not telling him about the freeway thing. I have to find just the right secret. Can't be gossipy and petty. Also can't be too deep or dark or messy or, for that matter, secret. This is giving me a headache. "Okay. Did you know I was named after Eudora Welty?"

Uh-oh. Did I detect a slight slur? Am I a little drunk? What the hell.

He smiles indulgently. "Oh, is that so . . ."

I know that look. He thinks I'm drunk.

"Yes. It is so."

"I'm not wild about the Southern women writers, a bunch of screwed-up old maids who lived with their parents and tended to their gardens."

"Nice, Fred." What a narrow-minded, chauvinistic, creepy thing to say. I attempt to temper my volubility. "You know, Welty was a brilliant writer. Reading her stuff is like watching slapstick—the timing is impeccable." I give an exaggerated kiss to my fingertips (the international sign for yeah, baby) and end with a flourish of my hand.

Fred is all insouciance. "I don't like slapstick."

"Did you read *The Ponder Heart* or *Why I Live at the P.O.?*"

"Maybe."

"No, you didn't. Otherwise, you couldn't feel this way. Next to Shakespeare, she has the best high comic dialogue I've ever read."

"Shakespeare? Come on, Dora. Let's not get too carried away here."

We're both quiet for a minute while I search for my next line. A-ha! I've got it.

"You know what Mencken said about Shakespeare, don't you . . . 'All he did was string together a lot of old well-known quotations.' " I think for a minute.

"So, what's your secret?" I give him a flirtatious, drunken wink.

Not missing a beat, Fred looks at me and says, "My secret is I really dig you, Eudora."

He laughs as he swivels me around, looks at me, and

plants his hands on my shoulders. I think he's going to kiss me, but instead he takes one of my ten napkins, wipes the chili off my chin, and says, "Now, this is my idea of a hoedown."

Later that night, when the fun and games are finally over, we crash in each other's arms too exhausted to speak. Well, not quite.

"Dora," he whispers. "Can you close the sliding doors?"

"What? Why? The breeze feels nice."

"I can't sleep. The sound of the surf. Too noisy."

"Oh. Okay."

I get up to close the doors . . . and think about this . . . he doesn't like the sound of the surf . . . doesn't like Eudora Welty and he still doesn't like my friends.

Oh well, nobody's perfect.

No Reliable Sense of Propriety

"Just the omission of Jane Austen's books
alone would make a fairly good library
out of a library that hadn't a book in it."
~ Mark Twain (1835–1910), *Following the Equator: A Journey
Around the World* ~

During the next few months, my life settled into a routine. Days I spent in a tired fog, reading novels and running only the most necessary errands, and nights I spent in bed with Fred. I juggled my friends and family, keeping them at bay, conceding an occasional lunch or dinner while I answered their questions concerning my whereabouts with blurry explanations. I wanted to keep my life with Fred completely separate. He had made up his mind that the differences between my friends and his life were irreconcilable, and I was determined not to ruin any more perfectly glorious nights by including them.

Darlene was the only one who crossed the line, periodically joining us for drinks or dinner, which she insisted we split three ways.

The job search went on the back burner. The editor at the *Times* told me he couldn't hire me right now, but I could freelance and he'd put me on the list for the first opening. He asked me what sort of stories I'd be willing to do and, of course, I said anything.

The evening began, as usual, at seven thirty, at the bookstore. Fred and I were planning dinner and a movie. As I enter, I can hear Fred and Sara squabbling in the children's section.

"Sara, this will scare the shit out of her." Fred grabs a brightly colored paperback edition of *Bluebeard* that Sara is holding and shoves it back on the shelf.

"What! I loved this book when I was her age."

"But you're warped," Fred concludes.

"That's true, but if it was up to me, I'd give her something that isn't constantly regurgitated by the media."

"Like what?" Fred asks.

"Like the original *Cinderella,* where the stepsisters lop off their toes to fit into the slipper and birds peck out their eyes in the end." She grimaces dramatically and then giggles.

"Come on, Sara. I don't want to spend the whole night doing this."

"Okay. How about *My Father's Dragon,* where the kid goes to an island to free a baby dragon enslaved by wild animals, or *The Princess and the Goblin*? But just forget about stuff like *The Little Prince.* It's so lame.

Saint-Exupéry was a total freak—he makes me want to vomit. Sunsets, conversations with flowers, crap words like ephemeral." She tops it off with a raspberry.

"It reminds me of the books they made me read in Mormon primary back in Utah, right after we baked Jesus cookies with Miss Evelyn and Miss Gwen. Like everyone didn't know they were gay.

"Oh hi, Dora," Sara says, and gives me the sweetest smile.

She is wearing a minidress, which she proudly tells me is a cut-off vintage gospel choir gown. It is bright sanctuary blue, has an enormous, starched white collar with an embroidered gold cross, and a friar's hood, which hangs down her back like a sweatshirt. It is cinched at her waist with a dark brown leather motorcycle belt and her hair, as usual, is a black clump of messy tangles. She smells faintly of mothballs and patchouli.

"You're from Utah?" I ask.

"Surprised? I grew up in Provo and went to Brigham Young, or Breed'um Young, as we used to call it. Lasted maybe two years."

"What's the matter, not enough lesbians for you?" Fred teases.

"No. Just family differences."

"I can imagine," Fred deadpans.

"Okay, Dora." Sara takes over. "Fred needs some books for his six-year-old niece and we're having a dispute here. He wants to give her *Little Women* and some Disney crap. And I want to get her something more substantial."

"By that, she means violent and scary."

"Well," I interject, "I have to agree with Sara on *Little Women,* but what about the classics? *Alice in Wonderland, Treasure Island, The Black Stallion, The Wizard of Oz, The Secret Garden,* or children's poetry like A. A. Milne or *The Owl and the Pussycat.*"

"One of my personal favorites," Fred interrupts. "Edward Lear hooks up a cat and an owl, archenemies, in a wildly romantic adventure. They fall in love, get married, and 'hand in hand on the edge of the sand, they danced by the light of the moon, the moon . . .' "

Oh shit, I'm thinking. He's at it again. I melt every time. "Let's forget the movie," I whisper.

He gives me a wink and says to Sara, "Okay, let's wrap this up. What about *Sleepy Hollow* or *Huck Finn?*"

Now, I have a definite opinion on this. "Your niece is how old, six? She's too young for *Huck Finn.* Most people view Huck as a lighthearted adventure for kids, but every time I read it, it hits me that the book is profoundly serious. I mean, when you're a kid, you cruise along expecting things to just naturally work themselves out and then all of a sudden, bang, horrible things start to happen. You find out life isn't one big party but filled with sorrow and pain and people who are stupid and prejudiced and hypocritical. Twain created Huck so he could say all that—a semi-illiterate boy who is funny as hell but whose life on the river is lonely and harsh. Jim is really his only friend, and even that is poignant because Huck believes he is morally wrong for protecting him."

Sara and Fred are looking at me in the way that people look at you when you've gone over the top. Freshman lit 101. Sara breaks the silence . . . in my favor.

"How old were you when you first read it?" Sara asks.

"I've read it lots of times. But the first time I was about eight, shortly after my mother accidentally drove our car off a bridge."

"Oops," Fred says.

"We were stuck in the pitch-dark, in the mud, and I was scared as hell. So when I read the part where Twain describes how Huck felt floating down the river on his raft, it was a revelation."

"I can relate to that," Sara says, with an easy glance of camaraderie. "My family threw me out when I was a teenager. I used to sleep under the bleachers on the football field. 'And it sure was dismal and lonesome out there.'" She smiles at me. I know she's quoting from *Huck Finn*. "I'd make up funny stories to amuse my friends the next day."

"I can't even imagine." I feel a wave of compassion. "I holed up in my room and read. Mark Twain made me laugh, but now I get it. His humor was based on sorrow. I loved his line 'There's no humor in heaven.'"

"That's what I kept trying to tell those missionaries who wanted to save me," Sara replies.

Fred looks pointedly at Sara. "Hemingway said that *Huck Finn* was 'the best book we've ever had,' and," he says, baiting her, "HE was a literary god."

Sara scowls. "Yeah, he's just my type, boozing, womanizing, chauvinistic jackass. The poster boy for our patriarchal literary society."

"Sara, my dear," Fred says in a condescending tone, "as you get older you will learn to separate the writer from the writing."

"You know," I interrupt, "after I read *Huck*, I decided I'd had it with Alcott and Austen. Austen's books were too much about the upper class and not enough about real people and Alcott said Twain had 'no reliable sense of propriety.' I never felt the same about her after that."

"Wait a minute. Wait a minute!" Sara butts in. "You never heard of Leona Rostenberg?"

"Well, no, I haven't," I say. Fred's smirking. He knows what's coming.

"She's dead now, poor thing. But she was the one who discovered a series of porno novels written by Alcott under a pseudonym. Blood, passion, opium dens, and other way-cool stuff . . . years before she wrote *Little Women*. What a hypocrite."

"God, Sara. Where do you get all this stuff?"

Sara is clearly pleased with herself. "I'm a literary sleuth, didn't you know?"

"So, what about Austen? Any dirt there?" I ask.

"No. She is what she is. Except Twain hated her. I think he said something like 'Jane is entirely impossible. It seems a great pity they allowed her to die a natural death.' "*

Fred lifts his eyebrows, looks at me, and says, "I would've thought you'd love Austen. Aren't you one of

---

* *Mark Twain-Howells Letters*, "My Mark Twain," by William Howells.

those cultlike Janeites? They're swarming all over West L.A."

"You don't know me."

Fred smiles and gives me a little punch on the shoulder. "I'm working on it. Do you want to come home and meet my mother?"

I laugh. "You're kidding, right?"

"No. I'd like you to meet her."

Whoaaa! Do I want to meet his mother? I don't think so. How do I get out of this? Would it be rude to tell him I don't want to meet her? Absolutely. I can't tell him that. I used to leave the house whenever Palmer's mother showed up. She was mean and bossy. And she borrowed my books and never returned them. It was always, "Oh, doesn't Palmer look nice," and, "Isn't Palmer brilliant" and on and on. You'd think she'd give me some kind of compliment even if she didn't want to, but it never entered her mind. She'd stay in our guesthouse for a month every January to escape the cold. I'd pray for a thaw. Palmer used to throw his hands up rather than confront the issue and say, "What do you want me to do?" Throw the bitch out is what I wanted to say but never did. I relented and served her breakfast in her room and dinner on a tray and listened to her scream back at the TV and drove her to her doctors' appointments and the YMCA, where she swam forty laps (she was as strong as an ox). I hated every minute. Enough!

"I'd love to meet your mother."

Mother's Day

> "Judge not a book by its cover."
> ~ Anonymous ~

*H*ermosa means "beautiful." And it is. A quaint little beach community seventeen miles from Los
Angeles, this small town of twenty thousand consists of
a fishing pier, a few parks, a volleyball court, some bars
and restaurants, a slightly run-down main street, and
not much else. Pacific Coast Highway (PCH to the locals) runs through the middle and divides the little town
like a caste system. West of PCH are expensive beach-
front apartments, condos, and upscale vacation rentals.
East of PCH, the hills rise into somnolent middle-class
neighborhoods with older, run-down tract homes on
tree-lined streets.

As we wind our way into the hills, we pass Ocean View Elementary School, obviously built in the twenties, and then an expanse of trees that all have that slightly askew, weather-beaten look from years of battling the constant ocean breeze. I notice that this is an old-fashioned neighborhood. A few houses down, a woman is watering her lawn in her robe and slippers, and a block farther off, two women talk over a hedge. So different from West L.A.

We pull into the driveway of a small, Craftsman-style bungalow. It looks slightly dilapidated, and probably hasn't been touched in decades. But in this case it's a good thing. The window shingles are displaced in some places but there is an earthiness and authenticity to the structure that I find appealing. To the side of the front door is a sleeping porch. Imagine, in this day and age. I live in a security building, my apartment has an alarm system that rivals any bank's, and still, sometimes in the middle of the night, I hear a noise and feel uneasy.

There is no traffic on the street as we park behind a six-year-old maroon Chrysler. I don't know anyone besides Hertz and undercover agents who buys this kind of American midsized car. The front yard has a well-tended "do it yourself" look. The grass has been mowed sporadically and on the porch there are unmatched terra-cotta pots with flowering plants and hanging fuchsias cradled in jute macramé holders right out of the seventies.

I pick up the bouquet of yellow jonquils I brought for Fred's mother and climb up the three wide steps to the porch. The house has large windows and peaked transoms and all of the woodwork, though peeling, has intricate details and trim. There is a sense of arrival. The doorbell is covered over with masking tape, so Fred knocks a few times on the screen door and opens the unlocked door. Are we in Iowa or what?

"Hey, Bea, we're here," he announces.

Ugh! I hate it when people call their mothers by their first names. It always makes me feel uncomfortable, and I know I'm not alone in this. There is something abnormal about it, like the state of motherhood is foreign to them or they dislike their mother or their mother is so vain that she doesn't want to admit she has a grown son. Even in my dysfunctional family, neither my sister nor I would ever think of calling our parents by their first names.

Bea is standing in the hallway squinting from the bright afternoon sun that is flooding the porch and the garden. The sounds of a muted television float from somewhere beyond the hallway and the smell of roasted meat wafts through the air. Fred gives her a perfunctory "let's get this over with" kind of kiss, then turns and says, "Bea, this is Dora." There is a look on Fred's face I've never seen before. And now it comes to me. The other reason people call their parents by their first name is because they're embarrassed by them.

Fred's mother is a tall, substantial-looking woman in her late seventies, with a wide handsome face, soft gray-green eyes, and a strong masculine-shaped jaw. She wears scuffed Easy Spirit sneakers, a long pleated skirt, and a crisp white long-sleeved blouse with a Peter Pan collar. Her thick gray hair is brushed back in a tidy bun and her hands are large and covered with age spots, but the skin is soft and plump, not at all like the skeletal hands of most women her age. The other thing I notice about her is that she smells like lavender, not the dried-out, faint purple lavender that you find in closet sachets, but fresh, wild, sweet lavender, the kind that grows in gardens and scents the air with faint perfume.

When she first takes my hand to say hello I can feel her plush, strong grip as she says, "Well, Dora. I'm so glad to meet you. Aren't you just a lovely girl." I hand her the flowers. There is a quiet, self-effacing yet watchful quality about Bea that I like immediately. "How nice. I have the perfect vase." We follow her into the cluttered, homey kitchen. The counters are filled with bright-colored jars and mugs and the refrigerator is decorated with a child's drawings held on with magnets. There are three parakeets in a cage in the alcove by the wooden table, and coupons are neatly cut out and stacked in a plastic coupon caddy by the telephone.

As Bea fusses with the flowers, Fred says, "So, where is she?" There is a barely perceptible note of disdain in his voice.

"In her bedroom playing."

Fred looks at her and says, "You know I mean Lorraine."

"Well, she didn't come home last night, but I'm hoping she'll be here soon."

"I won't hold my breath," says Fred, his voice dripping with sarcasm.

Bea looks toward the door. "Hush, Harper'll hear you."

"You know she's going to be disappointed. You never prepare her. We've been over this a thousand times."

"No. She told me she'd definitely be home for Mother's Day and she told Harper that too."

"And you believed her? She'll be home if she happens to need money or her connection splits or she needs a place to crash for the night."

"Well, what do you want me to do?"

"Tell Harper the truth so she doesn't just sit here waiting for her. Again."

"She knows the truth. Don't you know that?"

I quietly back out of the kitchen as Bea looks up sheepishly, embarrassed to be having this conversation in front of me.

I walk down the hall until I see a child's room to the right. The sun is streaming through the crisscrossed white cotton eyelet curtains and there is a twin bed with a faded Little Mermaid bedspread and an old painted wooden headboard. Harper is sitting on the shag carpet in front of ten elaborately dressed Barbies forming two lines in some sort of processional. In the center is a Barbie carriage with a Princess Barbie sitting inside wearing a white satin wedding gown. A Ken doll sits beside her in a crown but no shoes. Thrown to the side are several nude dolls who evidently haven't been invited to the nuptials.

Harper is around six years old, with medium brown braids and a shiny pink clip holding back bangs that are half hanging in her eyes. She is wearing jeans and a hot pink T-shirt that has pastel rhinestones across the front.

"Hi! You must be Harper. I'm Dora."

Harper doesn't look up. "I know. You're Uncle Fred's friend."

"That's right. What beautiful dolls!"

Harper still doesn't acknowledge me. "It's a wedding."

I smile. "Of course."

"Prince Eric and Princess Ariel are getting married."

"Isn't that wonderful, and they have so many nice friends."

Harper's face brightens as she crawls over to one side of the processional and starts pointing to each doll. "This is Princess Lea and this is Princess Jasmine and this is her little sister, Kelly."

She introduces me to each doll. They all have names and stories. I ask a million questions and at one point Harper races out of the room to get the Barbie dog that she left in the living room. I tell her, "My sister and I only had Barbie dolls. You're so lucky you have all this other stuff."

Harper looks at me innocently. "They had Barbie dolls in the old days?"

"Geez, do I look that old?" I laugh.

"Oh no, you're beautiful." She smiles. No front teeth. How adorable. Just then we hear Bea's voice from the kitchen announcing that lunch is ready.

Harper yells back, "We can't come now. We're playing."

Bea yells back, "Right now, Harper. It'll get cold."

Harper reluctantly puts down the dolls and starts to get up. She grabs my hand and pulls me into the dining room.

Fred greets Harper and tussles her hair. "Hi, Cookie, brought you a present."

"I know what that is . . . more books!" she says with a grin.

Fred hands her the books and we sit down at the table. Bea starts making small talk, obviously trying to avoid the issue of Lorraine's absence. Harper doesn't mention it and neither does Fred, although he is hunkered down in an uncharacteristic sulk. The air in the dining room is stifling and Bea gets up to turn on the fan. A welcome breeze moves through the room.

The lunch consists of brisket cooked in dried onion soup mix, fresh green beans, and old-fashioned whipped mashed potatoes that never come out this way when I do them. Bea has baked a peach pie for dessert and obviously has spent a lot of time and effort on this meal.

"It's such a treat to have a great home-cooked meal," I say to Bea.

Bea gives me a deep, low belly laugh and says, "Fred thinks it's too heavy. But I think it's comfort food."

Bea has this way of talking in sentences that end with a sigh or a "my, my, my." She also uses gospel chorus-like asides such as "amen" or "all right" or "yes, indeed." At several points during the meal, Harper asks if she and I can be excused so we can "play some more." Bea smiles at her indulgently and tells her to wait a few more minutes.

I'm amazed that there is still no mention of Lorraine. I say to Harper, "What a beautiful name you have. Were you named after the writer of *To Kill a Mockingbird*?"

Harper looks puzzled and turns to Bea. "Was I, Grandma?"

"Harper, you know how you got your name."

"Do we have to go into this right now?" Fred asks.

Bea ignores him. "My daughter named her after my profession. I was a Harper Lady."

I am about to ask her what that is, when the telephone rings and Bea's shoulders tense. I get the feeling that when the telephone rings around here it's not good news.

Bea gets up, goes to the kitchen, and answers the phone. It's uncomfortably quiet as we listen to her side of the conversation.

"Oh, dear. Oh, no. Okay, okay. We'll come get you." Fred jumps up and goes into the kitchen. Bea hangs up. We hear Fred's angry voice.

"I'm not getting her."

"Please, Fred, I told her we'd come," Bea pleads.

"Let her take a taxi."

"She doesn't have any money and I can't get ahold of her now."

"Jesus, Bea. It's the same old shit around here. How do you expect her to ever get any better if you constantly bail her out?"

I look at Harper's stricken face. "My mommy must be sick again."

"Yes, I'm so sorry. Let's go play some more." I take her hand and lead her back into her room. She sucks her thumb as we walk. As soon as we get to her bedroom, she grabs her small pink blanket off a chair.

I try to divert her attention. "Is that your special blanket?"

"Yes, Bea calls it my pinky dinky."

"That's a good one. I like that." I look up and see Fred in the doorway.

He motions for me to follow him down the hall. There's something amiss, that's for sure. He's holding a cigarette that has been smoked right down to the filter.

"What's going on?" I whisper.

"I'm stalling," he answers with no emotion.

"Are you going to go get her?"

"Of course. It's Mother's Day."

"Do you want me to come with you?"

"Why would I want you to come with me?"

"I don't know. Moral support?"

"Yeah, right. Believe me, I've done this so many times I could do it in my sleep. I'm in a shitty mood and I'm lousy company. Look, Dora, I'm sorry about all this."

"It's fine. Really."

He softens. "This may take a while. Do you mind waiting here?"

"No problem." What can I say?

He's relieved. He kisses me on the cheek and says, "I owe you."

The Woman with
Phenomenal Tresses

"Wisdom is not wisdom when it is derived from books
alone."

~ Horace (65–8 B.C.) ~

It's a long afternoon. I help Bea with the dishes while
Harper watches TV. After that, I read Harper *The
Magic Finger* by Roald Dahl while we sit in plastic
chairs on the porch and watch clouds appear on the
horizon. Bea's backyard at twilight seems almost like an
enchanted garden. There are homemade birdhouses
crafted from petrified gourds hanging in the trees, and a
pair of small bamboo wind chimes faintly tinkle in the
breeze. Just before sunset, gulls circle the neighboring
houses and call to each other in guttural deep-throated
tones. I love this time of day. The colors in the sky are
rich and luminous like stained glass scenes in a cathedral

and Harper and I watch as the light fades and the vibrant reds and pinks in the sky grow weak and anemic. Someone is barbecuing next door and the smell of Matchlight and mesquite perfumes the air. When the sky finally darkens, Harper and I retreat inside.

I help Harper take her bath because Bea's back is acting up, and amazingly enough, Harper is hungry again. There is something wonderful about the way a child smells after a bath, moist, fresh, flowery, and taley, and I inhale the sweet aroma as Harper slips into her robe and heads for the kitchen. Bea still isn't feeling well, so Harper and I make little tea sandwiches and bring them to her room, where we have a Barbie tea party. At seven thirty she starts to rub her eyes. I was a teenager the last time I babysat for a child this age, but I still remember what that means. I watch her mechanically brush her teeth and tuck her into bed. Bea comes in and gives her a kiss good-night and I do too.

"Why don't you lie down too? You must be exhausted," Bea says to me as we turn out the light.

And I am. I go into the guest bedroom and pull a paperback out of my bag, the new David Mitchell book, *Cloud Atlas*. It's all about the transmigration of souls across four continents and three time zones, but I quickly decide that it is totally unreadable. I lie on the bed and watch the fading sun filter through the window, casting shadows on the oversized bureau, the rocking chair, and the side table.

Outside in the yard, I see a clothesline and a long covered sandbox. When I get up to wash my face in the bathroom, dust speckles dance furiously in the gauzy light. Maybe I should just call a cab and go home. How far from civilization am I really? Twenty minutes? I guess I shouldn't do that. It would be so rude. I know, I'll just pad my way down to the kitchen and see if I can find a bottle of something. Bea served sherry at lunch, but hopefully I can find something with a little more teeth.

As I start down the hall I hear a dog bark and someone, maybe Bea, cough and then yawn. There is the muffled sound of a TV sitcom with canned laughter coming from her bedroom. When I reach the kitchen, the birdcage is covered with a dishtowel, and I'm aware that any noise would start them chirping. Where to look? Maybe the cupboard? Bingo. Two bottles of Paul Masson chablis and a pint of Cutty Sark. Normally, I'm not a Scotch person, but I don't want to open the wine, so I'll just take a little nip. I pour it into a plastic cup and take a swig. The alcohol burns up into my center forehead and warms my solar plexus. I take one more swig, rinse out my mouth with a Diet Coke from the fridge, and head back to my room. I look at the clock. This is taking longer than I thought. What could he be doing? I turn back to my book and decide to hunker down and wait it out.

Later that evening, with Fred still gone, the house quiet and dimly lit, Bea lightly taps on my door and says, "Knock, knock." I jump up to let her in.

"I didn't mean to disturb you, Dora." She is carrying what looks like a heavy brown leather satchel stuffed with brushes and plastic bottles along with rollers and combs. The satchel looks ancient, like something from a seedy port town. The leather is cracked and noticeably water stained, and it has the stale, musty smell that always seems to go with used-clothing stores.

"Would you like me to brush your hair?"

"What?" I answer, confused.

"Would you like me to brush your hair? I used to do it for a living when we all lived in Delaware, a hundred years ago. Before we moved to New Orleans." She laughs nervously.

"Oh, I see. Why not? Were you a hairdresser?"

"Not really. Not the way you mean it today. I was a Harper Lady."

"A Harper Lady," I repeat. I have no idea what she is talking about, so I just smile.

"Yes, I used to do the loveliest ladies. It was such a joy. Yes, indeed. The DuPonts and the Rothschilds. I did them all. And they all had such lovely families."

I watch as she pulls out her brushes one by one and then her tortoiseshell combs and bottles of castile soap, tar shampoo, and white vinegar.

"I guess I'm not exactly sure what you did, but I'd love for you to brush my hair," I say, trying to sound enthusiastic. Frankly, I thought it all sounded a little weird, but I was loath to let her know it.

Bea tells me the Harper method was an in-home hair treatment embraced by the social elite that involved neck and shoulder massages along with a special shampoo concocted with natural ingredients and a long brushing-dry session. The business was started by a Canadian woman named Martha Harper who had such gorgeous chestnut hair that P. T. Barnum tried to sign her up for his circus as "The Woman with Phenomenal Tresses."

"Oh, all the celebrities and first ladies had Harper Ladies come to their homes," says Bea. Apparently, the emphasis was on healthy hair, and the trained ladies used natural hair dyes, special tonics, and other methods of stimulating the scalp and hair growth. "Beauty comes from cleanliness and good circulation. That's what we all preached."

"Where did you learn all this, Bea?"

"Oh, well, there were these training salons all over the country, but they all died out eventually. I had a girl-friend who used to work in one downtown and she helped me learn. I had some customers for twenty-five, even thirty years. Every night, Monday through Friday, I'd drive up to Wilmington and even to Rittenhouse Square in Philadelphia to do my ladies. My Whiz, that was my husband, Whizwald, he's passed on now, used to wait for me until I got home. Then we'd sit down to dinner at nine thirty or even ten. He was a good man, my Whiz. He was an electrician by trade, but he had a green thumb and he was a fine dancer. I guess you noticed I'm not such a success with my garden out there."

"Not at all, Bea. It's charming. Did you really go dancing?"

"Oh, yes. We were the oldest charter members of the Delaware Square Dancing Society and we'd go to their socials once a month and dance all night. I had a closet-ful of the most beautiful outfits and so did Whiz. He looked so dapper back then."

Fred never told me this. Any of it. His mother was a hairdresser to society mavens and his father an electrician. They went square dancing on Saturday nights in those insane, garish costumes with corny rickrack and silver fringes that seniors wear to hoedowns. No wonder he left for New York at seventeen. A mortifying combination of factors for a young intellectual who viewed himself as an artist. Still, there was something so lovely and decent and pure about Bea. You'd think by now he'd appreciate her.

"Come sit here, Dora. I can reach your head easier," she says, motioning me over to the rocker. "I have such bad arthritis in my fingers and joints, I can't do the job I used to . . ."

"Oh, that's okay, Bea, you don't have to. Really."

"No, I like it. It keeps me calm, gets my mind off my troubles. I worry so about Lorraine. We've tried everything, god knows. She's been in and out of rehab a dozen times, but after a few days she gets desperate and calls me. I always go fetch her and bring her home. I can't help myself. She sounds so pitiful. It's the devil, that drug. Her boyfriend got her into it and then he up and leaves her when she gets pregnant. I thought if I moved out here, I could help her. But she just keeps getting worse. It's just Harper and me most days, and that's the truth."

Bea is quiet for a minute as she brushes my hair. I can't think of a thing to say.

"Harper loves for me to do her hair. It's our way of comforting each other. Gee, Dora, you have such nice hair, so thick and healthy. Good for you."

Bea brushes my hair with a natural boar's bristle brush imported from England. Her movements are firm and strong, and soon my whole head starts to tingle as the circulation in my scalp is stimulated. Every so often, she dabs what smells like a combination of tar and vinegar on my head, rubs it in with her fingers, and brushes my hair again in long, methodical strokes. First this way, then that. Then she flips my hair over my face and brushes in a circular motion at the nape of my neck. I think this is the next best thing to my Thai masseuse who comes over to my apartment and charges ninety-five dollars plus tip. No. This is better. This is nirvana. Mrs. DuPont was a cagey old broad.

"How much did you charge for this, Bea?" I ask, clearly in bliss.

"My fee was thirty-five dollars to come twice a week, but on their birthdays and Christmas, I'd do it for free. They liked that."

"Did you get a tip?"

"Shhh, Dora, you're supposed to relax."

"I know but, Bea, this is brilliant. I absolutely adore it."

Bea keeps brushing until the streetlamps outside the window flicker on and I can see the domed rings of light reflected on the pavement. She pauses briefly to switch on the bedside light and to check on Harper.

When she comes back, I stand up. "Bea, that was hypnotic. Thank you so much."

"Oh, don't thank me. I loved doing it. Maybe you'll get a good rest now. It's good for that. That's why I always did my ladies at night."

After Bea leaves, I lie in bed in the dark and watch the headlights of passing cars dance across the ceiling. When I was a child, I remember doing the same thing and then listening to the far-off sound of the local train roaring through the station, its whistle blasting through the distant neighborhood. I turn over on my side and thread my fingers through my hair. It feels silky and thick and squeaky clean. For the first time ever, I don't pick up my book to get to sleep. I just drift off in a daze.

Along Came a Spider

"... out of the darkness came a small voice ..."
~ E. B. White (1899–1985), *Charlotte's Web* ~

I wake up to see Fred standing stiffly at my bedside, staring down at my face. The early morning light is filtering through the bedroom window and I feel like I've been sprinkled with angel dust. I haven't been this relaxed in years. He leans over and gives me a perfunctory kiss on the cheek. He has dark, puffy circles under his eyes and he looks like he's slept in his clothes.

"What time is it?"

"Nearly six."

"Did you find her?"

"No. By the time I got there she was gone. I looked for her in the usual places, but I guess she got a better offer. This happens all the time, Dora. Let's get out of here."

I pull myself together, go into the bathroom, and notice that my hair is gleaming. As Fred and I quietly start to walk out, Bea appears in her bulky lavender chenille bathrobe. The pockets are stuffed with Kleenex and there are a few coffee stains on the lapel. Harper is still asleep.

"Oh. You're leaving? Can I fix you some breakfast? How about some fried eggs?" Bea asks.

"No thanks, Bea," Fred says. "I have to get back."

"So, what should I do now, do you think?" Bea asks carefully.

"They'll call when she turns up. You know the drill," he says, brushing her off. I'm a little embarrassed at his abruptness.

"I hope everything works out okay. Thanks again for the, you know." I touch my hair.

"Oh, for goodness sakes, it was my pleasure, dear." Bea gives me a hug. I really like this woman. She stands in the doorway and watches us leave.

Fred's pretty silent on the ride home.

"Maybe you should have stayed to help Bea," I suggest.

"Dora, do you have any idea what it's like to live with someone like Lorraine?" he says angrily, cutting me off.

"No, I guess I don't," I reply, feeling that I've overstepped my bounds.

"She hacks through your love and the love of everyone who knows her. You plead with her to stop, you drive her to therapists, AA meetings, probation officers, doctors' appointments, you lend her money, you lend her more money, you take away her keys, it just goes on and on. She's indifferent to your appeals. And, finally, you throw her out of the house and tell her not to come back until she's sober. And then you're grateful that the whole ordeal is over until the phone rings in the middle of the night and someone's found her on a street corner and she's incoherent and dirty and helpless. And she needs to come home. Bea has run through most of her savings paying for all this stuff. The private rehab places cost thousands of dollars up front and Lorraine doesn't even stay a week. The first time she went she couldn't handle the detox or the rules, so she called Bea screaming in pain and agony. Bea freaked out and picked her up. Then the courts sent her to a lockdown for a month, and as soon as she got home, Bea gave her some cash for the market and that was it. You can't reason with Bea when it comes to Lorraine. She gives in every time, it turns into a disaster, and then Bea comes crying to me for help."

"I had no idea."

"It's worse when Lorraine just holes up in her room, locks the door, and won't let Bea or Harper in for days and days. Then she'll come out and tear up the place looking for money. She's stolen Bea's jewelry, her silver, her camera, anything she could hock. She even wiped out Harper's piggy bank. Bea finally found a great facility, which is where Lorraine was supposed to be now. But, as you heard, she's obviously bolted."

"Why don't you get Harper out of there?"

"Harper won't leave Bea. And Bea won't leave Lorraine. So there you are."

"How long has this been going on?"

"Since Bea moved here five years ago. Harper thinks her mother is sick," he says with disgust. "And I've had it. It's just too draining. Anyway, what can I do?"

"I'm so sorry, Fred." But I'm thinking, isn't there always something you can do? We arrive at my place. He gives me a weak kiss good-bye, says see you later, and leaves.

As I walk into my apartment, I am reminded of an old adage my mother was fond of repeating. If everyone's problems were hung out on a line, you'd pick your own.

I'd planned to use today to make some calls about my job. I'm not exactly in the mood anymore, but I've put it off long enough. I clean up and decide to put together another version of my portfolio. I've heard that the *Santa Monica Tribune* is looking for a metro reporter. These little newspapers don't seem like much, but the editors at the dailies read them religiously and scan them for scoops and newcomers. I guess I'm in that category once again.

I met with my accountant the other day and he delicately suggested for about the ten billionth time that I scale down my spending. He inquired as to whether I had any other sources of income, I guess meaning Palmer. When I said no, he helpfully suggested I speed up my job search. I know he thinks I'm in another world as far as finances are concerned. And I must admit, I barely look at my investment statements or my checkbook balance, for that matter. My sister uses quaint terms such as "the chickens are coming home to roost," to motivate me to take charge. I've pretty much ignored her until last week when she started referring to me as "the poor relation."

I like to blame my cavalier attitude about money on my father, who would compensate for his absences by periodically sending us large checks. The checks were especially generous when he missed milestones like birthdays, school plays, Christmas, and father-daughter dances. I knew that when the envelope showed up, he wouldn't. My mother's drinking would get worse, and the whole cycle would begin all over again. My sister and I took care of ourselves until her binge was over and then she would blithely try to pretend that this was just a temporary situation. Many times she would say, "When your father gets back" but my big question would be, "When?" Sometimes I would sink into a morass of vague anger and resentment. It's strange that Harper doesn't seem to feel that way about Lorraine, although it's hard to know what the child was thinking last night.

I lay my portfolio on my desk, pull out all the supplies my sister brought me, and juice up my laptop. That's when the phone rings and Fred tells me the news. They found Lorraine on the beach, wrapped in a sleeping bag. She'd been dead for about six hours according to the beach patrol, who called Bea shortly after Fred and I took off. Fred's voice is strained as he tells me he's heading back to Bea's and then to the morgue.

There's something excruciatingly quiet about bad

news. All the noises of normal human behavior suddenly cease, but it's the oddest thing—you can still hear the sound of the faintest clock ticking, the wind sighing through the bushes, a far-off bird trilling, or the hum of a refrigerator motor in the kitchen. Human voices sort of . . . fall away . . . like the false veil of protection and comfort we all seem to take for granted in between life's inevitable disasters. I've had this feeling before. One minute you're full of trust and affection, and the next, you feel as if you've been yanked out of your world and are careening somewhere treacherous and unknown.

Fred tells me that Lorraine overdosed on a mixture of heroin and cocaine. He is surprisingly clinical and unemotional as he goes through the details of how they found her and what they are planning to do. He also informs me that Bea is grief-stricken and they haven't told Harper yet. With a feeling of dread, I offer to drop off some food and Fred says something noncommittal like "whatever you think."

I drive to the little toy store in my neighborhood to pick up some things for Harper. Then I stop at a French children's clothing boutique and get Harper an expensive fuzzy pink sweater with a flannel skirt and tights to match. I have it all wrapped and put in the trunk of my car. It's funny how one's mind flashes on events that took place years ago, especially when you least expect it.

My mother woke me up one morning when I was ten and told me that my girlfriend's father had shot himself in the head the night before. He sat in his car, in front of his large Tudor house at twilight, just like the Beatles song, and the whole family heard the bang inside. Anyway, my sister and I went back to her house after the funeral and the only thing I remember was the pile of presents by the door. They were all for my girlfriend, of course, and I was insanely jealous, the way children get when they are totally oblivious to the crushing sadness of something that takes place outside of their universe. I remember thinking that my dad was also gone, never mind that he was living someplace else, and didn't I deserve something too?

I pull into Vicente Foods, pick up a honey-baked ham, lasagna from the deli counter, a chocolate layer cake, a large bottle of Scotch, and several bottles of wine. I'm just going to drop the stuff off and leave.

It's almost dark by the time I pull up to Bea's place. I'm surprised that there are no other cars lining the streets or in the driveway. In fact, the place looks deserted and the front door is slightly ajar. Harper greets me in her pajamas with an expectant smile.

"Are you here because of my mom?" she asks.

"Yes, Harper. I am. I'm so sorry."

"She's in heaven and in my heart," Harper repeats in a practiced, almost singsong voice and I wonder who has coached her.

"That's good," I reply. Definitely at a loss for words.

"Are those for me?" Harper suddenly exclaims with a wide smile.

Bea comes up behind Harper and wraps her arms lovingly around the child's neck.

She's wearing a housedress and slippers and her silken, silver hair is pulled back in a haphazard way.

"Bless your heart, Dora. You didn't need to come back all this way. Look at you. Oh my, and all these groceries and things for Harper. You're such a jewel."

I am about to say something polite like "it was nothing," when I suddenly realize that Bea is weeping and awkwardly trying to dab her cheeks with an embroidered old-fashioned hankie. She has another in the pocket of her dress, with dainty little daisies needlepointed around the edges, and I feel so helpless.

I put my arms around her and feel her heavy frame trembling through her limp, wrinkled housedress. Her face is hot and moist and I can smell that faint touch of lavender on her neck. We stand in that embrace for a few moments like long-lost friends, and I am overcome with feelings of sadness and loss. "I'm so sorry, Bea."

"I know, dear. Thank you."

Somewhere from behind us, I hear Harper's tentative voice.

"Can I open them now?"

"Of course," I answer. How can I leave? I guess I'll stay for a while. At least until some other people arrive.

Harper rips open the presents. Her face brightens when she sees the pink prima-donna sweater. She puts it on over her pajamas and runs to look at herself in the mirror. Then she comes back and proudly says, "I look just like a teenager."

I look at Bea, who's clearly distraught and distracted,

and I say to Harper, "Why don't you go play and I'll fix dinner."

I walk into the kitchen and see half-eaten breakfast dishes still on the table and a lukewarm quart of milk on the countertop. Bea was apparently in the middle of breakfast when she got the news. I start cleaning up and Bea comes in. Her face is drawn and her hands are shaking.

"Do you feel like talking?" I ask. "Is there anyone you'd like me to call?"

"No, thanks. Some things don't bear going into. She couldn't be saved, you know. I don't believe you can save anyone, really. She had to do that herself and the drug took that will away from her. You never knew her, but she loved Harper and me and her brother and her friends. I know she knew we were praying for her. And I know she felt awful about disappointing us all the time."

There is a tone of finality in her voice as she adds, "You need to eat more, Dora. I bet you're one of those girls who eats all day and still looks like a sparrow." She gives me a ghost of a smile. "Do you need some help here?"

"No, you go get some rest, Bea. I'll call you when it's ready."

"That would be real nice, dear. I'm dead on my feet. Thank you."

I watch her drift into the hall and then I slice up the ham, throw a salad together, open the wine I brought, and down a few slugs.

I put everything on the table and call Bea and Harper.

Harper comes running in the way kids do. She asks if she can have some cake and I tell her dinner first. She sits down, half off the chair, and starts wolfing down the ham. It's obvious she hasn't eaten since breakfast. Bea walks in, her eyes red and swollen. "I don't know what in the world is taking Fred so long. Good heavens, why isn't he calling?"

I'd like the answer to that myself. "You know, Bea, sometimes these things take a while. You're dealing with the city and I'm sure there's a lot of paperwork."

Bea sits down heavily and stares off into space. Then she closes her eyes for a moment and clasps her hands in her lap. I can't tell if she is dozing or praying. "Can I get you something to drink, Bea?" Silence.

She slowly opens her eyes. "I tried to get her to come to church. They have a group of young people there that could've helped her. 'For it is written, he shall give his angels charge over thee. And in their hands, they shall bear thee up.' "

Harper is eating, not seeming to hear. I don't know how to comfort Bea. Where are all the other people? Neighbors? Friends? I guess nobody knows yet.

There is a knock on the door. Bea jumps up. From the corner of my eye, I see two uniformed policemen and Fred follows them in. When Bea sees Fred, she erupts into a pitiful, wailing sound and falls into his arms. I feel like I shouldn't be here intruding on their most painful, private moments. I should have waited.

Harper pulls on my sleeve. "Can I have my cake

now?" She either isn't aware of the scene going on at the door or she's had a lot of practice dealing with terrible moments. I quickly tell Harper, let's have the cake in your room. I grab the cake, a couple of plates, and hustle her off down the hall.

We pass Lorraine's room and Harper darts in saying, "I left my blankie in here." As I stand at the doorway, she turns on the light.

"Do you want to see a picture of my mommy?"

"I'd love to," I answer. Oh god.

She takes my hand, leads me into the room, and shows me a small, framed photo from the bedside table. The picture is of Harper and her mother standing on the beach. Lorraine looks shockingly young, a dark-haired, solemn girl in her early twenties with her arms around Harper. The room is poorly lit, with Indian madras fabric sewn as curtains and an Indonesian caftan on the bed. There are carved, wooden gargoyle-shaped candle-holders on a small bookshelf and heavy silver cross necklaces hang over the sides of the headboard. The bedside table is cluttered with a dirty ashtray, a crushed box of Camels, packages of gum, and an open can of Diet Coke. On the floor next to the bed are some well-worn Doc Martens and a pile of dirty clothes. It's clear that Bea doesn't come into this room. Harper's blanket is on the bed next to a few Barbies, some glitter nail polish, and a can of Aqua Net. There is a small TV in the corner with some children's tapes on top.

"Do you want to wait here for my mommy to come

home?" Harper asks as if I'm one of her playmates. I've been told that it takes some time for children to comprehend the finality of death. Harper clearly doesn't understand.

I say, "No, sweetheart. Let's go to your room."

I cut her a large piece of chocolate cake, sit her next to me in her overstuffed chair, and grab one of the books Fred bought for her. *Charlotte's Web*. "Let's read, Harper."

She snuggles into me, balancing the cake on her lap and folding her blankie over her.

" '. . . out of the darkness, came a small voice he had never heard before. It sounded rather thin, but pleasant. "Do you want a friend, Wilbur?" it said. "I'll be a friend to you. . . ." ' "

I remember from my childhood that this book is about life and death, the passing of time, friendship, and miracles. My favorite passage is "Human beings must always be on the watch for the coming of wonders." The sound of my voice lulls Harper to sleep, but I keep on reading . . . right up to the end.

Funeral

"Dying is an art, like everything else."

~ Sylvia Plath (1932–1963), "Lady Lazarus" ~

Lorraine didn't have a normal funeral. Fred and Bea agreed on cremation at Bunker Bros. Mortuary near their neighborhood mall and then, afterwards, threw a sort of afternoon tea at the house. If truth be known, I felt uncomfortable going but Fred took it for granted that I would be there, and I did think I could be helpful.

I drive up to the house on a bright, temperate Sunday afternoon. A bunch of old junky cars line the street in front of Bea's house. A few of them have Haitian liberation or Deadhead bumper stickers and a Ford truck has a silhouette of a naked woman on the passenger door. The Sunday *Times* is still sitting in its plastic wrap on the driveway and the potted plants have taken a turn for the worse. Leaning against the wall of the screened-in porch are a stack of brightly colored surfboards and a pile of duffels. "That's odd," I think.

I walk into the too-small, stuffy living room, which at this point is filled with people, and Bea greets me at the door. I hand her a bottle of wine and a large coffee cake. She is wearing a long, white, starched organza apron with a wide sash, a simple black, tentlike dress, and shiny black ebony beads. Her silver hair is pulled back in a tight plaited bun and she is in her stocking feet. She looks tired and a little out of it.

"Oh, Dora. Come on in. Can I get you a drink?"

"No thanks. Can I help you? With the food or with Harper?"

"That's nice of you, dear," she says, jamming a wet hankie in her apron pocket.

"But there really isn't much to do. I ordered most of the platters from the supermarket up there by the mall. I don't usually do that, and that's a fact, but my heart wasn't in all the preparing. You know when Whiz died, my neighbors took care of everything. Oh my, we had every kind of casserole you can think of and more alcohol than you can shake a stick at. In those days, you had to get your liquor up there at the state blue store and it wasn't so easy to just run out and get a nip. It's different now, of course. My uncle Albert, he got so plastered . . ."

"Hey, Dora. Glad you could come," Fred says in an impersonal, formal way, stopping Bea in midsentence. He looks stiff and uncomfortable.

"How are you holding up?" I ask.

"Good," he says, giving me a peck on the cheek, and then whispers, "Glad you're here."

"Thanks . . . well, I'm sure you have a lot to do," I say as some guests approach. I walk over to a card table where the makeshift bar is set up and pour myself a juice. Harper comes running over to me. She is wearing the outfit I gave her last week, the tights, skirt, and fuzzy pink sweater. She introduces me to her friend from school and the two of them hold hands and disappear down the hallway.

I sit down on the sofa and look around. There is a large manila envelope stuffed with official-looking papers on the coffee table and several large leather-bound photo albums. On the mantel above the fireplace is a modest-looking pewter urn with two candles flanking it, and the same photo of Lorraine and Harper I saw the other night is sitting beside it.

There is something disturbing about an urn. I hate looking at it, although it sure beats an open-casket funeral. I went to one of those once, when my uncle died. We all stood in line to pay our respects and when it was my turn, I noticed that his glasses were slightly askew on his overly rouged face. My aunt reached in the casket to adjust his glasses and I noticed a smudge of makeup came off on her hand. I've never understood the need to have an open casket. I know that people want to say good-bye, but it seems like added torture to have that last glance of your loved one in macabre maquillage. When my dad died and the creepy funeral director suggested an open casket, we all agreed that a large photo was as far as we wanted to go.

I remember at his funeral, people would say things like "He's in a better place" or "He's at peace." I hated all of that because if you asked him, he wouldn't want to be there and neither would they.

Lorraine's friends start to straggle in. There are two tall, dark-haired women in their twenties who look as if they have been sleeping in a very dark room and someone suddenly switched on all the lights. They keep blinking in the afternoon glare and they are both exceedingly pale. It is about seventy-eight, maybe even eighty degrees, but the taller one is wearing a heavy black winter coat with ratty fur trim and black high-heeled ankle-length boots. She wears heavy black eye makeup and black lace crocheted gloves with the fingers cut out. Her name is Violet. Her friend wears a black wool morning coat over jeans and heavy black boots, a kind of Goth, stylized gloom. When Harper sees them, she grins, and both girls give her a long, warm hug. Heartening rather than depressing.

"Hello, precious," croons Violet. "Oh, my baby. I love you so much. And I am soooo sorry. Your mother would be so proud of you today. You look totally dope."

"Dora brought me this. It's for the party."

"You look amazing," echoes the friend, who has dragonfly-blue streaks in her hair and some kind of a tattoo on her wrist, which I can't quite make out. Then they both embrace Bea. These girls could have been close friends of Edgar Allan Poe but somehow, standing next to the regal Bea, it's more like a twisted Thornton Wilder scene. The three of them make a surprisingly good match. Granted, Lorraine definitely had a messed-up life, but she did have some good friends who seemed to adore her.

I flip through the photo album in front of me. Lorraine as a toddler in a swimsuit and flippers, Lorraine and Fred whirring around on an amusement park ride, Lorraine with a wide "happy childhood" smile standing bow-legged on a beach in a floppy hat and sunglasses. When was it, I wondered, that she fell into the abyss? No photos of Lorraine with a man, or for that matter, a baby.

More people now pile into the stifling living room. There is a tall, grizzled man with limp shoulder-length hair named Ish and a few older, dressed-up couples in their sixties and seventies who introduce themselves as Bea's church friends. Most look slightly ill at ease and are carrying small bouquets of flowers or bottles of wine. Hanging around the doorway are a few gaunt, un-shaven guys in their twenties who look wasted. Bea greets each guest with a warm, ardent smile as if they are old family friends. The emotional toll on her is clearly apparent, but she is still hospitable.

"Nice of you to come, dearie."

"Have you seen her album?"

"Please sit down, sugar."

The pastor from Bea's church is also here. I see him take her arm and lead her to the corner of the room, where they sit across from each other in straight-back chairs. Bea bends her head and lowers her eyes as the man takes both her hands in his and talks softly to her as if she were a child. The shadows are lengthening outside the window as I overhear him saying that it wasn't Bea's fault, there was nothing she could have done that would have made a difference. "What you have to understand, my dear, is that everything you did was done out of love and God knows that." Bea shakes her head and starts to sob.

Harper tugs on my arm. "There's some big plates of sandwiches. Do you want one? We have lots of food."

"You are a wonderful hostess, Harper. But I'll help my-self."

I go into the kitchen where I find a few people talking quietly in the corner and Fred sipping Scotch. His eyes are weary and he's looking flushed but more relaxed.

"We're going to the beach now for the ceremony," he tells me, and I'm thinking, What ceremony? I guess they're going to have a memorial service after all . . . that's nice. He walks out and as I'm getting something to eat I hear the woman in the corner whisper, "It's for the best. It was no good for the child. No one will tell Bea that to her face, but everyone's thinking it . . ."

Fred makes the announcement in the living room and then goes up to the mantel, lifts the lid to the urn, and removes a small plastic bag, the contents of which look suspiciously like kitty litter. People start piling in their cars and Harper excitedly asks Bea, "Can I ride with the big girls?" One of the Goth twins says, "Cool, Harper. Come with us."

"Dora, just wait. You'll come with Bea and me," says Fred.

The young men grab their surfboards and throw them

into their cars. A few of them have long boards with eucalyptus tied to them, and in most cases, the boards stick out the window like a dog catching the breeze. They tie a red flag on the ends and take off. We weave our way down the hill, cross Pacific Coast Highway, and drive up the coast a bit until we hit a somewhat deserted beach.

By the time we get there, most of the guests have already arrived and are walking on the sand to the water's edge. The girls carry bunches of carnations and sage and someone holds a large conch shell.

The guys then pull wet suits and rash guards out of their duffels and strip down to their boxers. No one is talking. Ish seems to be leading the proceedings. He suits up and swings the backpack with the bag over his shoulder. They all slide into the ocean after him, carrying the eucalyptus and carnations.

It's one of those perfect California sunsets—the wind has stopped, the sky is slashed with oranges, purples, and reds, it could be a poster from *Endless Summer*. They paddle out into the chilly Pacific in formation until they are well beyond the surf. At this point, like synchronized swimmers in the Olympics, they form an almost perfect circle, boards pointed in like a giant pinwheel. One of the girls burns sage on the beach, telling us it's an ancient Chumash Indian custom—cleanses the soul and banishes sorrow.

Ish straddles his board, says something inaudible, opens the bag, and dramatically sweeps the ashes out to sea. Someone blows the conch shell and starts to beat on the drum. Everyone on shore is quietly weeping. I look over at Fred, stoic, eyes cast down. He has his arms around Bea, who is sobbing. Harper is standing next to Bea with a bewildered look on her face.

After the surfers return, the guests take turns giving impromptu tributes to Lorraine. I learn that most of these girls are fairly new friends and that Lorraine bounced around a lot, that she came to California six years ago and got a job working as a bartender at a local restaurant. She apparently had a boyfriend named Bobby D, who doesn't seem to be here. Now Ish stands up, puts on his black sunglasses, and speaks.

"Lorraine, honey. I didn't really know you but I told Bobby D that I would stand in for him today on account of he's been pretty fucked up since you, you know, gave it up. I'm not sure if you can hear me up there, but if you can, I have a few things to say . . ."

I'm thinking to myself, I can't even imagine. . . . I look over at Fred and he's shaking his head in disbelief.

Ish goes on, "We know you are going to a better place and that things got pretty messed up for you toward the end. But honey, we love you. Just remember that. And we aren't gonna ever forget you. And you left a beautiful baby doll here on earth and I know Bobby D is thinking about you right now and will always love you. Amen."

The sounds of the highway rise and fall with the eternal rolling of the waves and I can hear the roar of a faroff jet somewhere in the clouds.

Bea goes next. She takes out a folded piece of lined notebook paper and clears her throat. Her voice is shaky but audible. Violet puts her arms around her as she reads and Harper, surprising me, edges up beside me and takes my hand. Her hand is so small and soft and smooth. And she is holding on so tight. I kiss the top of her head as Bea starts to read, "Lord, now lettest thou thy servant depart in peace, according to thy word: for mine eyes have seen thy salvation which thou hast prepared before the face of all people. For all flesh is as grass and all the glory of man as the flower of grass. The grass witherist and the flower thereof falleth away."*

Fred is the last speaker. He recites from memory, of course, and his voice is clear and strong and mesmerizing. He starts out by saying, "This is called 'Love Song' by William Carlos Williams.

> "Sweep the house clean,
> hang fresh curtains
> in the windows
> put on a new dress
> and come with me!
> The elm is scattering
> its little loaves
> of sweet smells
> from a white sky!
>
> Who shall hear of us
> in the time to come?
> Let him say there was
> a burst of fragrance
> from black branches."

---

* Luke 229–232, Peter 123–124.

Dr. Seuss Doesn't Like Kids

> "It had been startling and disappointing to me
> to find out that story books had been written
> by people, that books were not natural
> wonders, coming of themselves like grass."
> ~ Eudora Welty (1909–2001), *One Writer's Beginnings* ~

You may be wondering why we're speeding down the 405 in Darlene's faded yellow 1963 convertible Thunderbird. I'm riding shotgun, Bea and Harper are in the backseat, the sun is beating down on us, and the windshield acts more like a funnel than a barrier. Darlene drives her ratty muscle car as if it were a Ferrari, and as she downshifts I hear something that sounds suspiciously like metal scraping blacktop. My thighs are stuck to the vinyl seat, the radio squawks an old Beach Boys song, the shocks are a thing of the past, and Darlene is in heaven.

"I love my 'bird," she yells at me over the wind. Sometimes you just need a party. And then you call Darlene.

It's been a month since Lorraine died. Fred and I have spent a lot of time helping Bea with all the formalities and paperwork. I usually played with Harper outside while they sat at the dining room table filling out forms and dealing with the mountains of official documents that needed to be filed.

After a few weeks of this, Fred told me that Harper was finally going back to school and Bea had asked him to come along for moral support. He added that Harper was less than enthusiastic and that Bea kept putting off the date of her return. On the day before he was supposed to take them, Fred got a call from Bea telling him not to bother. We had just eaten breakfast and Fred was getting ready to go to work. The two of them had been getting on each other's nerves lately and it was obvious, at least to me, that Bea felt she had disrupted Fred's life long enough.

"She doesn't really mean it," I said to him. "She just doesn't want to impose. I still think you should go."

"If you think it's so important, why don't you go?" he snapped.

"Okay, I will," I said. Boy, is he in a bad mood. But now I'm stuck. I AM right, though. Someone should be with them.

I called Bea back and told her I'd like to go instead of Fred and was that all right. I had bought a few things for Harper's room and I was planning on bringing them this weekend anyway. Bea, ever gracious, said she'd be delighted. Fred grumbled and left for work.

The next morning, I held Harper's small, delicate hand as Bea and I walked her into her second-grade class. The teacher, a young woman in her mid-twenties, gave Bea and Harper a hug and told them how much she missed having Harper in class. There was a poster on the blackboard signed by all the children welcoming Harper back, and I noticed her trying to wiggle out from the glare of all the attention. No kid wants to be different.

The teacher took Bea and me aside and reassured us that the counselor was standing by to help. It seemed as if the school had it handled. As we were leaving, Harper, whispering in my ear, asked me if I'd be there when she got home.

"Yes, of course," I answered. She wrapped her thin arms around my neck and buried her head in my shoulder. Then she whispered something to Bea as well and clung to her until Bea gently pulled away. "Now, you're my big girl and you're going to be just fine."

I had bought a pink satin poufy comforter with matching sheets and pillows for Harper's room and a pretty round braided area rug to put by the bed. When Bea and I got home, we set up Harper's room and then spent the rest of the day taking boxes of Lorraine's stuff to Goodwill.

When Harper got home and saw the room, her eyes widened and she covered her face with her hands. "I love it," she said shyly.

Later that night, when I told Fred about the day, he admitted that it was good I had gone and thanked me. He said Harper was bouncing off the walls and it was about time she was back in school.

In the weeks that followed, Harper resumed her usual activities, including Bible studies and an art class after school. Someone else took over Brownies and a few of the other things that Bea used to do. Every time I visited the house with Fred, Harper seemed busy and remarkably well-adjusted, considering the situation.

Then it was June and the pace of things shifted. Harper's school let out and her schedule loosened up. Fred and I tried to stop by as often as we could, but the last time we went over, Bea seemed tired, Fred detached, and Harper was unusually withdrawn.

We were in the midst of a terrible bout of June gloom, the California phenomenon where the cold marine layer collides with the hot inland air and creates a blanket of thick morning fog, which can last all day. Harper's spirits, which had been pretty stable, took a sudden turn for the worse. I don't know whether it was depression or grief or boredom or a mixture of all three, but Bea was starting to worry and so was I. Harper just seemed like she was at loose ends. She would lie limply on the couch in her heavy flannel pajamas, afflicted with a kind of inertia that left her staring out into the emptiness, uninterested in whatever activities we suggested.

At about the same time, Fred got a call from New York regarding his play. This had been a bone of contention with us because he still hadn't let me read it. He said it was because I wouldn't like it, but I think he was afraid of my reaction. Whatever. An agent in N.Y. had shown some interest and wanted to meet with him. Fred was cautiously optimistic and we celebrated at dinner the night before he left. He took me to one of our favorite places, Paddy's Crab Shack. I wore a black chiffon see-through blouse and a sexy, tight A-line skirt. This was our first real date since Lorraine's death, and we were both thinking that we needed this night.

Fred looked weary and he wasn't as talkative as usual. It was okay by me. Totally understandable. At least he wasn't as depressed as he'd been. We both threw back a few and started to relax. He told me he was reading a fantastic, slim little novel by DeLillo called *The Body Artist,* about a woman who lives alone and encounters a strange, ghostlike guy who knows all about her. Weird. He then amused me with the latest dumb bookstore customer story. Several times I had an urge to bring up Bea and Harper, but I caught myself. He always seemed to brush off any of my concerns.

After dinner, Fred took me in his arms and we danced to Johnny Hartman and John Coltrane's "You Are So Beautiful." I just love the way he dances. I love the way he feels and smells. He did that thing I really like, brushing up against my ear with his mouth. He still does it for me. That's all there is to it.

The next morning, I told Fred I would check in with Bea while he was gone. When I called her later that afternoon, she told me that the situation with Harper had deteriorated. Harper had a meltdown the day before when a friend came over to play and she was refusing to go to Bible studies or anywhere else for that matter. She just wanted to sit in Lorraine's room and watch TV.

Darlene happened to call right afterwards and when I told her what was going on, her response was, "Road trip! I'll drive."

At first I thought, well, that's a dumb idea, but then I

remembered it's what my mother used to do when things got really bad at home. A literary road trip. Why not?

So now we are heading for La Jolla. Often referred to as the best place to live in America, the draw is that it was the home of Theodor Geisel, better known as Dr. Seuss.

We get off the freeway at the tony seaside town of La Jolla. We drive past golf courses, restaurants, and low-key shops like Cartier and Ralph Lauren until we reach a gas station. Bea and Harper get the key and head for the restroom while I fill up the car and hand Darlene some bios of Dr. Seuss I found on the Internet.

When my mother used to throw out historical facts during our literary trips, my sister and I would zone out. But because this is Dr. Seuss, I'm hoping to pique Harper's interest.

"Darlene, pick out a few facts for me to tell Harper," I say as I swipe my credit card.

"Not gonna happen. This is booooring. . . . Let's go to Sea World."

"I am NOT going to Sea World. And you're wrong. All kids like Dr. Seuss. *The Cat in the Hat, Green Eggs and Ham, The Grinch.*"

"Okay. If you say so." Darlene starts to paraphrase the articles in a singsong voice. "It says here, Dr. Seuss's real name was Theodor Geisel and he moved to La Jolla in the early fifties with his first wife. Published forty-four children's books. Invented the name Dr. Seuss when he published *And to Think That I Saw It on Mulberry Street*. Seuss was his middle name and he just gave himself the doctor title. Uh-oh! Listen to this. Met his second wife, Audrey, eighteen years his junior, when they were both still married to other people. In the wake of their affair, Seuss's first wife, Helen, committed suicide. Audrey divorced her husband, married Seuss, and sent her two daughters away to boarding school."*

"What?! Where are you reading this?"

"*The New York Times.* You couldn't make this stuff up. Listen, quotes from the wife, 'He was very happy without children. I've never been very maternal. There were too many other things I wanted to do.'† God, who are these people?"

"This isn't exactly what I had in mind."

Harper and Bea appear from the bathroom. Harper's hair is a windblown mess. She's wearing a white *The Cat in the Hat* T-shirt that I bought her and a denim skirt with ruffles. Bea has a floppy cotton hat tied under her chin and they are both excited to finally be here.

"Are we almost there?" Harper asks in a thin, expectant voice. Her eyes are wide with anticipation.

Darlene and I look at each other. "Oh yes!" I say with forced enthusiasm.

We drive up to the summit of La Jolla's Mount Soledad, where a row of twisted and bent eucalyptus trees line the street. The house is a two-story structure surrounding an old observatory tower, which was Seuss's studio, and there is a picture window that offers a com-

---

* *The New York Times,* November 29, 2000. "Mrs. Seuss Hears a Who, and Tells About It," by Joyce Wadler.

† Ibid.

manding view of the Pacific Ocean. Parked out in front is a 1984 Cadillac with the personalized license plate GRINCH.

As we approach the house, Darlene points her index finger to her head and dramatically pulls an imaginary trigger, the universal sign for blowing your brains out. "Pow!" she mouths as she races past Geisel's house.

"Dear, could you slow down a little?" Bea asks Darlene. Darlene grudgingly slows down.

I whisper to Darlene to cool it and quickly give Harper my own version of Geisel's life. What a bust.

Normally, I would have gone into a whole thing. We would have parked a couple blocks away, walked to the house, and talked to a few people in the neighborhood. Then we might have looked up at the room and described what it must have been like to sit at those magnificent windows and write some of the most beloved children's books of all time. I would have told Harper how Seuss started out as a cartoonist and his first children's book was an ABC book. How before his books were published, children's books were dumb little Dick and Jane readers that droned on and on and bored kids to tears. But my heart just wasn't in it.

Instead I say, "We can't go in because the widow still lives there."

"Speaking of wicked witches, can we go to Coronado now?" Darlene asks. Our next stop is the home of L. Frank Baum. Thank god we have something else planned today.

Halfway to Fairyland

"There is no frigate like a book
To take us lands away."
~ Emily Dickinson (1830–1886) ~

We are now speeding across the Coronado Bay Bridge, where, in the distance, the grand old Hotel del Coronado rises up like Oz above the Pacific shore. It's been said that this flamboyant Victorian monument, with its cupolas, red-shingled turrets, and whimsical architecture, was the inspiration for the Emerald City, and I tell Harper that the author of *The Wizard of Oz* lived in a now-famous house down the street.

As we pull up to the hotel, Harper catches her breath. "Are we going in there?" she whispers with wonder in a hushed, cathedral-like voice.

"Yes," I answer. "We're staying here tonight."

"It's all planned. Leave it to your Auntie Darlene," Darlene crows, as if she had anything to do with the hotel.

"My goodness. Doesn't it look just like a wedding cake, Harper? Dora, my dear, this is too much," Bea says.

"Oh no, Bea. I'm doing this for me too. I've wanted to come here. It's nice to have company . . . wait until we get inside . . ." I say. Harper is now pulling my hand and excitedly running into the formidable, wood-paneled lobby.

I can hear her giggling as Darlene and I check in and the receptionist confirms our connecting rooms. When they ask me if I want a cot for Harper, I say yes.

"Make sure they don't charge you for the cot," Darlene adds in a too-loud voice. "These places always try to gyp you on the extra stuff. And don't give Harper the key to the mini-bar. The Cokes are like ten dollars."

I ignore her and take the keys to the room. She sneaks a look at the price and says, "The motel across the street is sixty bucks a night and you get breakfast. This is why you never have any money, Dora. You could've snowed Harper with a tour of the hotel and then moved over to the Cozee Cottage."

It's always such a delight to travel with Darlene. "Cut it out, Darlene. The whole point is to spoil them."

"Okay. Never mind. This is really nice of you, Dora."

They are now serving high tea in the Crown Room and I think, why not? I understand that Baum actually designed the crown-shaped chandeliers that drop from the domed sugar-pine ceiling. We sit at a table next to the window and gaze out on gardens bursting with bougainvillea, hibiscus, and birds-of-paradise. I remember when I first moved out here, I was amazed to see birds-of-paradise growing like weeds next to gas stations—back East they are so expensive and rare.

We go for it and order the whole thing: scones with strawberry preserves and Devon cream, cucumber sandwiches with the crusts cut off, pastries, chocolate-dipped strawberries. There are five different kinds of imported tea, but Harper has her heart set on hot chocolate so we order that as well.

The presentation is lavish and Harper nods earnestly when a waiter asks her if she wants whipped cream. "Yes, please," she says, her mouth open, eyes bright, as he leans over her shoulder and spoons out mounds and mounds into the white porcelain cup. He leaves the steaming sterling silver pot on the table next to several three-tiered silver servers laden with sweets.

It is twilight now, the darkness encroaches on our little tea party, and the warmth from the room, the tea, and the company wash over me. I watch Harper demurely reach for a tart and then eat it ever so slowly, one bite at a time.

"My goodness, how fancy," beams Bea. "This is like a dream."

"It sure is," Darlene says, helping herself to some of the child's whipped cream. "What do you think of all this, kiddo?"

"It's really good," Harper says self-consciously.

"Tomorrow we'll go on a little field trip, see the house

of the man who wrote *The Wizard of Oz,*" I tell Harper, pulling some research out of my purse.

"Put it back, Dora. Don't ruin this! I don't want to know anything about him. I loved that movie," Darlene hisses.

"Geez. Relax. Baum loved children. He was a good guy."

"Well, I don't know what other junk you might dig up and, frankly, I'd rather not hear it," Darlene says as she motions for the waiter to come over.

The waiter appears instantaneously and Darlene says, "Any chance of a little high-octane stuff for the tea? It's five o'clock somewhere." She looks at her watch with a flowery gesture of surprise. "Oh my! It's five o'clock here!"

The waiter, a twenty-two-year-old college student stuffed into formal attire, smiles, and is clearly getting a kick out of her.

Darlene flashes a flirtatious grin. "Just look at these fellows." She points to a group of middle-aged business-men at the next table. "I'm sure they're dying for a little hooch. Aren't you, guys?" They seem more than agree-able. My lucky night.

Bea and Harper are watching in amazement. Harper's hand flies to her face, covering her mouth, hiding her smile, like kids do when they're hearing something they're not supposed to, and I quickly decide it's time to reel Darlene in before this goes any further.

"Okay. Time to check out our rooms," I say with gusto. We head upstairs, passing an antique caged elevator in the middle of the lobby, which is manned by an old-fashioned uniformed operator in a pillbox hat. Harper is thrilled. "Grandma, can we ride in that?"

"We're on the fourth floor and that old thing only goes to the second. Let's just take the regular one," says Darlene.

"Oh no. It'll be fun. Let's take this one," I say.

"You're such a pushover, Dora," Darlene whispers fondly. "I can tell what kind of mother YOU'RE going to be. Your kids will get away with anything."

Our connecting rooms have large balconies fronting the white sand beach. Bea and Harper are staying in one room and Darlene and I share the other. We unpack and settle in for the night. Darlene is very busy in the bathrooms collecting all the amenities: soap, shampoo, conditioner, body lotion, shower caps, and she even throws the candle in her bag. I tell her to at least leave some soap for the shower. And if she swipes the robe, it'll cost us a hundred bucks. She breezes past me and flashes a heads-up sign. Then she switches on the satellite radio and turns to a rock station. Black Eyed Peas are playing "Let's Get It Started" and she proceeds to talk about the latest film she saw—something the critics call a religious-horror-satanic spectacle, which I concluded was a terrible movie.

Around eight, she wanders into Bea and Harper's room and I hear the two of them laughing and carrying on as though they were best friends. The conversation gets around to Bea's Harper Lady days and Darlene flips out.

"You are such an amazing woman, Bea," Darlene gushes, loopy and endearing all at once. If Darlene likes you she'll hang on your every word, in a guileless, completely sincere way. Suddenly, Darlene jumps up and yells, "Bea, it's starting!" What a coincidence that some campy nighttime soap is "can't miss TV" for both of them. Darlene flops on Bea's bed and the two of them become thoroughly engrossed.

That's when I hear a light knock on the connecting door. Harper is standing there in her pjs and terrycloth hotel slippers that are much too large for her thin bare feet. She is holding her blanket in one hand and a toothbrush in the other. "Can I come in?" she asks tentatively.

I lay her blanket on the bed and give her a big hug. Her body is warm and slight and her wet hair smells like Bea's castile shampoo.

"Of course," I say with a smile.

"Bea says that I can only stay for a little while because I might bother you."

"No, I want you to stay," I say, closing my book of short stories and laying it on the bedside table.

She smiles and jumps on the bed, slipping under the covers next to me. The hotel sheets are bright white and heavily starched. They feel cool, crisp, and luxurious.

"This bed is nice," says Harper, pulling the fluffy down comforter right up to her chin.

"Shall I tell you a story?" I ask. She nods and cuddles closer.

"Hmm," I say, stalling, mentally sorting through all the old stories I read as a child.

"Once upon a time—"

"Not scary," she interrupts.

"Okay," I say. "Once upon a time—"

"And not sad . . ."

"Okay," I say again, smiling. "Not scary. Not sad. Got it."

Harper sighs and I feel her body relax.

I tell Harper the story of *The Water Babies* by Charles Kingsley. I remember most of it but change it around, especially the part about the poor little chimney sweep who was beaten by his master. I'm pretty sure she's never heard it before because you can't even find the book anymore. It's probably because it's too old-fashioned and the language is difficult.

Harper loved the part about the Irish fairy godmother who changed children into water babies and how they swam around in an ideal world where the sun was never too hot and the frost was never too cold and they had nothing to do but enjoy themselves and look at all the pretty things.

After that, I tell her the short version of *The Borrowers*. She hasn't seen the movie, thank goodness, so all the charm and mystery of things just disappearing are fresh and new to her.

But then something happens. I'm describing to her how things you love are never really lost, they are just borrowed by magical fairies, when suddenly, I see tears rolling down her cheeks. Her shoulders are heaving up and down as she buries her head in the pillow.

"I miss my mommy," she cries.

Oh god. How stupid I am for telling her that story. I pull Harper up in my arms and set her on my lap on the edge of the bed. She leans her warm moist cheek on my shoulder, still sobbing, and I pat her back and stroke her hair.

"Gee, Harper. Such a lot of troubles for a little girl, and you are so brave and wonderful."

"Why can't my mommy come back from heaven? Maybe the angels just borrowed her for a little while and they'll bring her back to Grandma and me and then we'll all be together again."

"Harper, baby, your mommy will come back in your memories and in your heart. All your life she'll be with you. I know it doesn't feel like that now, but it will happen." I wonder if what I'm saying is making her feel better. She's quiet for a while as I rock her back and forth. If this gets any worse, I'm calling Bea.

"Do you want to tell me something about your mother? Something you remember?" I ask.

Her brow furrows. "Grandma and I would sometimes wait for Mommy to come home and we'd be so worried. When she came home, even though it was really late, we'd have picnics on the rug in front of the TV and eat jelly sandwiches with popcorn."

"Sounds like fun."

Harper smiles. "Yes. And then she'd tell me stories about her boyfriend and how we were all going to take a trip someplace soon."

"I bet she was really looking forward to that."

"And then she'd let me put on her eye shadow and lipstick and we'd dance to teenage music."

They could have been sisters, poor kid. Harper gets

back into bed, I rub her back, and she falls asleep almost immediately.

In the movie version of *The Wizard of Oz,* Dorothy's adventure is just a dream. In Baum's book, Oz really exists, a magical land over the rainbow, where a child can escape all of her problems and sorrows. So now she sleeps. Frank Baum believed in the power of fairy tales, in the power of a child's imagination to heal and comfort. To pull them out of dark places and carry them to a distant land. I hope she's halfway to fairyland.

Lost Days and Knights

"You should only read what is
truly good or what is frankly bad."

~ Gertrude Stein (1874–1946) ~

Fred seems stern and aloof as he walks out of the baggage area lugging his computer bag and a small duffel. His hair is messy, he has a two-day growth of beard, and he's wearing jeans, a rumpled, untucked linen shirt, and a black leather jacket. When he first catches my eye, he says, "Hey," with half a wave. But he doesn't give me the usual warm hug. I can't really read his expression, it's remote and closed. I gather things didn't go well in New York.

We chat about a few innocuous things until we get into the car. "How was the trip? Was the weather okay in New York?" His answers are clipped, almost snippy. Something's up.

"Not only were they total assholes but they were all of twenty-two years old. What do they know about what makes a good play? I mean, how can you be in this business and not have read Albee or Strindberg or even Sartre, for god's sake?" he rants.

This isn't sounding good.

"Well, they must have liked it. They brought you to New York," I say, trying to stay upbeat.

"First of all, they didn't 'bring' me, I went. And I don't know why they said they liked it, because they wanted to change everything."

"Well, couldn't you work with them on it?"

"They were impossible. Anyway, they called me the next day and passed. The whole trip was a complete waste."

"I'm sorry, Fred. At least your family was taken care of . . ." He nods mechanically and then falls silent.

"Yeah, Bea told me all about it." He holds my gaze a minute and then looks away.

"And . . . ?" I ask.

"What's going on here, Dora? What do you think you're doing?" What is he talking about?

"Well, what I thought I was doing was showing Harper and Bea where the Oz books were written," I reply, swallowing hard. I am baffled and can feel my stomach tensing up. I know he had a tough time in New York but this is ridiculous.

"That's not what I mean," he snaps. "You take them on this lavish trip as if they were your little pet foster foundlings who come from nothing and you shower them with bullshit, expensive stuff like you're the fucking good fairy. They're not your problem, you know?"

"I'm speechless." I feel as if I've been slapped.

"Listen. I don't want to hurt your feelings," he says, softening a little, "but I've done my bit. They're not my responsibility. And, frankly, they're not yours."

"They're your family. They need you."

"Bea can handle it from now on. She knows how I feel. Anyway, I wouldn't be any good for them. I'd just end up resenting the whole deal. They're okay now," he rationalizes, "and I'm not going to disrupt my life anymore." I am stunned at his selfishness.

"You really feel that they're okay now? How can you be so cold?"

I am trying hard to control the tangle of wounded feelings and disappointment twisting through me. I look over and catch him giving me an insolent stare. It's so strange to be totally caught off guard. This has happened to me just a few times in my life and, afterwards, I'm always amazed at the complete lack of understanding and communication. It's almost like you're speaking two different languages and neither one of you can make any headway. Sometimes I hear a little voice saying, "Just walk away, Dora," but you need the other person to understand. Trying to explain yourself just escalates the situation as you get more and more frustrated and angry.

"What's this all about, anyway? Maybe you just don't have enough to do. Maybe you're just bored."

"Is that what you think? I like Bea and Harper. Anyone would like them. What's wrong with you?"

"Don't throw this guilt thing on me. I don't have to spend my life taking care of my mother and my sister's kid."

"You have no heart." A little dramatic, but that's how I feel.

"Oh, like you're Mother Teresa in your fucking Prada dress and your five-hundred-dollar Gucci shoes."

I pull the car over to a gas station and say, "Get out!"

•　•　•

What was I thinking? Maybe Fred's right. Just because someone in your family needs help, does that mean you have to drop everything and take over? How much do you have to give? How much does your family deserve to get? I mean, some people end up devoting their lives to someone else out of obligation and guilt. And you only live once. I had an aunt who spent her whole life taking care of a sick husband and then a sick daughter. Well, her husband finally died, her daughter finally got better, and now she's seventy-five and alone and bitter. Maybe that's what Fred's afraid of, looking back on lost opportunities, a half-lived life filled with regrets.

But how can he just abandon them? How can he live with that? And what about the notion of doing something out of love without worrying about the consequences? Just feeling good that you can help them and make them happy.

Okay, maybe I did overdo it with the gifts and the hotel. But that wasn't the point. He's had it with them. I
understand how these things work. Sometimes you just
want to walk away.

Oh damn! I feel it coming. Yes. It's definitely coming.
I turn off my cell phone, turn on my answering machine.
Put on my junky sweats. This is going to be an epic
binge. I don't care if I ever emerge.

What to read? I examine my bookshelf. Nothing
grabs me. It all looks so depressing and self-important
and the print's too little and the books are too big. I
want to be entertained. I want a page-turner. Maybe
something to fit my mood . . . hard-boiled, gritty, something with guns, murder, body parts, and women getting
back at selfish, mean, small-time hoods. Okay. I got it.
Sam Spade. I go to the mystery section. (Yes, I do have a
mystery section. Macdonald, Hammett, and Chandler
were great American novelists.) I start out rereading *The
Maltese Falcon*. Perfect. Spade has a relationship with a
woman but doesn't think twice about turning her in.
People who do bad things deserve what they get. Yes!

I settle myself on the couch and move on to the
intellectual—Ross Macdonald. I start to read *The Chill*.
Nah, a little too psychoanalytical for my mood. Moving
on to, oh yes, my favorite, Raymond Chandler. Where is
Philip Marlowe when I need him? A dick with honor. A
modern-day knight with a college education. Gray eyes,
a hard jaw, listens to classical music. Rescues women
from terrible situations.

I curl up, grab my bottle of wine (which I notice is

half gone), and prepare to steep myself in Marlowe's romantic presence. I read and read and doze and read. When I finish the last one, *The Lady in the Lake,* I am momentarily content. The story is damn good but I've had my fill of the genre for now. I'm almost yearning for something gentler, more escapist.

What's this box on the bottom shelf? Oh. Darlene's gift. It's still wrapped in red-and-green-striped paper with goofy Santa Claus faces all over it. Handwritten on the lid: "Dear Dora, Merry Christmas. I know you're going to love these books! Just try one! You'll see. Love, Darlene."

It's July. Think I can open them now. I rip open the package and pull out the paperbacks. Must be twenty of them. Hmmm. Looks like romances. Fred would be appalled. Well, fuck Fred! *The Paid Companion* by Amanda Quick, *Lady Be Good* by Susan Elizabeth Phillips, *Forbidden* by Elizabeth Lowell, *Paradise* by Judith McNaught. *The Reluctant Suitor* by Kathleen Woodiwiss. *The Heiress* by Jude Deveraux. I read the blurb on the back, something about a majestic knight falling for the beautiful, rich heiress, Axia, who, alas, is betrothed to someone else. Okay. I'll start with this one. I grab the box and head for the tub.

I throw off my clothes and sink in. Nirvana. I turn on the radio and start the first book. Wow! This shit is good. Why haven't I ever read this stuff before? A sympathetic heroine. A hero she can love. A crisis they overcome. Torrid love scenes with none of those nasty clinical details of lovemaking. Happy endings (not like any relationship I've ever had). I power through the first one in about an hour. And grab another. Angry young man, passionate artist, virginal heroine, unaware of her intense, sensual nature until miraculously awakened by the man of her dreams. I start the third. Wild woman captures the heart of a fierce warrior. A lingering, unforgettable kiss. A rebirth that brings true love. And then another. Julia is beside herself with rage. She's fatally attracted to a gorgeous, infuriating man who turns out to be her betrothed. A dark period when things may not work out but then the lovers see the light, climb the mountains of despair, and fling themselves into each other's arms . . . all for love. I want more.

I buzz Victor downstairs. Up till now, I've been disdainful of tenants who use the guys downstairs to run their dumb errands. But this is important.

"Hey, Victor, could one of the guys run over to Trader Joe's and pick up a couple bottles of wine and some cocktail nuts?"

"No problem. Having a party?" he says.

"Um, oh yeah. I am." That's what I'm having. A fucking party.

I go to the desk to get my credit card, when the phone rings. Damn. My stomach turns over when I hear Fred's voice on the answering machine.

"Dora, why don't you give me a call? We can work this out." He sounds cheerful. That's weird.

No way.

• • •

Okay. It's been two days and I've only scratched the surface. This stuff is like heroin. I can't get enough. And so distracting. I think I prefer the historical ones with knights and ladies-in-waiting and carriages and kings. It's all there. Vikings, Saxon warriors, Norsemen, good-hearted trolls, sorcerers, drop-dead gorgeous Robin Hood types, passionate struggles. I'm into it. It's all fantasy. Fairy tales for the modern woman lusting for people who don't exist. No one can stop me now.

The phone rings. It's Palmer on the machine. "Your sister called me. She's out of town and she's been calling you for days. She's worried. I know you're there, Dora." He chuckles. "Okay. You want to play that way. I'm coming over."

I pick up. "Hi!" I say, trying to sound normal and happy.

"Virginia thinks you may be on another one of your benders."

"Why would she think that . . ." I don't sound convincing. I have to sound convincing. It's Palmer. He knows me. "I've just been doing a little spring cleaning."

"Oh, I know how you love to do that." He laughs.

"Okay. I've been a little down. I'm dealing with it."

"Really?"

"Yes. Really."

"Can I take you out and feed you at least?"

"You don't know what I look like."

"Oh, I can imagine. It's the way you always look when I see you."

"No, it's really, really bad this time. My hair's dirty

and I'm seriously sleep deprived, I just couldn't possibly—"

"I'm downstairs," he cuts me off.

"Okay." I look around. My place is a shambles. "I'll be right down."

I throw on a pair of jeans and a sweatshirt, pull back my hair into a ponytail, and meet Palmer in the lobby. He's dashing in a dark suit and I feel like the over-the-hill shriveled sister of the lovely and enchanting Lady Victoria who's been hidden away in a tower for twenty years.

He clutches my shoulders in a bear hug. "You're trapped," he laughs.

"I'm starved," I reply.

"Okay, let's call your sister, tell her you're still breathing, and then let's eat."

I order two appetizers and a steak, but Palmer doesn't make any stupid jokes and he doesn't press me for any information. I can tell he's trying to keep things light. We talk about my job search. He offers to make some phone calls for me. Then things take a serious turn.

"Dora, I'd like to be your friend. No demands. I've missed talking to you."

Oh. "Really? I mean, thank you. That's nice of you to say." What does he mean by this? Does he mean he misses talking to me or does he mean he misses me? I'm not going to make a big deal about this. This is just two people who are talking about how they miss talking to each other. That's all this is. "I miss talking to you too."

He smiles. "So, what's up with you, Dora?"

"Well, if you really want to know, I've just broken up with someone and it's complicated."

"It's always complicated." I noticed he doesn't offer up any info in the Kimberly department.

"But this is really complicated." I decide to tell him about Bea and Harper. A couple of times I can tell he is surprised and unprepared to hear what he is hearing. I think he was expecting the "my boyfriend doesn't treat me well, he's seeing someone else, he's noncommittal" kind of story.

"Fred has made a decision about himself, but you can do whatever you want, Dora. If you want to keep on seeing them, you can. He's not going to stop you. It sounds to me that he just didn't want the relationship to turn into a foursome."

"It's more than that. It really didn't have much to do with me. He wants them out of his life."

"That's too bad. For him. What are they like?"

I think for a moment. It's hard to explain. A therapist would probably say that Bea is the mother I never had, and Harper? I don't know.

"You'd like them, Palmer."

"I'm sure I would."

Dog Duty

> "Outside of a dog, a book is Man's best friend.
> And inside of a dog, it's too dark to read."
> ~ Groucho Marx (1890–1977) ~

When I get home, I see that I have six messages on my cell phone from Darlene and a dozen roses waiting for me at the front desk.

"I guess they're not from Bea and Harper," Palmer says wryly.

I shove the card in my pocket without reading it as Victor catches my eye.

"Someone named Darlene has been trying to reach you. She's in the hospital. Here's her number." He hands me a piece of paper with the number of a hospital in the Valley.

I quickly call her on my cell. "Darlene? What's wrong?"

"Oh, hiiii. I'm sorry to bother you. Am I bothering you?"

"What's happened, Darlene?"

"I don't know. I guess I just collapsed. My neighbor found me and drove me here. They say I have some kind of a monster virus that's going around and I need to stay on an IV for a few days. Where have you been?"

"Never mind. I'll come right over."

"What I really need you to do is bring me a few things and take care of Brawley. He's been trapped in my apartment for two days and no one has fed him or anything. The neighbors are complaining about the barking and this one guy upstairs who hates me says he's going to call the cops. God knows what the place looks like." The place didn't look so great before.

"Oh, Dora. I hate it here. It's so awful and the nurses are so mean. As soon as they get me off this thing, I'm going home."

I look at Palmer, who has overheard the whole thing.

"Do you want me to drive you out there?" he asks.

"It's okay. Really. You've done enough. I'll call that driver I use."

"Just let me take you out there."

"But I need to go to the hospital too. It's going to be a whole thing."

"I'm a full-service rescue operation. . . . It's no big deal. I know how much you like her."

We get in the car and just as we're pulling out I say, "Wait a minute." I run back in and grab the roses. Darlene will love them. Palmer smiles when I get back in the car. "Don't tell her," I say.

When we get to her apartment, I retrieve the key from under the doormat (I've told her not to do this) and slowly open the door. Brawley knows me, but I'm wary of just barging in on him. I'm sure he's hungry and crazed and in a really bad dog mood.

I peer in. He is sleeping on the couch, dog dreaming, his head nestled between his paws. When he sees it's me, he leaps off the couch, tail wagging wildly, and lunges at me with joy. His two enormous front paws slam on my shoulders and we sort of dance around the room that way. Then he races to the door and sits at attention. He really needs to go out. Palmer and I find his leash and when the dog spots it in my hand he twirls around three times in excitement and then grabs it in his mouth. Palmer laughs and starts roughhousing with him, rushing around his blocky body and swinging the leash over his head. Brawley suddenly bolts around the apartment in a frenzied gallop, up-ending chairs and lamps in the process. We finally get the leash on him and lunge out the door and down the stairs.

He drags us down the beach boardwalk. It's a balmy summer's night and I breathe in the humid saltwater air.

"What luck," he says as he casually caresses my neck. "This is turning into a great date—dinner, romantic stroll by the ocean, beautiful woman . . ."

I'm embarrassed and fall into my usual trap of ruining the moment with my weak attempt at humor. "Well, you know what they say about luck, it wasn't so good for the rabbit."

He raises his eyebrows.

"You know, the rabbit's foot . . ."

"I get the joke, Dora."

When we get back, I clean up the mess in the corner of the room (I would only do this for Darlene), scrounge around the kitchen looking for dog food, and fill Brawley's bowl as he drools in front of me. I gather some things to bring to Darlene, but I know what she misses the most is her Vaseline. (Darlene uses this for everything. I once saw her rub it on her face, hands, and feet and then polish the table with it.) There are giant jars of the stuff stacked up like toilet paper under the sink, so I throw one in the bag.

We try to sneak out while Brawley's eating, but even though he's starving, he follows us to the door and sits at attention. Palmer stares down at his upturned muzzle and looks at me.

"My apartment doesn't allow dogs."

"Well, we can't leave him here. I'll take him, and Darlene can pick him up when she's better."

"He pees on people, Palmer."

"Anything else about him you want to tell me?"

I think about telling him that Brawley, like Darlene, is a survivor. She found him several years ago near a gas station, tied to a lamppost with a heavy chain, no collar, no tags. The cashier in the office told her the animal had been sitting there for at least eight hours, so, in a moment of weakness, Darlene took him home. The dog is a big, shaggy version of a Rottweiler mix with hip dysplasia and cataracts. And Darlene was thrilled to discover he had been trained by someone, somewhere, to sit, speak, roll over, and play dead.

His only failing is that he is definitely the alpha when

other dogs are around, which has led to several unfortunate attacks on other dogs, including one where someone's
Lab lost half an ear. (Thus the name, Brawley.) The Lab's
owner sent Darlene a vet bill for five hundred dollars and
ever since then she has walked him late at night or at
dawn. When she's not working, the dog goes everywhere
with her. She jokes that when he dies, she'll put on his
tombstone, "Here lies Brawley, a bad but beloved dog."

"No. That's about it. It's really nice of you."

The three of us head for the hospital. The dog is still
panting from the walk and his foul, stagnant doggy breath
fogs up the windows of the car. Palmer switches on the de-
frost as Brawley leaps from the backseat into the space between our two front seats and lays his head on Palmer's
lap. Dog hair flies everywhere and he leaves a slobber trail
across Palmer's khakis. Palmer strokes his head affectionately and says, "You're a real charmer, Brawley."

We pull into the hospital visitor parking. The place
is deserted. What a dump. The waiting room smells of
institutional-strength disinfectant and has the humming
lights and glaring neon emptiness of a late-night lounge.
Palmer looks around and concludes he'd rather wait in
the car with Brawley.

"I might be a while, though."

"That's okay. I'll try to find a Starbucks or something."

I walk down a few stark, empty hallways and find
Darlene in a semi-private room with two other beds that
have the curtains drawn around them. She is sitting up
sound asleep with her glasses slipping off her nose. Her
book has dropped onto her lap.

Someone moans from the next bed. Darlene opens her eyes and sees the roses.

"Oh, Dora," she says in a hoarse, groggy voice. "You didn't have to. Really. They're so expensive."

"Don't be silly. It's nothing," I say. Literally.

There is desolation to this scene. Darlene keeps apologizing profusely for imposing but it's understood that she has no one else to call. Her mother is in a wheelchair and lives in Fresno and her father is ninety-six with Alzheimer's. Her sister lives someplace up north, but I don't think they're close.

The harsh reality of a single life is painfully evident here. There's a line from a Jim Harrison book where Dalva, the main character, says, "I've always found the term 'lonely old woman' appealing." I used to love that line. It sounded so peaceful and relaxing. But the truth is, as I stare at her fragile figure in the bed, it's no damn fun being sick and alone.

The moaning gets louder. Darlene whispers and points to the next bed, "I think she's crazy, she keeps calling 911 and telling them to take her to the hospital."

"How are you?"

"I was feeling really lousy before; now I'm okay but they won't release me until I'm on this thing forty-eight hours." She shakes the IV stand.

"Well, we've got Brawley. Palmer says he'll take him until you feel better."

"Palmer?" She looks at me, puzzled.

"It's a long story. He's waiting outside. . . ."

"Wow."

"I'll tell you later, although there is nothing to tell, I mean, nothing about Palmer."

"If you say so . . ." She winks.

"I don't want to get into it."

I put some of her things away and then tell her I'll be back tomorrow.

Outside, Palmer, holding a Starbucks cup, is walking the dog in the shrubs by the parking lot. As I approach, Brawley emits a low growl, like an electric toothbrush.

"That's gratitude for you." I smile.

"I was getting asphyxiated by his breath, so I thought we'd take another little stroll."

Brawley's intelligent brow furrows as he sits down on Palmer's foot.

"I think he's in love, Palmer."

"Well, he's a good judge of character."

When we get back to my place, Palmer parks by the valet and walks me inside. Brawley sticks his head out the window and starts to howl as Palmer leaves the car.

"Always a pleasure, Dora."

I'm about to say something when he leans in and kisses me on the mouth. I'm startled and a bit flustered. Now what . . .

He casually says, "See ya." And leaves.

A Christmas Carol

"A Merry Christmas, Uncle! God save you!" cried a
cheerful voice . . .
"Bah!" said Scrooge, "Humbug!"
~ Charles Dickens (1812–1870), *A Christmas Carol* ~

I watch Palmer drive away. How did we get to this
point? I remember the last straw—a formal YPO
Christmas party held at a ranch near Santa Barbara.
Palmer and I had been arguing about it for weeks and, I
must say, I tried my best to back out. But I finally agreed
to go, on the condition that we take our own car and
leave shortly after dinner.

I can safely say that the evening was a total disaster
from the word go. As we were headed for the hotel
parking lot that fateful night, Palmer in a designer tux,
me in a holly-green satin suit, we were whisked into a
sleek chartered bus by a group of already half-ripped

YPOers. Palmer looked at me and shrugged. He just couldn't let on that I was a closet party pooper who didn't want to join in all the fa la la la la. I shot him one last desperate look before we were herded on the bus, but he didn't respond.

Now, I always get carsick in the back of a bus, a holdover from my schooldays. So I ended up sitting in the front row next to Nan Price, a diminutive woman with too much Eau de Joy and a pained look on her face. Palmer caught my eye and winked as he strode to the rear, where the Mistletoe Bar was surrounded by a bunch of beefy-faced men with very loud voices. I was just about to order a drink when a buxom elf with black patent-leather boots passed around giant mugs of caramel-colored eggnog so strong that the "egg" was beside the point. A few sips of that and good ole Nan started pouring out her heart to me. Seems that at the pre-pre-cocktail party back at the hotel, a woman named Marge (the wife of the ex-YPO president) announced that two seasons ago she bought the same sparkly St. John knit that Nan was wearing and it was now in storage. Nan further confided that her husband was going bankrupt and she couldn't even pay her son's private school tuition. She continued with her sad, sad story, as Palmer's happy, animated voice boomed from the back. I held her limp, damp hand as she confided she wished she were dead.

Three eggnogs later, we finally arrived at the Spanish estate and were greeted by a jolly group of Christmas carolers dressed in Victorian velvets and those Scroogey black velvet top hats, singing "I'm Dreaming of a White

Christmas." (What a joke. Irving Berlin wrote this while lounging in his backyard on a brilliant sunny day in Beverly Hills.) We all paraded inside, past a roaring fire in a huge stone fireplace and a towering Douglas fir that just grazed the massive, beamed ceiling. Someone said they had imported the distressed wood from a nineteenth-century farmhouse they'd dismantled in Provence. Palmer, evidently in fine humor, gave me a "Buck up, dearie" peck on the cheek as he handed me a flute of champagne and moved into the big-game trophy room.

I wandered after him, watching in horror as the host gingerly tugged on the tongue of a seven-foot-tall, stuffed, matted-haired grizzly standing on its hind legs in attack position.

"Here," he said, as he pulled the tongue out, showing it to a group of admiring guests. "You wanna feel it?"

On the walls, in between the twisty-horned goat heads and antlered elks were huge rococo gold-framed oils of dogs ripping apart fox carcasses. I grabbed another drink off the tray of a passing elf as I maneuvered past a set of impressive leather furniture with animal-limb legs. That's when poor, beleaguered Nan cornered me, two sheets to the wind.

"Guess what, Dora," she said in a pinched, trembly voice. "They've seated me next to Marge and her husband. I don't think I can stand it."

She looked as if she had fallen asleep in the bus. Her lipstick was dried-out and feathered into the lines around her mouth. Her hair was askew and she seemed on the verge of a major breakdown.

Okay, I'm not excusing myself for what happened next. I just couldn't help it. I strolled into the tented dining area with Nan to casually check out the ornate, calligraphed place-cards, and I did it. I switched them. I must say I was ever so pleased with myself.

"It's nothing," I announced smugly. "They'll never even notice."

"God, Dora, you're so sweet," she slurred.

We were about to join the party when the hostess, an elegantly dressed woman with a huge diamond brooch and an upturned nose, ambushed us. It took her about two seconds to sniff out the crime.

"You know, I spent a lot of time doing the seating and I don't appreciate you switching everything around," she said imperiously. Nan immediately explained it was all my idea. Just goes to show you, no good deed ever goes unpunished.

"Gosh," I said ingenuously. "I'm really sorry."

She could tell I didn't give a shit. Shooting me a dirty look, she switched the cards back and, without another word, departed. What a jerk. Nan slinked out after her while I grabbed a champagne glass off the table and helped myself to the Moët chilling in the nearby ice bucket. I gulped it down, poured myself another, and another, and suddenly realized the room was spinning. Whoops. I sat down carefully and tried to keep my equilibrium.

It was at this point, I noticed Palmer walking in, obviously wondering where the hell I'd been.

"You're drunk," he said. He could always tell.

"So is everyone else," I replied. But probably everyone else didn't feel like vomiting.

"I think I have to go home. I'm sorry, Palmer. Those eggnogs were lethal." (And the champagne didn't help either.)

"How come I'm the only one with a drunk wife?" he shot back unsympathetically.

Why is he so pissed? "You don't have to leave. You stay here and I'll call a cab," I offered, trying to defuse the situation.

"Right. How embarrassing. In front of all my friends. You did this on purpose. You didn't want to come to this party in the first place. Next time, do me a favor and stay home."

It was a grim scenario after that. I called a cab. Palmer insisted on leaving with me, holding me steady as we weaved past the massacred animals, the enormous glass gun case, and the still-joyful carolers.

"Christ, Dora. What were you thinking?"

"I don't know," I replied, fighting back the tears. "Marge was such a shrew to Nan and I just felt sorry for her."

"Who cares? It's not your problem. Anyway, everyone knows Nan's a pain in the neck. You're the only one who takes her seriously."

"Well, it sounds like she has serious problems."

"This isn't a therapy session. It's a party and you're supposed to have fun," he said, shaking his head in frustration.

"Well, ho, ho, ho!" I said defiantly, the tears starting

to stream down my cheeks. Palmer was unmoved. I hate that.

"You know, you don't give a shit about anything, including our marriage."

There it was. He was quiet for a minute waiting for me to deny it, but now I was angry. He could have been more understanding, he could have been a lot of things. But maybe we were too far gone for that. Palmer and I split up a few weeks later.

As for Nan, I never heard from her again. That's how life goes sometimes.

The Piper at the Gates of Dawn

"Ask a toad what is beauty. . . . He will answer
that it is a female with two great round eyes
coming out of her little head, a large flat
mouth, a yellow belly, and a brown back."

~ Voltaire ~

I drag through the next few days, avoiding any contact
with Fred. On the third day, I sit down at my computer and open my mail. I see that I have seventeen
e-mails, two of them from Fred. I open the first one.

"Hast thou no care of me? Shall I abide in this dull
world, Which in thy absence is no better than a sty?*
Fred."

There is a faint touch of humor and pathos in the second one. "Dora, be nice. At least answer my phone calls.
I'm dying here. Let's make up. Fred."

---

* *Antony and Cleopatra*

I fight the urge to delete and instead reread the message a few more times. Then I make a decision. I decide to procrastinate. Clean up the kitchen. Make a few calls to the bank. Check my bills. Call Darlene to see how she's doing—she's going home tomorrow. I ask her about the dog and she says that Palmer's already called to check on her and told her to not worry about Brawley. Palmer has it handled, as usual.

Then, out of the blue, Brooke calls and offers me a freelance assignment. No one on staff wants to cover it. Evidently a man has a pond in his backyard filled with bullfrogs. As if that wasn't noisy enough, now it's mating season, the bullfrogs are bellowing to each other in the moonlight, and the neighbors are threatening to have animal control come down and bludgeon the little suckers. She tells me the owner is a wacko and all the neighbors are wackos but, without hesitating, I say yes. In fact, I'm thrilled. In the old days, I would have turned up my nose, but now it's a chance to write again.

Here's the deal. The deadline is tomorrow, so I need to interview the guy at his home tonight and hear the racket for myself. This freeway thing is really starting to handicap my life. I can't have a limo taking me to my assignments. That's absurd. Darlene's still laid up. No one to call. And I have to be in Riverside by six. With the traffic, I'd need to start out pretty soon. I can do this.

I call the Frogman, Mr. O'Connor, to get directions. He can't wait to tell me his side of the story. His voice sounds like Chuck Yeager, slightly Southern, earnest, and reassuring, like all pilots. "Nothing to worry about . . .

just a little turbulence, we'll be through this in a couple a minutes. I'm going to ask all the flight attendants to please sit down . . ."

I get into my old Mercedes and jump on the 10. Well, not exactly jump. I hesitate at the top of the on-ramp until some jackass behind me honks impatiently. I place my foot on the accelerator and slowly speed up to fifty-five (and I'm not going one bit faster). My car hasn't gone this fast in four years and the engine strains and sputters like an old lawn mower. My hands are sweating and I hunch over the steering wheel, gripping it tightly, as if it were a lifeline. I feel slightly dizzy. I keep saying to myself, focus, focus, sixteen-year-old kids do this, people with an IQ of 12 do this, eighty-five-year-old deaf people do this . . . I can do this.

I stay in the far right lane, the worst lane to be in because everyone exits and enters from it, but I'm not moving. I want to be able to get off at a moment's notice. I think of Edvard Munch's painting *The Scream*. That's me. Silent hysteria.

It takes me over two hours because of traffic, but I show up at exactly the right time. I'm bedraggled and I need a shower. But I did it! Do they give out merit points or medals for this? I'll celebrate later.

The guy lives in a slightly cockeyed, ramshackle California hacienda that looks as if you'd have to hack your way through with a machete to get to the front door. Large banana trees and thick bushes are everywhere and there is a narrow walkway that goes around the house into the backyard. He hears my car pull up and yells, "I'm back here."

I venture into the backyard, where he stands next to an amoeba-shaped, scum-covered pond surrounded by overgrown, weedy-looking grass and reeds. Dragonflies and mosquitoes are skidding across the surface. There is a hand-carved wooden birdhouse hanging from a crooked old oak tree and some white iron benches under it.

O'Connor is a guy in his early forties. He's wearing a floppy canvas hat tied under his chin and a pair of green Wellies. He apologizes for his appearance; he's been cleaning the pond. He tells me the story. When he first moved in, the pond was choked with weeds and algae and he spent weeks clearing it out and replanting. A few months later, he heard the first "Jug-a-rum" mating call of a male bullfrog. Female bullfrogs, he informed me, do not call, but the males are aggressive and their voices can be heard for almost half a mile. It didn't take long, he says, for a few more frogs to join in and soon the backyard became a cacophony of bullfrogs croaking and physically wrestling with each other, the way they do when they are actually mating.

He goes on, "I'm not a nature freak, but this is their habitat. I didn't put 'em here. And I'm not gonna move 'em. These people even checked into relocation. Cost about five thousand dollars and no one wanted to pay. Can you imagine? Neighbors don't complain about the crickets. And they're much louder. We're pretty near the freeway, they don't complain about that. Jets fly over all the time from the Ontario Airport, they don't complain about that. And hell, it's only a few months out of the year."

"What do you do for a living, Mr. O'Connor?"

"I'm a computer technician, worked for Lockheed for fifteen years."

As he's talking, I'm thinking, this is a great story. This is what America's all about. Suburbia encroaching on nature and squeezing it out.

"I mean look at this guy," he says as he bends down, searches through the rushes for a minute, and grabs a large, brownish-greenish, splotchy bullfrog with smooth moist skin. "Isn't he handsome?" He goes on, "In the old days, people used to make up songs about these guys, you know, 'froggy went a courting he did ride, uh huh.' They loved the way they serenaded each other. Now all these people want to do is nuke 'em."

"Well, hello, Mr. Toad," I say, and think of Toad dressed in a dapper plaid three-piece suit with a silk cravat casually peeking out of his pocket and a watch fob draped around his chest.

"So, they'll start their ruckus in a little while. Have a seat. My wife's bringing out some iced tea." At this point a pretty, natural-looking woman wearing a calf-length flowered dress comes out carrying a tray with an icy pitcher and two glasses. She sweetly says hi and walks back into the house.

The humidity has now reached mythical proportions and I feel little droplets of sweat trickling down my back. We chat for a while longer until it is pitch-dark. A cool breeze hits my face, gently rustling the reeds by the pond.

And so it begins. A single baritone note heralds the start. Other deep melancholy voices join, ushering in a symphony of enchanted music. There is a furious double fugue tempered with delicate, lyrical shading and then, suddenly, the voices soar and a burst of sound erupts like thunderous, cosmic cannon fire. I am spellbound as I listen to this majestic amphibian requiem with its triumphant grandeur.

I think back to *The Wind in the Willows,* when Rat passionately reacts to the music of Pan, "So beautiful and strange and new! . . . Such music I never dreamed of, and the call in it is stronger even than the music is sweet!"

Save Me!

"... always read stuff that will make
you look good if you die in the middle of the night."
~ P. J. O'Rourke (1947–), American Political Satirist ~

How could I think that I'd just get on the freeway and all my fears would be gone? The glaring headlights from oncoming cars are blinding, like hot, laser streaks of white flashing across my vision. I've slowed down to forty and I'm still totally freaked out. I can't do this! I have to get off! I was so elated when I left the O'Connors'. I knew exactly what I was going to write. I even had my lead. But now, it's all turned to shit.

I need intensive therapy. . . . A lot of good that does me now. Oh, thank god, there's an exit. Hell, no one's letting me in. What rude people live in L.A. In Nebraska, they probably slow down for you. I should live in Nebraska or Kansas or some other place you fly over where it's mostly one-lane country roads.

What's this semi doing? Aren't they supposed to stay in the far lane? Jesus! Now he's tailgating me. His headlights look as if they're two stories high. "Just go around, you moron!" Damn! He's still there. He lays on his air horn, which sounds like the USS *Liberty* approaching port.

I put on my blinker. Great. He changes lanes and blocks my exit. I'm trapped. I can truly understand road rage. If I had a gun I'd shoot out his tires, all twenty of them. Then I'd aim for his head. There, thank god. He's gone. I've had it. I'm just going to pull over onto the side. But weren't all those girls raped and murdered when their cars broke down on the freeway? Guys impersonating police officers with giant nightsticks approach the car and then it's all over. The next thing you know, your corpse is found stuffed in the trunk of your car. Or thrown in a deserted ditch. I think I can hang on until the next exit. I slowly drive down the off-ramp to safety.

It takes me a few minutes to calm down and stop shaking. I pull into the 7-Eleven and do what I always do when I hit rock bottom. I call my sister.

"I need you to come get me," I say, my voice audibly trembling.

"What's happened? Where are you?" Virginia says. I can hear Camille squawking in the background.

"I'm in San Bernardino somewhere. And I can't drive home. I tried but this big truck bullied me, well, I was scared before that, but that didn't help and it's dark . . ." I'm starting to lose it.

"Okay. Calm down. Tell me where you are. I'll throw Camille in the car and come get you." She doesn't hesitate when she says this. I love my sister for that.

I glance at my watch. It's almost nine p.m. Way past Camille's bedtime. I'm relieved but depressed. I'm awash with failure.

By the time Virginia pulls up, it's after ten and I've eaten at least two Little Debbie sweet rolls, nachos with melted cheese, and a frozen cherry Slurpee. I tell the young Indian cashier about the car and he says it's okay to leave it until tomorrow. I'm going to call my driver to come pick it up with one of his people.

Camille is asleep in the car seat in the back, her little body swathed in a stretchy sleeper and covered with a pink-and-white-checked blanket. I open the car door, get in, and immediately burst into tears.

"Oh, sweetie. Come on. It's not that bad."

"I've been sitting here for two hours because I'm too psycho to drive home. I thought I was over this. I'll never be able to do this job. I have no life. I'm totally fucked." The tears are streaming down my face. My clothes are stuck to my body. I smell like a mixture of mulch and sweat and rancid cheese. Virginia looks at me. She's clean and crisp and together.

"Don't be so dramatic. You were a little unnerved on the freeway. That's all. It's a process. You can't expect to be normal overnight. Well, not normal. I don't mean normal. But you know what I mean. Anyway, your job isn't about driving. It's about writing. You can work out the other stuff."

I'm quiet for a minute. I take a deep breath. Maybe she's right.

"Dora, where have you been for the last three days? I must have called you a dozen times."

"I was reading." I sniffle.

"That's what I was afraid of. Why do you do this? You make everybody crazy."

"Sorry, Ginny. Really. I didn't mean to worry you."

"Everybody has problems. Everyone's been disappointed. They don't sit around for days doing nothing, bingeing on books."

"Everyone does have problems, but this is the way I deal with mine. I'm happy sitting alone in my room reading."

"No you're not. Anyway, books can't fix your life. You should know that by now."

There is no way to answer this, because no matter what's going on in my life, I will always need a book. Nevertheless, after all that's happened to me this past year, I've come to the conclusion that for me, reading is not purely an escape. It's more of a search for some kind of meaning in this world. Now when I read, I think I might open to any page and find the truth. I just can't stand the fog of not knowing. Whether you love someone or not, what you are willing to do to make it last, how you come to terms with the people who leave you or disappoint you, or how you deal with people with whom you feel a deep connection but who ultimately may not have anything to do with your life. I don't know. The answers are there. Somewhere. Each author has their own vision, whether it be transforming, un-nerving, inspiring, or devastating. It's comforting in a pathetic sort of way and I have wallowed in this comfort for most of my life.

But now it's different. Something's shaken me up, skewed my priorities, and it's not so easy to disengage and let the world be damned. Like Fred. Enthralling, infuriating, disappointing Fred. His insular behavior toward Harper and Bea really makes me mad. And to further cloud the issue, along comes Palmer, who is, I re-mind myself, now unavailable. And the damn dog. How do I explain all this to Virginia?

"So, did Palmer reach you?" Virginia probes.

"You know he did."

"So. How was that?"

"He was great. He picked me up. Fed me. Saved me. Everyone is saving me. I'm a worthless human being."

Virginia starts laughing. I start laughing.

"You'll be happy to know that there's a new book* out that says there's no correlation between high self-esteem and being a good person. Juvenile delinquents have high self-esteem. Sociopaths have high self-esteem."

I'm looking at her like she's nuts. "So, you're saying it's a good thing I think I'm worthless?"

"Oh, forget it. All I'm saying is you're terrific but you've been in a coma for the last year. Ever since the split with Palmer. And we all want the old Dora back. You used to be fun. Like Dad. Now you get into this

---

* Christina Hoff Sommers and Sally Satel, M.D., *One Nation Under Therapy*.

negative, downer stuff . . . and the whole scenario is not flattering, Dora."

"So, what do you want me to do? Like poof? Everything is okay now?"

"Why not? Palmer is back in the picture. Sort of. You're getting a job. Sort of. You're driving on the freeway. Sort of."

"Okay. I'll try to be sort of less depressing for everyone."

Just as I feared. I'm turning into my mother. Even though there have been times when I drop out and read, I could always get back my momentum. Palmer used to say that despite all my quirks and weirdnesses, he thought I was funny and endearing. Endearing. Can you imagine? I wonder what he thinks now.

We pull up to my apartment. Luckily, no one is taping my comings and goings. I grab my notebook. The story is due tomorrow. Even if I have to work all night, I'm going to make it a damn good one.

Princes and Toads

"I can resist everything but temptation."

~ Oscar Wilde, *Lady Windermere's Fan*

After a glass of wine (or two) to quiet my nerves, I write furiously until midnight, decide I hate every word, throw it out and start over. I used to bang these stories out in an afternoon, but there's a lot at stake here. I finally finish at god knows what hour, wake up early, revise it again, and e-mail it to Brooke on deadline, 9:00 a.m.

An hour later the phone rings. It's Brooke.

"Is this Dora? RIVET! RIVET! Hey, it's not easy being green—get it?" I hear her collapse in laughter and other people in the background laughing as well. This doesn't sound good.

"Does this mean you hated it or what?"

I hear her clearing her throat. "Oh, excuse me, I have a FROG in my throat." She snorts. "Maybe it was the GRENOUILLE I had for lunch." She can hardly talk, she's laughing so hard.

"Okay, cut it out, will you?"

"You're right, I better stop before I CROAK."

"Brooke, that's not funny."

"Oh, yes it is. But I'll tell you anyway. Here's the story. The editor said too much frog, too little people. Well, what he said exactly was 'Frogs 10–People 0,' but don't take it too hard. He also said it was a well-written piece and he wants to use it. You just have to tweak it."

"Meaning what?"

"Meaning, more neighborhood reaction, not so toady, maybe put a call in to the conservation board. You know what to do. Got to run. Hey, Dora. One more thing . . . don't WARTY, it'll be all right." She starts laughing again and hangs up.

It takes another hour to make the calls, plug in the changes, and it's gone. They liked it this time, but they still couldn't resist throwing me a last-minute Kermit joke. Who knows what the guys on the headline desk are going to do with it.

Okay, I can't put this off any longer. Time to call Fred. What to say? Maybe he'll do all the talking. I call him at the bookstore.

"Hi, Fred. Thanks for the roses. They were beautiful." (Darlene liked them a lot.)

"Hey, Dora." He's obviously happy to hear from me. "We need to talk. Can you meet me for a drink later?"

I guess I'm stuck. I say okay and he tells me to meet him at the Brentwood Grill at six. At least it's not coffee.

He gives me a faint smile as he walks in the restaurant and orders a bottle of wine. Looks like we're going to be here a while. It starts out with small talk. I tell him about Darlene being in the hospital, leaving out the part about Palmer. He tells me he's been reworking a few scenes in his play and maybe the New York people had a point. He's feeling better about it.

Then he cuts to the chase.

"I'm sorry, Dora. I had an awful time in New York, and the family stuff has been stressful. I didn't mean what I said. Can't we just kiss and make up?"

I take a sip of wine.

"How're Harper and Bea?" I say.

"They're fine. They're still crowing about what a great time they had with you and Darlene. And I was wrong. I AM glad you took them. It was a big help. Can we just forget about what I said in the car?"

I look at him. I want to forgive him. I'm not one for confrontations. And he WAS tired and pressured. And he had just come back from a rotten trip. I'm still attracted to him. It's his shoulders this time. Everyone deserves a second chance.

"How about dinner?" he asks.

What's this? He lays his hand ever so lightly on my thigh. How crass. It's burning a hole through my dress. Well, I do have to eat. And I know where this is leading.

In my experience, makeup sex has nothing to do with making up. It's all about pent-up passion and unresolved issues that are temporarily put on hold—the fierce, false ardor of a one-night stand culminating in waves of remorse the next morning. That's when those nagging thoughts, those doubts, those worrisome intrusions insinuate themselves in the afterglow as he rolls over to stroke your back and whisper sweet nothings. It's not a resolution, more like a truce, a white-flag night of passionate sex.

Last night I was insatiable. Everything he did made me want him more. I wouldn't say he roughed me up exactly, maybe we roughed each other up. "Come here," he said as he grabbed my wrists, pinned me down on the bed. "Talk to me. Tell me what you like," he whispered. And I did. I wanted this fuck. I slammed against him, yanked his shirt open, and felt his skin on mine. Mouth to mouth. My nails digging into his back. I could have gone on for days. I was wet before he even started to caress my neck, my breasts, my abdomen, his tongue moving up my inner thigh, back and forth, up and down, flicking over me, until I couldn't stand it anymore, my moans lasting longer and louder until I could hear myself scream. When it was over, we collapsed against each other, heaving and panting and not talking. And then a flash of something plowed into me, Palmer caressing my neck as we walked along the beach. I tried to will the memory away; I closed my eyes, he was still there.

A guy once told me that it isn't true that men avoid women with baggage. In fact, they look forward to it. There's a tacit understanding that the sex is better, hotter, more erotic when the woman is beleaguered with rage and bitterness directed at someone else. Why does sex have to be so complicated? Why CAN'T you have a night of total abandon without consequences, feelings, and self-analysis? Why can't it just be fun, like it used to be?

And now, here I am, on the cusp of dawn, with the same issues I had before. I'm certain Fred wants me. And I want him. But has anything been resolved? Well, he apologized . . . I don't want to think about this anymore.

"Let's get out of here," he says as he smoothes back my damp hair. "Let's go to Mexico, spend a week, just you and me. See what we have without the outside world intruding." He is looking at me, waiting for an answer.

"I'll have to think about it."

He traces my lips with his fingers. "My friend has this place in Cabo. Right on the beach. We'll take walks, make margaritas, I'll work on my play." His fingers teasingly trail down my neck. "You'll work on me."

I'm at a disadvantage here. He's cute. He's sly and charming. He's used to winning over women like me. "Okay," I say. I'm not exactly sure what I'm doing. But okay.

Drop Dead. Strong Letter
to Follow.

"It is seldom indeed that one parts on
good terms, because if one were on
good terms one would not part."

~ Marcel Proust (1871–1922), *Remembrance of Things Past*, "The Fugitive" ~

Michael Kors has a great white dress with coral beads on top that would be perfect for dinner in Cabo. I looked all over for sandals to match and finally ended up with these fantastic gold ones from Valentino next door. Then there's the two Eres strapless tank suits that look great as long as I wrap the pareo around my butt. Why stores have three-way mirrors I'll never understand, particularly stores that sell bathing suits. Unless you're sixteen, no one wants to look at the back of their thighs.

I've been shopping for two days and the booty is spread all over my bed, ready to throw in my duffel. I am really looking forward to this trip. I can't remember the last time I went to Mexico. It sounds so loose and cool and sexy. Maybe the Kors is a bit much. Fred will probably show up in wrinkled khakis and an aloha shirt. I hold up the white linen dress. It is gorgeous. But maybe a little too Southampton. I put the plastic back over it. I'll wait until the salesgirl is off and take it back. She spent hours helping me. Oh well. I think of my sister's only useful fashion advice: less is more.

I finally decide on a cotton skirt, a racerback T-shirt, and gold flip-flops. I fold everything and throw it in the duffel. I don't have the patience to seal it in separate, gallon-size ziplock baggies like my sister always does. Not that it matters with her raggy clothes. So now I'm ready to go. Three hours early. Fred is meeting me at the airport at one. He's coming from Bea's because he needed to sign some papers for her.

I decide to call Darlene to say good-bye. She's home but feeling funky and weak. Palmer still has the dog.

"I hope that's okay," she says in a scratchy voice. "What are you doing, anyway? I thought maybe you and Palmer were working things out."

"Palmer has a girlfriend, remember?" I say coolly.

"Yeah, I remember," she replies in a dopey, well-meaning tone that makes me suddenly feel guilty for some reason. "Don't get mad at me, Dora. I'm only trying to help."

"I'm not mad. I just don't want to get sidetracked here. I think this is going to be fun."

"Good, then. I'm happy for you. Have fun. I love you."

"Me too," I answer, then hang up.

I sit down on the bed, suddenly disoriented. The image of Palmer with the damn dog is jarring and confusing, and the fact that this IS an impulsive move puts somewhat of a damper on my mood. I decide to call Bea to say good-bye and check on Fred.

When Bea answers, I can tell she's upset.

"Is there something wrong?" I ask.

"Things have gone to hell in a handbasket over here, honey."

"Is Harper okay?"

"We're all a little shaken. Hasn't Fred told you?"

"No." Shit. This sounds bad.

"Well, it was bound to happen, with Lorraine's lifestyle and all. It seems she had some debts going with this boy Bobby D. He asked us to pay him back, but I don't have that kind of money. And neither did Lorraine. I don't know. I just told him to go away and he got mad."

My heart is racing. "Did he hurt Harper or you?"

"No. That wasn't it. He waited until we went out and then he and his friends smashed through the window with the old broom we have out there and tore up the place. Oh, and Harper's new bedroom. It's all such a mess."

"Goddamn it, Bea. When did this happen?"

"Last night, when we were at Bible study. You know, with the trip and all, Fred probably thought it was better not to upset you. He went home to pack."

"I'm coming right over."

"Wait. Harper wants to talk to you."

"Dora?" Harper says in her reedy little voice. There is a pause. "Don't be mad. They messed up all my stuff you gave me. My bed is bad now. They were mean." She starts to cry.

"Don't cry, honey. I'll fix it. I'm coming there now."

"Okay." She sniffles.

I drive over there as fast as I can. I don't even think about the freeway thing. I pull up to their house and see a broken glass window with masking tape and another window entirely missing with a piece of plywood covering it. There are shards of broken glass in the screened porch and thick black swirls of spray paint smeared like a hex across the front door. It looks like a house that has weathered a hurricane, except for the graffiti. Then Bea opens the door and I give her a hug. The scene inside is unreal. The vandals had evidently used some sort of blunt object to shatter Bea's lamps, TV, and pictures, and the hall mirror has intricately designed cracks spreading across it like a web. The drawers to her sideboard have been yanked out and the contents dumped in a rubble on the rug. The floor is caked with a thick, dried-up coating of what looks like ketchup, maybe mud, I'm not sure which, and the whole place reeks of liquor mixed with detergent or possibly vinegar. The devastation oozes into the kitchen, where the walls are streaked with dirty handprints and the refrigerator door is hanging half off its hinges. A bunch of broken bottles and smashed dishes are piled up like a heap of garbage in the corner where Bea has apparently swept them.

I am speechless. Harper appears and runs into my arms.

"Come see what they did to my room."

I try not to look aghast as she leads me to her room. I can already see before I get there that the bedsheets have been yanked off the mattress and dragged into the hall. Slashed-up clothes are sitting in a heap on top.

"You know what, Harper," I say, looking around at the havoc, "I'm going to get you new stuff, okay? You and Bea are all right and that's what counts."

Bea seems overwhelmed and disoriented. As she absently sweeps the debris, she tells me the police were here last night and already have an idea of where to find the guys. She couldn't reach Fred last night, but he came early this morning to help fill out the police reports.

"There was the nicest young man down the block, Eddie, I think his name is, who helped us board up the windows and sweep around a bit." Bea goes on, "I want to send him a little something, what do you think is nice? Maybe a bottle of wine or some chocolates?"

My mind is racing. Where the hell is Fred?

I tell Bea that she and Harper can stay at my place tonight and that I'll get on the phone and call a cleaning crew and glass company to repair the windows. She resists my help, but I can see that her hands are shaking and I'm insistent. She is relieved but reluctantly agrees.

"All right, dear. But it's just for the night. And I'm paying for all this."

Bea and Harper gather a few things as I step outside to call Fred.

He's already in the car on the way to the airport.

"Hola, my little margarita baby," he chirps.

"I'm here at Bea's house."

Silence.

"What are you doing there?"

"I called to say good-bye and heard what happened. Why didn't you tell me?"

"It's not your problem. We've been through all of this."

What a jerk. "I don't understand how you could just leave them like this. Bea's a total mess. The house has been trashed."

"Calm down. I've got it handled. I have a friend coming over this afternoon to help Bea clean up. Come on, Dora, we can fight about this on the plane. Don't ruin everything."

Is he serious? "I'm not going."

"Are you kidding me?"

"No. What's the matter with you?"

"Oh, now I'm some kind of a monster because I don't drop everything and hold their hands."

"Fred, there are times in life when you do drop everything, and this is one of those. I can't believe I even have to tell you this."

"Well, I'll tell you what, Dora. I'm going with you or without you. And I'm going to have a good time. This is the only weekend my friend can give us the place and I'm not going to fuck it up because my sister is still leaving a trail of shit for me to clean up."

"No, excuse me, Fred. Not for YOU to clean up. For your seventy-five-year-old mother and your six-year-old niece to clean up."

"If I remember correctly, you have your own mother and sister and niece. You don't have to adopt mine."

"Well, somebody needs to take care of them." I am outraged. What a piece of shit. I hang up. He calls back. I see it's him and don't answer.

It rings and rings again. I still don't answer it.

Bea and Harper come out of the house. I turn my phone off. Harper rolls a bright pink Little Mermaid wheelie suitcase. She's holding her nose. "It smells yucky in there. Can we have pizza for lunch?"

I'm shaken up. I can feel my cheeks start to burn. This always happens when I get really upset. The big question is, will that motherfucker get on the plane or will he do the right thing and come home? The right thing—there are so many different choices when it comes to that issue. I know that there are times when you are willing to give it all up for someone you love and times when you are not. The times you are not often call everything into question and define what type of person you are. My view is, can you live with yourself when you make those choices? And Fred seems to be just fine.

Maybe Fred's right. Maybe I have no business meddling in his family's problems. But I know that I can't get on that plane. So I'm just going to go with that and take care of Bea and Harper and let Fred do whatever he's going to do. Maybe when I get back to my apartment, he'll be standing there waiting for us. I actually hope he's not.

Border Crossings

"Where am I going? I don't quite know.
What does it matter where people go?"
~ A. A. Milne (1882–1956), *When We Were Very Young*, "Spring Morning" ~

Normally at this point I would go on yet another self-indulgent book bender. Hell, there's sure reason enough to do it. But I just don't feel like it, even if I could, which I can't, because I have houseguests.

On the way home, I tell Bea that, as it turns out, I can't just pick up and go to Mexico on the spur of the moment. Bea is silent for a minute and then says, "I hope I'm not the cause of troubles between you and Fred. We could have gone to a motel." How can I tell her what's really going on—that her son's a jerk. Maybe the truth is best.

"I just got an assignment and can't leave. I've worked

it out with Fred." I bat away my mother's old rhyme in my head. Oh, what a tangled web we weave when first we practice to deceive.

"Well, I'm glad things are okay. Lord knows, along with everything else, I wouldn't want that on my head," Bea says.

"Absolutely. You're going to love my place."

Bea makes herself right at home. She offers to go to the market and make Salisbury steak and mashed potatoes, but I don't have the strength for it. So she's making pasta for dinner. She doesn't have a lot of options. I have some spaghetti and canned sauce, but she's added onions and garlic and the whole place smells great. I'm tempted to open a bottle of wine. Maybe later.

Just as I'm about to collapse on the couch, the doorbell rings. Who could that be? Why didn't Victor buzz me? There's only one person who has a pass and key to my apartment. Virginia rings the doorbell as a courtesy, but in about two seconds the doorknob is going to turn. Either Virginia or Camille is having a meltdown. As I pull the doorknob she's pushing from the other side. I can now hear the screams loud and clear. Not a good day for baby Camille. And I'm so drained. But she did just rescue me.

"What's wrong with her?" I ask. Virginia enters in her usual exasperated state when her child is inconsolable. All her paraphernalia is hanging on the stroller; Camille's face has turned purple and tears are streaming down her face.

"I feel so awful. I banged her head when I was getting

her out of the car and she was so cranky anyway. Andy's been working late so he's no help." She hands me the baby. "I'm getting some ice."

Then she sees Harper and Bea. "Oh, I'm sorry, I didn't know you had company. You never have company." Nice, Virginia. I do the introductions.

"This is Bea and Harper, FRED'S mother and niece." Code to Virginia to keep her mouth shut about Fred.

"Oh, so nice to meet you both . . ." She looks at me like "what's going on?"

"They're having a few problems with their house, so they're staying here tonight. Fred had to go out of town."

"Oh, I'm sorry," Virginia says, trying to be polite, but she is distracted by Camille's incessant screaming. Meanwhile, Harper is edging closer and closer to the baby until she timidly reaches out her hand and strokes Camille on the shoulder. Camille gazes at her with wonder, fascinated. Babies always seem to respond to young children's faces. Harper starts giggling and smiling and Camille makes a few little hiccups and then stops crying.

"Can I hold her?" Harper asks. Virginia nods okay, grateful to have someone else take over. Bea fusses around, adjusting the baby in Harper's lap as Harper holds out her finger and Camille grabs it. "Look, Grandma. She's holding my hand."

It is now almost dinnertime. Camille is quietly playing with Harper on the floor and Virginia has just had an in-depth conversation about organic hair dyes with Bea. They've gotten to the whole Harper Lady method thing and I can tell Virginia is digging it. I'm setting the table when I overhear words in whispered tones like "trashed," "all my dishes," "Harper's bedspread," "druggies." The whole dreadful story.

"Oh my god," Virginia responds. "I have a whole set of dishes in my garage I can lend you." Yes, indeed. Now is the time to open the wine.

I wonder what Fred is thinking right now, if he's had a flash of conscience. I check my e-mail. Nothing. I check my cell phone. Nothing. This whole thing is pretty incredible. Fred always takes care of Fred. Oh, maybe that's not fair. He did help Bea. But I keep asking myself over and over, how could he just abandon them now?

After my third glass of wine, Camille falls asleep and, as we all sit down to dinner, Bea raises her glass and says, "I'd like to propose a toast. To Dora. For taking us in. The Bible tells us that a faithful friend is the medicine of life. And that's what you are. And we love you." I am touched, a little drunk, and a little depressed. It's starting to hit home about Fred.

Virginia, who's also a little smashed, chimes in, "To Harper and Bea, wonderful new friends. We love you too." What is she doing? It's not like her to be this effusive.

After dinner, Virginia and I clean up while Bea gives Harper a bath.

"Now I see what you like about her. She's so unusual and lovely. By the way . . . where's Fred?"

I knew she'd corner me sooner or later.

"He's a piece of shit. He left them to deal with all this stuff. Can you believe it? It's over for me, that's for sure. And don't say you're glad."

"I'm really sorry, Dora."

"I hate him."

"Okay. I got it."

I go on, I can't stop myself. "You know where he is right now?" I whisper loudly, "He's sitting on some beach having a margarita. That's what was so urgent. He's a selfish pig."

"Oh, dear. He has such a nice mother. And Harper is so unspoiled."

"Yeah, he's the black sheep. I guess every family has one."

Virginia gives me a knowing look. In our family, Dad's the mutton.

Meanwhile, I hear loud whining coming from the guest room. Harper, clad in pink thermal jammies, runs into the kitchen, with Bea following. She clutches her blankie and looks unhappy.

"Are you okay?" I ask Harper.

"My head hurts." She pouts.

Bea strokes Harper's head. "It's been a long day, sweetie. You need to go to bed. Say good-night and thank Dora."

"No." She drops on the floor.

"Now, Harper. You're nice and clean and the floor's dirty. Get up and let's get to bed." Bea has a slight panic in her voice. She knows what's coming.

"No. I'm not going to bed. I'm not tired."

"Honey, it's nine o'clock. Way past your bedtime."

"No."

"Okay. I'm counting to three and then you lose TV for a week."

At this point Harper starts wailing.

"No. I don't want to lose TV."

"Well, then get up and let's go to bed."

"No! No!" She's wailing and tears are streaming down her face. I don't know why, it's insane, but strains of the saccharine good-night song from *The Sound of Music* dance in my head as I envision the Von Trapp children merrily pirouetting off to bed one by one. "So long, farewell, auf Wiedersehen, adieu . . ."

Bea tries to pick up Harper, but it seems she's made of lead. Bea can't budge her. The baby wakes up and starts to scream. I try to comfort Harper and she kicks me in the shin. Virginia rushes over to Camille to pick her up.

"Now look what you've done, you woke up the baby!" Bea says, mortified. "Why are you being so naughty? I don't know what's wrong with you!"

"I want my mommy," she sobs. "I don't like you. And I want to go home!"

All of us look at each other. It's obvious now what's going on. Bea melts. She starts to cry as well and sits on the floor and hugs Harper.

"We all miss your mommy. And we'll go home tomorrow. You'll see. Your room will be perfect in no time."

My god, this has turned into a catastrophe. And that bastard just left them like this.

"Do you want me to read to you?" I say. "You can

come into my room and sit on my bed." No reaction. She's still crying. "I have jelly beans. All colors."

"Okay," she says as she starts to get up. Bea is still on the floor, her eyes filled with tears, and Camille is still howling.

"I think we'll be going now," says Virginia, holding the screaming baby and pushing her stroller out. "Really nice meeting you, Bea. I hope everything works out. I'm so sorry."

"I'm the one who's sorry, Harper isn't usually like this," Bea says, getting up.

"I think she's very brave," Virginia says, looking at Harper.

"Bye, Ginny. I love you, see you later," I say.

Harper is standing next to me sucking her thumb. I put my arm around her and we walk into my bedroom.

"Where are the jelly beans?"

"Right here." I grab a jar from my dresser. Do these things get old? I think they've been here since Easter. Too late now. I open the jar and hand her the whole thing. We settle on my bed with the jar between us. They taste okay to me.

I have a shelf in my bedroom filled with special books from my childhood, and before dinner I grabbed a few, thinking we could read them later. I pick up *Now We Are Six,* tossing aside Virginia's dog-eared, high-school copy of *Winne Ille Pu,* for Latin junkies.

It's so strange about Milne. He was a sourpuss like Dr. Seuss. I've decided that from now on I'm going to ig-nore disappointing autobiographical details. I'm not going to let the fact that Christopher Robin thought his dad was a stiff take away from the charm and gentle humor of the verse. His poems are funny, reassuring, and comforting. Not at all "quaintsy-waintsy," as Dorothy Parker scoffed in one of her *New Yorker* reviews about A. A. "Whimsey-the-Pooh" Milne, who apparently was her "literary mortal enemy."

I read a few lines to Harper and then she says, "Let me." I hear her little wispy voice as she reads, "The End."

"But now I am Six, I'm as clever as clever.
So I think I'll be six now for ever and ever." *

---

* A. A. Milne, *Now We Are Six,* "The End."

Ripping Off Rudyard

> My little old dog:
> A heart–beat
> At my feet.

~ Edith Wharton (1862–1937) ~

The next morning, Bea and Harper are up by seven. I can smell coffee brewing in the kitchen before I get out of bed, and then Harper lightly taps on my door. She says they're ready to go home whenever I'm ready to take them.

Bea has found my flour and meager cooking supplies and has thrown together an impressive breakfast of hotcakes and powdered sugar.

"I'm sorry there's no syrup," I say to Harper.

"That's okay. Grandma found sugar." She's clearly delighted.

After breakfast, Bea washes and puts away all the dishes while I get dressed. I find her sitting out on my terrace squinting into the glaring sunlight. The potted pink and white peonies, my favorite flower, are exploding in extravagant, frilly blooms and are lined up like Easter bonnets along the wall. I tell her that she can stay with me until the mess is cleaned up. Bea smiles at me kindly.

"I have friends who will help us through this. You don't need to worry so much, Dora. I didn't get to where I am without a little vinegar in my veins. But yesterday, I tell you, I don't know what I would have done without you."

"Have you talked to Fred?" I ask. It occurs to me that maybe Bea knew the situation with Fred all along.

"No. I haven't. But I know you two had a disagreement and I'm sorry about that. I hope we can still be good friends."

"I'd like that, Bea. I'll get the keys and take you home."

I have a hard time dropping them off. The place looks like a disaster and the cleaning crew still hasn't arrived. I can tell Harper is hesitant as I hug her good-bye. I ask Bea again if she'd like me to stay. She says no. It's obvious she doesn't want to impose any more. I hope they catch those bastards.

I get back into my car and try to figure out the route home. I can't face getting back on the freeway today. Then Brooke calls.

"Hey, Dora. Good news. You have another assignment. It's Top Dog Poetry Contest on Venice Beach and the editor wants you to cover it."

"Now, why would he pick me . . ." I say knowingly.

"You got it. You're our shaggy dog stringer. You've found yourself quite a little niche—no one here gives a shit about animals, and you know how people are about their dogs."

I briefly think about Brawley and Palmer. Not in that order.

"Let's see. *'Plus je vois l'homme, plus j'aimie mon chien.'* " Okay, I'm showing off a little.

"What the hell does that mean?"

"It's Pascal. It means, the more I know of man, the more I love my dog."

"Like my date last night, and I don't even have a dog."

"Want to hear another one?"

"Save it for the piece. I'm up to here with dogs. My neighbor's Lab howls all night and I'm seriously considering dog court. Or poisoned meat."

There's no time to change my clothes. By the time I get to the Dog Beach Zone near the boardwalk, a crowd of people are already shepherding their dogs to a small, flagged-in arena flanked by dozens of booths selling pet-related paraphernalia. It's like a canine revival meeting minus the hallelujahs. The event organizer is a preppy young man in his early thirties with a Lands' End kind of look. He is rousing the crowd with invocations to dogdom using buzzwords like *common bond, devotion, bravery,* and *unconditional love.*

I meet my photographer, a wiry, chain-smoking, balding loser with three cameras slung around his shoulder and a bulging dirty canvas camera bag hanging on the other. In the *Times* hierarchy, a freelancer, such as myself, is lower than dirt and the assignment is filler at best.

This guy is making it clear that he's just here to get a token shot. I introduce myself and he looks around.

"This is stupid. I'm outta here."

"You need to stay at least until they start reading. It's a poetry contest," (you slob).

"Looks like a bunch of fleabags to me." He snorts.

I ignore him as the organizer steps up to the podium.

"Welcome, ladies and gentlemen, mutts and hounds, puppies and pointers, and all the rest of you highfalutin, verse-spouting, muzzle-faced mongrels. Ha, ha, ha. I know you've all worked very hard on your poems, so I'll just get the ball rolling. Here goes. 'Ode to Rose.' 'Good dog, good dog, you make my days complete . . . I think of you in the morning and when I go to sleep.' "

Oh my god. Is this for real? The photographer snickers and shoots a couple pictures.

"That's it for me," he states.

I look around at the waiting contestants with their dogs. A young woman's trim little Doxie with a glossy chestnut coat has dropped to the ground and is furiously scratching his neck and ears. Nearby, an elderly man's cloddy English sheepdog has his head planted in a schnauzer's butt. The schnauzer's neck and back hairs start to bristle and then he whips around and clamps his jaws on the dog's neck, at which point the owners leap into action, trying to separate them.

The organizer ignores the scuffle, finishes his poem, and introduces the next entry. This poem is just as maudlin as the one before; the dog's cute though. It's kind of a short, stocky terrier mix with a Fu Manchu mustache trailing on either side of his snout. He sits at attention and gazes adoringly at his owner while she reads her embarrassing poem. I'm thinking that I can't possibly quote this in the article. I'd be the laughingstock of the newsroom. On the other hand, that's probably what they want. I'm not making fun of these people. No, I'm not. Even though they can't write their way out of a paper bag.

I endure four more moronic odes to Buddy, Gypsy, a mongrel named Elmo, and a whippet named Stick. Then, what turns out to be the winning poem knocks me for a loop. An elderly woman leading an enormously fat, wheezing English bulldog starts to read.

> "Brothers and sisters, I bid you beware.
> Of giving your heart to a dog to tear."*

Wait a minute! What is this? I know that poem. It's Kipling! It's Rudyard fucking Kipling! I look around. No one's saying a word. She reads on and finishes the poem.

There is wild applause, barking, yapping, straining on leashes. It seems I'm the only one who knows. Now what? I'm obliged to interview her because she's the first-prize winner (a twenty-five-dollar gift certificate to PETCO), but what to say? Do I turn her in? Do I give her a knowing wink? She looks so nice and honest and sweet. She's crying as they hand her the award. Now she's giving her acceptance speech.

---

* Rudyard Kipling, "The Power of the Dog."

". . . And I want to dedicate this award to my late husband, Charles, who wrote this poem and who loved this dog more than his life."

Okay. I need this story to be good. I really want my job back. If I out her, will it make this a better story? Probably. But I can't do it. Who could do it? Brooke. Brooke could do it. Fuck Brooke. I'm not doing it.

I briefly interview the woman, who tells me about her husband, who taught high school English for thirty years. Makes sense. And then I go home to write the story. It would be so easy to belittle these people or to turn this into a hokey, small-town Garrison Keillor vignette. Then again, I hate Garrison Keillor and his faux, twangy down-home voice. I decide to try a different tack. I go to my bookshelf and pick out a collection of poems by Thurber, Lord Byron, Elizabeth Barrett Browning, John Cheever, John Updike, and others, all of whom were well-known dog lovers and praised the legendary relationship between dog and master. The material is rich with sentiment and humor, like Byron's epitaph to Boatswain, his dog, born 1803, died at Newstead Abbey in 1808. The last two lines of his tribute are

"to mark a friend's remains these stones arise;
I never knew but one—and here he lies."

Browning's poem "To Flush, My Dog" is next. Brother, a little over the top, but that's the point isn't it?

"Leap! Thy broad tail waves a light,
Leap! Thy slender feet are bright."

E. B. White's graceful obituary to his dog, Daisy, is my favorite. She was hit by a yellow cab in University Place in 1931 and had a "quirkish temper . . . she suffered from chronic perplexity."

My lead for the article is that poems dedicated to dogs have been around since the seventeenth century and convey the faith and companionship of man's best friend. In order to temper the mundane verse I heard today, I intersperse quotes from the contestants with those of the masters. I describe at length the poetic attributes of the dogs present, and after rereading my article, I am feeling more of a connection to the likes of Brawley than I care to admit.

As for the plagiarist, I end the piece by quoting the woman's description of her husband's devotion to the bulldog that survived him.

When the editor's desk calls to ask for a copy of the winning poem, I simply tell them it sucks. That seems to satisfy them and they print the piece without it.

What a day! I take a bath and decide to check my e-mail. See if that jerk has sent me anything. Okay. There it is. FredFitzG . . . how pretentious. When you like someone you tend to overlook these little things. I almost open it and then I think, no, I'm not ready, I need a glass of wine. . . .

I do the same avoidance dance with my bills. They sit around like dust-balls in a corner until I get the second notice. Then I stack them in a pile on the bathroom sink so I'm forced to deal with them.

I empty the first glass of wine and then fiddle with the stem, deciding whether I need another. I stroll back over to my computer. Yep. E-mail's still there. What am I afraid of? In the beginning, Fred seemed so perfect. His lust for literature, his passion. And those nights. Maybe you never get over nights like that. But the fact that he was so willing to blow off Harper and Bea just pushed my buttons. He's an abandoner. Not a good thing in my world.

I'm going to delete it. There, it's gone. He's gone. I'm done. I have another glass of wine. Shit. I'm depressed. I wonder what he said. The insane thing about a computer is that nothing is ever gone. Not like in the old days when you'd fling unwanted correspondence dramatically into the fire. In cyberspace, every bit of minutia of the human mind and heart is swirling around out there somewhere, suspended in eternity like a prayer. You can find anything if you want to. Okay. Enough foreplay. I'm going to retrieve it. There it is, recently deleted e-mails. Talk to me, Fred.

Dear Dora, I'm sitting on my balcony looking at a very blue Pacific and a very cold Pacifica—that's a local beer, my sweet, and I've already had at least four of them.

(Oh good, now we're both drunk.)

Even though I'm way over the legal limit, I'm more clear-minded now than I've been in years.

(Right.)

It's hard to know where to begin. So let's start with the fact that

I've finally figured out the answer to your question, "What's wrong with me?" The long and the short of it is, I've been a miserable failure.

(He's definitely drunk.)

Notwithstanding my swagger in the bookstore and my appeal to women of a certain age,

(Jesus, I hate that.)

my career trajectory has been abysmal, which might explain my antisocial behavior at your friend's birthday party. Up until now my life has been a series of pedestrian efforts and undistinguished accomplishments.

(At least he's honest.)

There's a reason I never let you read my play. It wasn't working and I knew it. But here, I feel like I'm on the verge of something great. I've been up all night writing and I can't tell you what a relief it is to finally feel creative again. So call me what you will, I've decided to stay here for a while and write. I do think about you but we're not kids anymore and at the moment we both know it's not working.

(Here it comes, the kiss-off.)

I'm sorry if I'm not the person you think I should be. Oh, I can see your face now, Dora. Your judgmental, disappointed, beautiful face. But this is who I am. So why don't you give me the benefit of the doubt. Let's take the high road here. I love Bea and Harper, I think I do enough for them. I'm sorry if it's not enough for you.

Take care. Love, Fred

I steeled myself for this and got exactly what I expected. How could it have ended any differently? Not after he skipped out like that.

This reminds me of an old cartoon my mother used to

love. It's a sketch of an over-the-hill cabaret singer seated at a piano in a late-night, partially deserted New York nightclub. As she introduces her next song, the caption reads something like this, "Ladies and gentlemen, sometimes the one you love disappoints you, and when that happens, it is very sad indeed. It happened to me, and I wrote this song.

"It's called 'Fuck you, Stuart.'"

Nightmare

"Last night I dreamt I
went to Manderley again."

~ Daphne du Maurier (1907–1989), *Rebecca* ~

I've never been the kind of person who talks about her dreams. The reason may well be that I rarely can remember what happens or who's involved, and a few hours past dawn, the fleeting images are lost forever.

My friends are just the opposite. Darlene says she dreams about her mother all the time, half the time she is in heaven and the other half in hell. She also says she has graphic "wolves at the gate" dreams where she's helplessly trapped, nowhere to run. Pamela's dream involves a carpenter who boarded up her whole house and she could never get into her closets again.

The few dreams I half remember are pretty standard.

I'm being chased by a man in dark clothes and my legs turn to mush and I can't move or Virginia and I are seated together in an airplane and suddenly the bottom falls out and we tumble through the air in slo-mo, falling, falling, falling. Palmer's dreams were classic too, in a male sort of way—he is eating a hamburger and all his teeth fall out or he is about to take an exam when he realizes, well, you know. Everyone's had this one.

But the dream I will never forget was different. It occurred in my childhood shortly after my father left us. I've never told another living soul about it except for my mother, and her reaction was so odd that I decided not to tell anyone else, ever.

The event that presumably triggered it was a road trip to the Amish country during one spring vacation. We passed miles of rolling pastures and scenic farms, but soon after cruising through a bucolic little town there was a potent, sickeningly sweet, unearthly stink that assaulted our senses like some grotesque pool of rot. Mother told Virginia and me that we were driving past a slaughterhouse. And I was fascinated.

"How are the animals killed?" I asked.

"They bash them over the head with a sledgehammer," Virginia taunted as she slapped me hard on the head with the back of her fist.

"That's not true, is it, Mother?" I replied in shock.

"I don't know," she replied, distracted, as usual. "I think they do something to that effect. It's a terrible thought, isn't it?"

I had the dream that night. It began with my father

telling Virginia and me that there was a carnival in town and that he was taking us all, including my mother. I should have been suspicious right away, because Mother never went with us to amusement parks. She just didn't believe in them.

When we arrived, she led Virginia off to the Ferris wheel and my father took my hand.

"Why don't you and I go over here to the bumper cars," he said. I was thrilled. Just him and me. We were a couple! I felt special and completely loved.

"If she doesn't want to go, don't force her," my mother said. But I was excited.

"No, I want to go," I answered.

We hiked for what seemed like miles in a dream forest, dimly lit with narrow, overgrown trails and darkening skies. Then we reached a clearing. There were banner-like streamers of little red plastic flags fluttering in the breeze like a used-car lot, and I realized it wasn't bumper cars at all but a large oval track where cars went around and around in a circle. The riders, all children about my age, wore helmets, and when they passed the front entrance, a giant robotic sledgehammer slammed down on their heads and killed them.

My father told me I had to trust him. That the hammer wouldn't come down on my head. That he wouldn't leave and that he'd be there to stop it before it was my turn. I cried, but I put on the helmet anyway and got into the car.

No matter how hard I try to remember, I'm still not sure what happened next. The images are shadowy with some suggestion of another ghostly presence somewhere, whispering, cajoling, insisting that I stay put in the car. Then I woke up abruptly.

I suppose any mother would be horrified to hear a daughter recount such a thing. I know I would. But I needed to tell her about the panic and heavy, numbing sadness I felt when I woke up. She grew very quiet and then asked me if I made this up. "You read that in Edgar Allan Poe or one of your mysteries, right?" When I said no, she asked me if I really believed that my father would do such a thing. I said no to this too, because I didn't.

"Then why did you dream this?" she puzzled.

"I don't know," I told her. I was shaken up and so was she. But it wasn't her style to comfort me. I have a vague recollection of her deliberately changing the subject in the way that she always did when painful issues cropped up. I needed something from her, maybe reassurance, maybe just a warm hug. But, as usual, we moved on.

Last Book Standing

"I like a thin book because it will steady a table,
a leather volume because it will strop a razor, and
a heavy book because it can be thrown at a cat."
~ Mark Twain ~

Every August since my father died, my mother spends a week in L.A. When I was married to Palmer, she stayed with us. He couldn't really refuse, considering I put up with his mother for the entire month of January. But Palmer and my mother actually seemed to get along. She liked his self-confidence, ease, and grace; he liked her independence, intellect, and patrician bearing.

Now that I'm separated, she stays with Virginia, to "help" her out with the baby.

"You have to come over here right now! She's driving me crazy. Maybe she could stay with you for a while," Virginia whines.

"She wants to be with Camille."

"Well, she makes her tense."

"She makes HER tense?"

"Okay. She makes ME tense. I don't do anything right. Feed her the right foods. Put her to bed on time. The baby's either too hot or too cold. She thinks I'm spoiling her."

It's the classic problem with mothers. They want to tell you how to raise your child—as if they did such a good job with you. I decide to give Virginia a break and take my mother out for the day.

"You don't have to entertain me, Dora. I'm just fine." Mothers always say this. What are you supposed to do? Throw her the *TV Guide* and say, "See ya"?

"I'd like to spend some time with you," I counter convincingly.

"Well, let me check with Virginia and see if she needs me." She puts her hand on the receiver as she yells to Virginia. "Do you need me here today, dear?" I'm betting she'll say no. Mother comes back on the line. "Virginia says she doesn't need me, so I'm all yours."

I tell my mother I have a great idea for a literary outing. For a long time now, I've been meaning to drive by Aldous Huxley's house on Deronda Drive in the Hollywood Hills. His original residence burned down in the early sixties, but I wanted to see where he and his second wife, Laura, lived until his death, the same day Kennedy was assassinated.

As we're driving through Beechwood Canyon, I point out that a biographer had described the Huxleys as oddly detached when flames destroyed their library, which contained, among other things, two unfinished novels, an original D. H. Lawrence manuscript, literary correspondences including Aldous's first wife's love letters, and his copiously annotated book collection. Evidently, they had plenty of time to rescue such irreplaceable treasures but chose instead to salvage some suits, Laura's Guarneri violin, and a Chinese porcelain statue. When asked how he coped in the aftermath of the fire, Huxley is said to have replied, "One goes out and buys a toothbrush."*

We decide to follow Huxley's daily routine. He wrote every morning, and in the afternoon he walked in Hollywood's immense Griffith Park. I love this park. When Palmer and I were dating, we would go to the Observatory, lie on the grass on our backs, and watch the constellations in the summer sky. It was very romantic.

We pull into the Beechwood Market, a popular hippie gourmet deli, and pick up some baguettes, chèvre, prosciutto, Pellegrino for her, and a bottle of Chianti for me. Then we head for the picnic grounds surrounding the famous deco merry-go-round. We sit close enough so we can watch the noble horses gracefully execute imaginary leaps and hear the organ piping out an unending series of marches and waltz music. The music brings back memories of utopian afternoons with my father at the Willow Grove amusement park. I decide not to share this with my mother.

We spread out our feast on a wooden picnic table un-

---

* Nicholas Murray, *Aldous Huxley, A Biography*.

der a grove of California oak trees and start to eat. I look over at my mother as she sighs contentedly, closes her eyes, and arches her long, graceful neck toward the sun. She has a beautiful, angular face with extravagantly high cheekbones and a long Roman nose. Her skin is still smooth and unwrinkled like a woman half her age and her thick auburn hair is styled in a chic wavy bob.

She seems so together and relaxed. The bitter, self-pitying, abandoned wife is gone, along with her periods of raging storms and melancholia when she prowled around our living room in her long pink housecoat, clinking the ice in her cocktail glass at noon.

Mother leans back farther on the bench and stretches out her long legs. She's wearing a pair of loose jeans, a long-sleeved cotton T-shirt, and Keds. As long as I can remember, she's preached to me about staying out of the sun, but she's clearly reached the stage in her life when she doesn't care. I watch her basking in the afternoon sun as if it were a forbidden pleasure. Her khaki safari hat is thrown beside her on the bench. She looks around and I think I'm going to hear something about the glorious day or the bucolic surroundings.

"You know, I never liked Aldous Huxley."

"What do you mean?"

"Well, he had one good book in him and after that he spent his life experimenting with drugs and women."

"So, why did you want to come here?"

"I thought you wanted to come here." This is so annoying. Oh well.

"Mother, did you know that Jim Morrison named his band The Doors after one of Huxley's books?"*

"Who's Jim Morrison?"

"Never mind, Mom."

We're quiet for a minute as we listen to the music and, when it stops, the breeze rustling the trees. She tilts her head and gives me a concerned look.

"So, what's going on with you, Dora?" My stomach tightens.

"Well, I'm trying to get my old job back."

She pauses, takes a sip of her Pellegrino, and gives me a rueful smile.

"And what about Palmer?"

"I don't know. It's complicated." I'm not going to get into this with her.

"I hate to dwell on ancient history, but I feel as if my problems with your father had a terrible impact on you girls. And I wouldn't want you to give up something good because of . . ." She pauses and breaks off for a moment in an attempt to gather her thoughts.

"Your father had a lot of very special qualities. And even though we had our differences, we worked it out."

Oh yeah, they worked it out. He was gone for eight years.

"I don't know exactly how to say this, but I hope you didn't torpedo this because of what happened between your father and me. When he left us, I think you girls reacted in different ways. I wasn't able to deal with any of

---

* Nicholas Murray, *Aldous Huxley, A Biography*.

it because of my drinking, so I'd throw you a book and you'd disappear. When I look back, I'm so ashamed."

This is unlike her. She's usually so stoic. The stone goddess barricaded in her bedroom.

"I should have held you girls close. I should have been more loving and more aware of your needs. The alcohol blurred my priorities and we lost a lot of good years together. It's completely my fault."

I can see tears welling in her eyes. I put my arms around her.

"Come on, Mom. You took us to the museum. You took us on literary trips. You did a lot."

"Not really. When I look back, I feel so sad and guilty. All I could think about was that your father left me." She starts crying. I can't remember ever seeing her like this.

"Mom, you were overwhelmed. There wasn't anybody there to help you. We got through it. Isn't that the important thing?"

"I just want you to be happy."

"I am happy, Mom." I'm ecstatically happy.

For some reason, I suddenly get a fleeting image of my sister and me as teenagers the morning my mother "ran away." At least that's the way Ginny described it to me one morning at breakfast before I left for school. My father, who had come back for a short visit, had left for the office before dawn to avoid any discussion or unpleasantness.

"What do you mean she ran away?" I asked, hoping she was kidding.

"Well, she left me a note on my desk telling me she was going to Atlantic City for the rest of the year and would I please tell Dad."

That night, she called at two in the morning to tell us that the screen door to her motel room wouldn't lock and the wind kept rattling the windows. She was scared and wanted to come home. She maybe lasted twenty-four hours. I remember saying that I wished she could have made it work because she would have been happier. Anyway, the next morning she appeared, as usual, and said, "It was a dumb idea. I don't know what I was thinking."

"Are you listening to me, Dora? I'd like you to have the security of marriage. Anyway, when people commit to each other, it's always a risk. But for you, I think, it became the overwhelming issue. Maybe you can't tell the difference between someone like your father and someone like Palmer." Mother composes herself as she wrings the handkerchief between her hands. She still finds it hard to embrace me.

"Have you been talking to Ginny?" Virginia always liked Palmer.

"Now, don't get mad at your sister. We're all concerned about you."

"Well, you don't have to be so concerned. I broke up with Fred." The memory of him, the physical sensation, abruptly washes over me. I take a large sip of wine. I'm getting a slight buzz.

"Good. And, by the way, you ought to watch yourself in that department." She nods her head toward the bottle of wine. "It creeps up slowly. Don't fall into the same trap I did."

"Okay, Mom. I get it." Her heartfelt apologies are clearly over.

On the way home, Mother confides that she is seeing a man named Thomas, a retired high school math teacher who also fixes clocks. All her widowed girlfriends adore him and he putters around their houses during Sunday brunches repairing their broken appliances and window hardware. The polar opposite of my father.

I drop her off and collapse back into my apartment. I start to pour another glass of Chianti and then think better of it. Fuck it. I pour it anyway. I pour two. Oh good. Now I'm feeling shaky. I flop on the bed and try to think about something other than what has just transpired in the park. Dammit. I hate thinking about those awful years. I hate talking about them. I hate analyzing them. I hate them! Hate them! Hate them! I go into the bathroom and wash my face. Maybe my mother's right. Maybe my whole life has been a reaction to my messed-up childhood. But everyone has a messed-up childhood. People get beyond it and lead productive lives. They don't float around. Shit! What's happening to me?

I walk back into the bedroom and eye the bookshelf. I pull out John Fowles's *The French Lieutenant's Woman*. When did I last read this? What was it about, anyway? Two different endings. One happy. One sad. The author is God. He gets to decide. I close the cover and hurl the book against the wall. The cover splays open and the pages crunch accordion-like on the floor. Gee. That feels good! I pick out another one. It's Henry James's *The Portrait of a Lady*. Isabel's life is ruined by the lowlife Gilbert Osmond. A big, fat hardback. Thud! It slams against the wall and chips the plaster. D. H. Lawrence. *Lady Chatterley's Lover*. Another depressing love affair. The husband brooding in his wheelchair. Slam! Iain Pears. Ick. Reminds me of Fred. I throw this sucker extra hard. I start grabbing the books one by one and pitching them like hardballs against the wall. John Updike. Slam! Henry Miller. Slam! Edith Wharton. Slam! Missed the wall and hit the lamp. The lightbulb explodes like a firecracker.

Books with broken spines are now heaped on top of each other like a literary junkyard. My bookshelf is almost empty. I'm feeling oddly empowered and liberated. I could just tip over the whole thing now and be done with it. How childish and what a mess. The tears are rolling down my face and I start to laugh. How ironic. The last book standing is *Huck Finn*. It almost makes me want to call Palmer because he'd laugh too. Instead, I dial Virginia.

"Virginia?"

"Yes, Dora." Her voice sounds really groggy.

"I just threw every book I own against the wall."

There is silence on the other end.

"Well, that's a start." She laughs.

Something Occurred to Me

"Books are good enough in their own way,
but they are a mighty bloodless substitute for life."
~ Robert Louis Stevenson (1850–1894) ~

The next morning at seven a.m. the doorbell rings. I stagger to the door with a major headache—must have been more wine than I thought. My mother's right, all I need is a fuzzy bathrobe, ratty slippers, and a cigarette hanging out of my mouth and I fit the image perfectly. The lush next door.

"Is everything okay in there?" It's Victor. I open the door.

"Hey, Victor. Everything's fine. What's up?"

"One of your neighbors called the front desk last night around midnight and complained of banging. She thought you were hammering something into the wall."

"At midnight? Come on. She must have heard my television."

"James came up and listened and it was quiet, so he didn't want to disturb you. As long as everything's all right."

"Definitely. Thanks for checking."

I shut the door and survey the damage. It looks like an earthquake in a bookstore. I glance at the gashes in the plaster. Or maybe more like one of those bizarre avant-garde installations at the Whitney. I bend down to pick up one of the books. Ugh. Maybe later. I need my coffee and aspirin. On the way to the kitchen, I check my e-mail.

Another message from Brooke. I hope it's good. A little more bad news will send me right over the edge. One might argue I'm already there.

Hi, Dora. Hate to HOUND you but just wanted to let you know the piece is DOGGONE good. An intriguing bit of DOGGEREL. (Sorry, I couldn't resist.) No kidding. They're impressed. Could get an offer soon.

P.S. The scuzzball photographer thinks you're cute.

I call Virginia. I'm sure I woke her up last night.

"Sorry about last night. I was a little overwrought."

"I'll say. Did you really trash all your books?"

"Uh-huh."

"God, Dora. What set you off?"

"I don't know. Mother and I had this heart-to-heart in the park and it was upsetting. She accused me of being emotionally handicapped because of our charmed childhood."

"Oh well. You know, Mother is into this whole AA thing now, where she's apologizing to all the people she's fucked over."

"A lot of good that does. Anyway, I'm worried she's right. Maybe I'll never be happy."

"Of course you will. You just have to think about what you want."

I did think about it. I thought about it all night. I thought about it as I hurled each book into the wall. I thought about it as I threw down a bottle of wine and then soaked in the steaming hot tub until it turned cold. I thought about it as I reread Fred's pathetic e-mail. I thought about it as I replayed the torrid nights that always seem to go along with weak, spineless, self-absorbed lying pieces of shit. I thought about it as I ordered Harper's new bedding online, pink, ruffled, dotted Swiss duvet with matching twin pillow shams and very expensive, imported boar's-bristle hairbrushes for Bea. Right before I passed out, I thought about what mother said in the park. About her wasted years. And my wasted years.

Then something occurred to me.

It occurred to me that what I really want is a mother like Bea and a daughter like Harper. Fred was right about something. I did want to adopt them. But it wasn't because of him or even them. It was because I wanted to be like everyone else. I picture my sister's face. My devoted, caring, nutty sister.

"I want a job. I want a family that's warm and that

loves me. I want to be normal and belong. I don't care if that sounds bourgeois. That's what I want. There."

"Oh honey. Just like when we were kids. You'll find that. I promise you, you'll find it."

I start to sniffle.

"Are you okay? I can come over."

"You'd freak out if you saw the mess here."

"I'll help you clean up."

"Virginia, I love you but I really don't want to deal with this now."

"Then maybe I should pick you up. We'll go somewhere fun."

"No. Really. I'm fine."

I pull myself together. "In fact, I have some promising news. I may get my job back at the *Times*."

"You're kidding. That's terrific!"

We talk a little more about the possibilities, when this could happen, and then we hang up.

Two minutes later the phone rings. It's Virginia again.

"I forgot to ask you. Did you get the invitation from Palmer?"

"No. Well, maybe." I look at the stack of unopened mail.

"He's being honored at the Museum of Contemporary Art and he's asked us to be his guests. I'd love to go . . . it's this Saturday night. . . ."

"Saturday! Are you kidding me? These things go out weeks in advance. You know what happened? Somebody probably canceled last minute or he just felt sorry for us."

"Whatever. It sounds like fun. Andy's out of town and I want to go."

"I don't know . . ."

"Dora, he's asking you. It's a big deal. It would be really rude not to show up . . . after all he's done for you . . . lately . . ."

So, what's he done? Just rescued me from my bender, treated me to a great dinner, drove me to Darlene's place to get Brawley, schlepped me to the hospital, and took care of the dog for a week.

"If you want to go . . . okay."

"Oh good. Why don't we go shopping? You like that. It's black tie and I don't have a thing to wear. Meet me at the mall around three, okay? And I'm not spending a fortune."

A fortune to Virginia is two hundred dollars. So this is going to be a long afternoon.

I hang up and decide to deal with the pile of mail sitting on the kitchen counter. Buried near the bottom is a calligraphy-embellished, cream-colored envelope. It's an invitation to a party at the Museum of Contemporary Art honoring Palmer and celebrating the new Warhol exhibit. It's addressed to me and a guest. And guest? Who should I bring? Virginia got her own invitation and Palmer's bringing Kimberly, of course. Maybe I can rent someone. Hah! Better yet, I'll call Darlene. She'll keep it light and funny and not let me spiral down into maudlin, negative thoughts.

●   ●   ●

We pull up to Grand Street. It's obvious the sponsors spared no expense. I heard the city and a lot of private organizations donated funds to the event with the hope that the exhibit would attract thousands of tourists to downtown L.A. Three city blocks have been closed and the street that connects them is tented with diaphanous, white, billowing fabric. There must be over a thousand people attending, from the looks of the valet line, which snakes around the corner and continues down the block.

Darlene is wearing what she calls "an homage to Warhol," which consists of a gold tulle miniskirt, platform shoes, and a silvery blue top with appliquéd planets and stars. And then there's Virginia and me. It took all day to find Virginia's outfit. She finally decided on a long black silk skirt and a white satin blouse. She now looks exactly like the musicians strolling through the cocktail area. I'm ready to hand her a violin. I'm in my usual long black dress, simple in the front, deep scoop in the back. Very sexy, I think.

The party planners have modeled the event after Studio 54 and hired tons of freaks and transvestites dressed up as disco dancers to greet the guests. Hanging from the ceiling are cages with go-go dancers, frugging away, while performance artists, sprayed silver from head to toe, do their thing on stages around the perimeter. Huge portraits of famous Warhols are projected on the walls and ceiling and keep changing like a slide show. It's all very dramatic and, for once, Darlene does not stand out. I hear a lot of jokes about "fifteen minutes of fame" as I scan the crowd for a glimpse of Palmer. It seems that every hip celeb in town has shown up.

We go to our assigned table, which is near the stage and definitely an A spot. My sister and Darlene are tripping on the famous VIPs surrounding them and all I can do is worry about whether this will be awkward. Oh. There he is. With Kimberly at his side. Shit, she looks unbelievable. I've seen that dress. It's an emerald-green Valentino that probably costs four grand. Maybe I should have worn a color. We're at a studio table and the two couples across from us obviously know each other. After a polite hello, they don't say another word to us.

The event begins with the head of the museum thanking everyone for all their hard work. He then introduces Dennis Hopper, who knew Andy Warhol when, and then rolls into Palmer's intro. Palmer's evidently getting the award for his fund-raising efforts on behalf of the museum . . . I didn't even know he liked art that much. Well, I guess when you're head of the studio . . . Dennis goes on, Palmer did this and Palmer did that, and by the time he's done, everyone, including Virginia and Darlene, is clapping wildly as he walks to the stage.

The audience quiets down as Palmer begins to speak. He always was a good speaker. Kimberly sits in rapt attention. Like Brawley. Wait. What is that on her finger! It's on her left hand, for god's sake. Virginia spots it at the same time. She puts her glasses on. It's a very big ring, an emerald with giant diamond baguettes.

"Do you think they're engaged?" Virginia whispers.

"What?" Darlene says. "Who's engaged?"

"Shhhh," I say. I'm mortified. The couples at our table are looking at us like "how rude."

Darlene leans over, points to me, and mouths, "Ex-wife."

"We're separated. How can he be engaged?" I hiss.

"Anyone can be engaged . . ." Darlene says.

"Or maybe it's just a friendship ring . . ." Virginia says hopefully.

"I'd like to be his friend," Darlene laughs.

"That's not funny, I can't hear his speech. Be quiet," I admonish them.

Palmer's winding up. He's looking at Kimberly, with a sickeningly sweet smile.

"And now I'd like to thank Kimberly, who worked so hard to make this evening a success, stand up, Kimberly."

How perfect. I smile and applaud like the rest of the audience. This is truly turning into a crap evening, not unlike the rest of my week.

They don't seem to be pouring refills on the wine. I need a drink. I go to the bar and order a vodka—straight up. When I get back to the table, Palmer's sitting in my seat talking to Virginia and Darlene.

"There she is," he says to me as he stands and gives me a warm hug.

"You look beautiful," he whispers.

The four of us talk about the event, we thank him for the tickets, he asks about the dog, blah, blah, blah. Virginia and Darlene are mesmerized by him and I'm feeling, well, I don't know what I'm feeling. Definitely jealous. Definitely insecure. Something's changed here. I'm thinking about my life with him. I hated these dinners. I wonder why I hated them so much. Phony and bullshitty. A waste of energy. No one ever had any fun. But these people look like they're having fun. Why did I make such a big deal about it? It's his business. I could have been more supportive. I bet Kimberly's very supportive. She probably even supervised the flower arrangements.

I hear him say, "Dora, give me your parking ticket. My secretary's going to give them all to the valet so you won't have to wait."

"Thank you. That is so nice of you," gushes Virginia.

I start scrounging through my beaded evening bag. I thought I put it right in the side pocket. Oh god. It's not there. Maybe in my wallet. Now I'm dumping things on the table. My lipstick, my mirror, my gum.

Palmer starts laughing.

"Please tell me you didn't lose it, Dora. There's like a thousand cars out there," Darlene moans.

"I lost it."

"Do you know your license plate, Dora?" Virginia asks.

"Of course she doesn't, do you, Dora?" Darlene challenges.

"Well, who knows their license plate number?" Nobody answers me. I'm fucked. Now what? Quite an impression.

To make things even more humiliating, the crowd is

starting to stream out and Kimberly floats up, a vision in green.

"Hi, hon. You about ready?"

Palmer tells Kimberly that he needs to help us get our car, like we're pathetic spinster hags. Then he asks me to come with him and he'll talk to the guy who's supervising the event. He takes my hand and leads me to the curtained-off area, which looks like a NASA control booth. I describe my car and they tell me to wait out front and they'll find it for me.

It's funny at events like this. One minute there's a thousand people crowded in the room, and the next, the place is deserted except for my sad little group. As we head for the table, he puts his arm in the small of my back and says, "There. It's all taken care of."

This gives me the courage to say, "Are you engaged?"

"What? How can I be engaged? We're separated, Dora. Anyway, would you care?"

"Yes. I'd care."

"Well, that's something. When we were married, I was always trying to figure out that question."

What do I say now? Do I apologize? Do I tell him I've changed? No one ever believes you when you say it. I know that I want him. Should I tell him? Okay. I'm going to tell him. I'd better hurry, here comes that fuckface Kimberly.

"Palmer, I want us to try again. What do you think about that?" I blurt out. I see his face register complete surprise. He's quiet for what seems like an hour, and then he says with half a smile, "I still find Shakespeare dull, Dora."

Now, I know you want to hear the end of the story. So do I, but Kimberly walked up and ruined the whole thing. Palmer politely said good-night, gave me a peck on the cheek. Always the gentleman. The valet guy ran up with my key. Virginia and Darlene came over and said, "Thank god, I thought we were going to be here all night." And everyone merrily headed for home.

Epilogue

One of the strangest things that happened in the days following my book rampage was that, somehow, I lost the desire to read. I dumped the debris of broken spines and disfigured pages into a box and delivered it to my neighborhood library. The librarian arched her eyebrows as I handed her my poor little darlings, but she didn't mention their wounded appearance. As I drove away, I felt a wave of remorse, the way a parent must feel when dropping off their child at boarding school. A mixture of freedom, guilt, and loss, tempered by the realization that I was doing the right thing. I must admit, my abstinence only lasted a few months and then I was back at Borders checking out the latest Booker Prize winners and National Book Finalists.

But it was different. Not like before, when my stupid, marathon zonk-out sessions plunged me into a deep and enthralling haze of complex, voluptuous portraits and mysteries, myths, dreams, deaths, human tragedies, ingenious plots, failed marriages, odysseys, ecstasies, meditations, hallucinations, and extended, strenuous, pulsating scenes of making love. But I do go on. That's what I'm prone to doing. Going on and on, devouring novels at an alarming rate and losing my way. I regret that now. I truly do. But big-deal realizations often elude you. In any case, memories of the past year are all jumbled together now with nostalgic whiffs of vinegar and bath soap and Palmer's tender calls and wounded bucks and tequila and a child's wispy little voice. I can tap into any of these sensations and come out with the blunt, hard edge of what actually happened to me and all the people I love.

As for my books, the pathetic, picked-over state of my diminishing library is only half the story. Speaking of which, I probably had you fooled about the giveaway book thing. I actually went back a few days later and told the same librarian I had changed my mind and could I just give a contribution instead. She pointed to the untouched box behind the counter and smiled an indulgent little smile. What was she going to do with a load of mangled, smashed-up-against-the-wall books? I took them to Virginia, who said she'd work on them when she could. Then she went into her whole "I'm exhausted, I have no free time, I'm so busy" routine and I felt better about everything.

I've driven by McKenzie's countless times in the past year since Fred and I stopped seeing each other but I still can't bring myself to go in. I'm pretty sure he doesn't approve of my relationship with Bea and Harper. They rarely talk about him, and I doubt if they even see him that often.

On Harper's last birthday, Bea and I gave her a tea party at Sally's, a Victorian teahouse in Santa Monica, and we invited all of her friends, along with their mothers. I sent Fred an invitation, never expecting him to come, but he surprised us all and showed up in time for the cake. As he flashed that grin of his at the gathering of attractive young mothers, Darlene leaned over to me, looked at Fred wistfully, and whispered, "Too bad he was a dud." Harper was happy to see him, though, and greeted him as one would a distant relative who sometimes drops in. She gave him a kiss and then ran off to play with her friends. He smiled. I smiled. It was awkward.

My advice to you concerning this matter is don't be snowed by a handsome guy at a bookstore who quotes Cicero and Proust. They are often not the real thing. As with so many fleeting pleasures—travel in their company, enjoy them every so often, and then get on with your life.

The other day, my mother called to tell me she's coming to L.A. to visit, maybe with Thomas. She suggested a literary trip to San Francisco to visit the old haunts of

Twain, Saroyan, and Steinbeck. I told her that I'd try, but I'm just not sure right now, what with my schedule at the *Times* and Palmer's obligations at the studio.

Ginny tells me I'm almost normal now. (Ha!) Well, compared to before, I guess I am. But every now and then, when I can't sleep, or when I'm at odds with the world, I have those urges. Sometimes I indulge. Sometimes I don't. In any event, books still quell the longing one gets in this world and can tell a simple story that helps make sense of things.

Some nights, you'll find me outside on our loggia, wrapped in my oversize terry-cloth robe, nestled in the big wicker rocker, with a steaming mug of hot choco-late—well, okay, laced with a little Kahlua—probably reading Alice Munro's latest collection of short stories, or rereading Vonnegut, keeping another stack of books on reserve, like a child hoarding Halloween candy. I can usually hear the distant hum of the freeway as I look out on the view—the lights of Century City and past that, on summer nights, the surreal silhouette of Dodger Sta-dium, floating on the horizon like a low-flying saucer.

Authors' Note

The authors would like to recognize a few other sources we consulted in writing this novel. In the chapter entitled "No Reliable Sense of Propriety" we used as a source *Mark Twain, An Illustrated Biography* by Geoffrey C. Ward and Dayton Duncan, including Ken Burns's preface to that book. In the chapter entitled "Halfway to Fairyland," we used as source material "The Man Behind the Curtain: L. Frank Baum and the Wizard of Oz" by Linda McGovern. We also would like to note that the chapter title "Where the Wild Things Are" is also the title of a Maurice Sendak book, and the chapter title "The Piper at the Gates of Dawn" is also a chapter heading in Kenneth Grahame's *The Wind in the Willows*.

Book List

Authors, artists, and works that are discussed or mentioned in this novel, listed in order of first appearance.

Ted Kooser, poet
Jorge Luis Borges, author
John O'Hara, author
Andrew Wyeth, painter/author
N. C. Wyeth, painter/author
Robert Frost, poet
Arthur Christopher Benson, author
Nicholas A. Basbanes, reporter/author, and *Among the Gently Mad*
Fourth Earl of Chesterfield (Philip Dormer Stanhope), author
The Member of the Wedding by Carson McCullers
John Coltrane, musician/composer
Paul Desmond, musician/composer
Shirley Hazzard, author, and *The Transit of Venus* and *The Great Fire*
Wuthering Heights by Emily Brontë
Dorothy Parker, author/wit
Jane Austen, author
The Optimist's Daughter by Eudora Welty

Gustave Flaubert, author, and *Sentimental Education* and *Madame Bovary*

Anna Karenina by Leo Tolstoy

The End of the Affair by Graham Greene

A Farewell to Arms by Ernest Hemingway

Evelyn Waugh, author

Michael Frayn, author/playwright

Mark Twain, author, and *The Adventures of Huckleberry Finn*

Henry James, author, and *The Portrait of a Lady*

Pablo Neruda, poet

Tuesdays with Morrie by Mitch Albom

The Scarlet Letter by Nathaniel Hawthorne

Thomas Carlyle, author/historian, and *The French Revolution: A History*

John Stuart Mill, author/philosopher/economist

Iain Pears, author, and *An Instance of the Fingerpost*

Charles Dickens, author

Cicero, Roman statesman/author

Francis Bacon, author/philosopher

Christopher Wren, architect/author

John Locke, author/philosopher

Voltaire, playwright/poet

Upstairs, Downstairs, British television series

Jonathan Franzen, author, and *The Corrections*

Alice Munro, author, and *Lives of Girls and Women*

Kate Braverman, author, and *Lithium for Medea*

Oscar Wilde, author/playwright, and *The Importance of Being Earnest*

William Shakespeare, playwright, and *The Tempest*
Emily Post, author
William Lyon Phelps, true crime writer
Buzz Aldrin, author/astronaut
T. S. Eliot, poet/playwright, and *The Waste Land*, "The Burial of the Dead"
Charles Lamb, essayist
A Wrinkle in Time by Madeleine L'Engle
Alice Roosevelt Longworth, author/political activist
Theodore Roosevelt, American president/author
The Swiss Family Robinson by Johann Wyss
Little Women by Louisa May Alcott
Eugene Ormandy, conductor/composer
Eudora Welty, author
Geoffrey Chaucer, author/poet
Virgil, Latin poet/author
William Butler Yeats, poet
Matthew Arnold, poet
Virginia Woolf, author
Leo Tolstoy, author, and *War and Peace*
"The Little Hours," short story by Dorothy Parker
Alain De Botton, author, and *How Proust Can Change Your Life*
Chicken Soup for the Soul by Jack Canfield
Atonement by Ian McEwan
Pam Keesey, editor
Jewelle Gomez, author
Nora Roberts, author
Graham Greene, author, and *The End of the Affair*

Georges Perec, author, and *La Disparition* (alternate
   title for the novel *A Void*); also *Life: A User's
   Manual*
Miguel de Cervantes, author, and *Don Quixote*
Henry Miller, author, and *Tropic of Cancer, Tropic of
   Capricorn*, and *The Rosy Crucifixion*
Margaret Oliphant, author
David Halberstam, journalist/author
A. Scott Berg, author
Frank McCourt, author
The South Beach Diet by Arthur Agatson
Sir Walter Scott, author/poet, and *Ivanhoe*
Christopher Marlowe, author/playwright, and *Dr. Faustus*
Bertrand Russell, philosopher/author, and *The
   Conquest of Happiness*
To the Lighthouse by Virginia Woolf
Ann Bannon, author
Willa Cather, author, and *My Antonia*
Anne Tyler, author
William Styron, author
William Faulkner, author
F. Scott Fitzgerald, author
Mary McCarthy, author
Logan Pearsall Smith, essayist
Julian Barnes, author, and *Flaubert's Parrot*
Edith Wharton, author
Christopher Morley, author, and *Kitty Foyle*
Duke Ellington, composer/author
Lewis Carroll (Charles Dodgson), author
Alexander Pope, poet

Ellen Bass, poet, and "Pray for Peace"

C. K. Williams, poet, and *The Singing* and "Scale: 11"

Frank Sinatra, singer/author

Lord Byron, poet

Billy Collins, poet, and *Sailing Alone Around the Room* and "Questions About Angels"

James J. Walker, former New York City mayor/author

Thomas Pynchon, author

Kenneth Grahame, author, and *The Wind in the Willows*

The Odyssey by Homer

T. E. Lawrence, author

The Life and Adventures of Nicholas Nickleby by Charles Dickens

Alfred, Lord Tennyson, poet

Tom Stoppard, playwright

Dante, poet

Allen Ginsberg, poet

Maurice Sendak, artist/author

George Orwell, author

Randy Newman, songwriter

Omar Khayyam, poet

The House of Mirth by Edith Wharton

"But the One on the Right," *The New Yorker* article by Dorothy Parker

Death in Venice by Thomas Mann

The Accidental Tourist by Anne Tyler

Thelma & Louise, film

Body Heat, film

Children of a Lesser God, film derived from play of same title by Mark Medoff

Christina Hoff Sommers and Sally Satel, authors, and
    One Nation Under Therapy
David Baldacci, author
Danielle Steel, author
Tom Clancy, author
Tender Is the Night by F. Scott Fitzgerald
Marjorie Kinnan Rawlings, author, and *The Yearling*
Where the Wild Things Are, illustrated children's book
    by Maurice Sendak
Harold Ross, journalist/editor/*New Yorker* co-founder
Philip Larkin, poet, and *A Study of Reading Habits*
    (poetry collection)
The Ponder Heart and *Why I Live at the P.O.* by
    Eudora Welty
H. L. Mencken, journalist/author
Following the Equator: A Journey Around the World
    by Mark Twain
Bluebeard, children's tale
Cinderella, children's tale
My Father's Dragon by Ruth Stiles Gannett
The Princess and the Goblin by George Macdonald
    and Arthur Hughes
Antoine de Saint-Exupéry, author, and *The Little Prince*
Alice's Adventures in Wonderland by Lewis Carroll
    (Charles Dodgson)
Treasure Island by Robert Louis Stevenson
The Black Stallion by Walter Farley
The Wizard of Oz and subsequent book series by
    L. Frank Baum
The Secret Garden by Frances Hodgson Burnett

A. A. Milne, children's author

Edward Lear, children's author, and *The Owl and the Pussycat*

The Legend of Sleepy Hollow by Washington Irving

Ernest Hemingway, author

Louisa May Alcott, author

Leona Rostenberg, author

Howells Letters by Mark Twain (Samuel L. Clemens) and William Dean Howells

To Kill a Mockingbird by Harper Lee

Horace, poet

Roald Dahl, author, and "The Magic Finger"

David Mitchell, author, and *Cloud Atlas*

E. B. White, author, and *Charlotte's Web*

"Lady Lazarus," by Sylvia Plath

Edgar Allan Poe, author/poet

Thornton Wilder, author

Endless Summer, film

William Carlos Williams, poet, and "Love Song"

One Writer's Beginnings by Eudora Welty

Don DeLillo, author, and *The Body Artist*

Johnny Hartman, musician/composer

The Bible

Theodor Geisel/Dr. Seuss, children's author, and *The Cat in the Hat, Green Eggs and Ham, How the Grinch Stole Christmas*, and *And to Think That I Saw It on Mulberry Street*

Audrey Geisel, author

L. Frank Baum, author

Emily Dickinson, poet

Charles Kingsley, author, and *The Water Babies*
The Borrowers by Mary Norton
Gertrude Stein, author
Edward Albee, playwright/author
August Strindberg, playwright/author
Jean-Paul Sartre, playwright/author
Mother Teresa, nun/author
Ross Macdonald, novelist, and *The Chill* and *The Lady in the Lake*
Dashiell Hammett, author, and *The Maltese Falcon*
Raymond Chandler, author
The Paid Companion by Amanda Quick
Lady Be Good by Susan Elizabeth Phillips
Forbidden by Elizabeth Lowell
Paradise by Judith McNaught
The Reluctant Suitor by Kathleen E. Woodiwiss
The Heiress by Jude Deveraux
Groucho Marx, author/comedian
Jim Harrison, author
A Christmas Carol by Charles Dickens
Irving Berlin, songwriter/composer
"The Piper at the Gates of Dawn," a chapter title from *The Wind in the Willows* by Kenneth Grahame
Antony and Cleopatra by William Shakespeare
Chuck Yeager, author/astronaut
Edvard Munch, artist, and *The Scream*
P. J. O'Rourke, journalist
Lady Windermere's Fan by Oscar Wilde
Marcel Proust, author, and *Remembrance of Things Past*

When We Were Very Young, poetry collection by A. A.
    Milne, and "Spring Morning"
The Sound of Music, film
Winne Ille Pu, Latin translation of *Winnie-the-Pooh* by
    A. A. Milne
Now We Are Six, poetry collection by A. A. Milne
Blaise Pascal, author
Rudyard Kipling, author/poet, and "The Power of the Dog"
Garrison Keillor, author
James Thurber, humorist/writer
Elizabeth Barrett Browning, poet
John Cheever, author
John Updike, author
"To Flush, My Dog" by Elizabeth Barrett Browning
Daphne Du Maurier, author, and *Rebecca*
Aldous Huxley, author
D. H. Lawrence, author
Nicholas Murray, author, and *Aldous Huxley, A Biography*
Jim Morrison, author/musician
John Fowles, author, and *The French Lieutenant's*
    Woman
The Portrait of a Lady by Henry James
Lady Chatterley's Lover by D. H. Lawrence
Robert Louis Stevenson, author
Andy Warhol, author/artist
Dennis Hopper, author/actor/photographer
William Saroyan, author
John Steinbeck, author
Kurt Vonnegut, author

About the Authors

Karen Mack, a former attorney, is a Golden Globe Award–winning film and television producer. Jennifer Kaufman was a staff writer at the *Los Angeles Times* and a two-time winner of the national Penney-Missouri Journalism Award. Both live in Los Angeles and this is their first novel.

Don't miss
the new novel from

Jennifer Kaufman & Karen Mack

A VERSION
OF THE TRUTH

On sale as a Delacorte Press hardcover
spring 2008

A VERSION OF THE TRUTH

on sale spring 2008

Chapter 1

I didn't intend to lie on my résumé. It just happened. It was after the icy reception I received at the last two employment agencies. The first time, a woman who looked younger than me suggested I try getting a job at a pet store—not that they handled small retail, no money in it. The next one walked me to the door of her office, after a sharp, measured glance at my résumé, and said the only thing she could possible think of was telemarketing from my home—check the classifieds.

As you can imagine I was feeling pretty deflated as I headed for yet another employment agency. This one had a bulletin board near the entrance, cluttered with notices including one that read "Accent Elimination" (as if it's some kind of disease): "Speak American, free consultation." I noticed no one had torn off the scrawled vertical telephone numbers from the fringed bottom. I sat in a cracked vinyl armchair still warm from the last sweaty bottom, filling out forms, but even in this dump the balding, unsavory proprietor couldn't get rid of me fast enough.

So here's my situation. Considering my educational background (a graduate of University of Nowheresville) and my age (34), I am now virtually unemployable. My years at the wildlife center didn't seem to matter to anyone, especially the employment agencies. They just whizzed right by them and focused on my education or lack of it. "Tell us again why you left high school?" As if I had no business even being there. My mother was always trying to buck me up, her optimism unflinching.

"They'll be sorry they didn't hire you. All the studies say that slow starters are more likely to become billionaires."

"What study was that, Mom?"

"I read it in the dentist's office."

It feels like I'm back in elementary school, where I had failure written all over me. I remember every Friday we would sit in the "Magic Circle" and go around the room reading aloud paragraphs from the "Fun Book of the Week." What seemed to come effortlessly for everyone else was torture for me. I was so slow that my classmates would make the most of my humiliation. One kid would fall over snoring as the other laughed or mouthed "Duh" or maybe "Dumb." I knew the words in my head; I just couldn't retrieve them from the printed page.

"Martha, try not to hold your pencil like a spike," the teacher would urge, breathing down my neck like a truant officer and wincing at my abominable handwriting. "And stop sucking on your lip so hard. Lord, you'll tear it to pieces. Why don't you just take a deep breath and start over."

That was the signal I eventually waited for—she gave up and so did I. You'd think she'd have put a stop to my misery, but the fact was she just didn't get it and neither did anyone else. The rest of the year I was either "sick" or late on Fridays, very late. It didn't make any difference, I was the dunce in the corner with a scarlet D on my chest.

Sometimes I'd hear a friend of my mother's talking about her child, little Stacy or darling Susie. "My daughter is amazing. She just woke up one morning and could read everything."

"Is that so?" my mother would reply in a monotone. "What a marvel."

I kept thinking, "Why didn't that happen to me?" When would I "just wake up" and be able to read? And then later, with each mounting failure, "What's so great about reading anyway?"

My mother would sit with me for hours reading things she thought I'd like. Her favorite was an illustrated anthology of Greek myths. We read about gods and heroes like Athena, Diana, Aphrodite, Zeus. The stories I liked the most were the ones where humans changed into birds or beasts or flowers. But my mother liked the stories where the gods shaped their own fate—all it took was magic. I guess that's what she was hoping for me when she'd hand me the book—but I still couldn't read a word.

In junior high, I made up the plots of the books I read based on the first and last chapters. As a result, my test scores on comprehension were all over the place. Sometimes I guessed right. Sometimes I didn't. I was a whiz at basic algebra, but if I had to solve how far Mr. Smith traveled on a train from his home in Phoenix to his regional office in Albuquerque, and at what velocity it collided with a freight train carrying textiles to Tucson—well, you get the picture. All through school, kids whispered "dim" or "dense" or "dumbbell." Not my friends, though. We never talked about my "problem." Mostly, they were oblivious. They'd always get rewarded with A's and I'd get my usual D's. You know the drill, A is for excellent, B is for good, C is for average, and D is just plain disgraceful.

"God, Martha, that test was so easy," they'd say incredulously.

"I didn't study," I'd laugh, like it meant nothing. *Heathers* became my favorite movie.

Eventually, I figured out the way to survive. Most kids do. I hid my tests and assignments like they were pornography. When my mother asked me how my spelling test had gone, I'd say "great," and if she questioned me about my homework, I'd tell her "I did it at school." "Doing it at school" meant shoving it in my desk along with a half dozen other worksheets I found impossible to complete. I'd always get found out, of course. The teacher would call my mother, who would angrily turn on me and say, "What's the matter with you?" We'd spend holiday weekends completing all the work that everyone else had finished during school. The threat of Special Ed. loomed over me like a death sentence. And the only consolation the teachers could offer was "Just give it another year. Some kids are slow starters."

So the masquerade went on. I made small strides. But mostly I feigned boredom or talked to my neighbor. In the meantime, my imagination soared. I made up words. I invented spelling. I created wild fantasies in my mind that were ever so much more entertaining than anything I tried to read at school.

"Once upon a time, a bunch of mean, foul-mouthed bullies wandered into the woods to gather berries . . ."

It was about this time my burned-out mother hired a beautiful silver-haired tutor named Janet Monroe. She lived in a lovely little cottage with a view of the ocean. The plan was for me to go to her house once a week over the summer. But, after an initial evaluation, she recommended two-hour sessions three times a week. In the beginning, I felt like a rich kid, although I was well aware that this was a serious financial burden on my mother.

Every afternoon, Mrs. Monroe would lead me through her house to an airy, sun-drenched porch filled with leafy palms, overstuffed furniture, and faded Persian rugs. You had to take your shoes off when you walked in and then say hello to her parrot—a magnificent African gray named Sam who imitated her voice and learned my name pronto. He gave me my first whistle and screeched a flirtatious "Hi, gorgeous!"

All through that summer I struggled with the process of decoding—learning how a written word represents a sound. It's something most kids take for granted, like swimming or riding a bike. But for me, it was hard work.

"This just happens sometimes to smart kids," Mrs. Monroe told my mother in a breathy smoker's voice that trailed off into nothingness. Then she did something even better. She asked Sam to tell her who, beside me, had trouble in school. That bird was so damn brilliant. He shouts back, "Einstein, Rockefeller, Edison, Picasso, Walt Disney, and John Lennon."

"There," she'd say when he was done. "You're in fine company. It's people like you who break through the barriers and discover great things. Anyone can learn to read."

We did a lot of workbook exercises and read out loud. Sam would imitate my labored, choppy voice when I read, memorize passages, and give me a beaky kiss when I was done. I got so I couldn't wait to see him. Then it was September, Mrs. Monroe went back to Nebraska to visit her family, and I went back to school.

Soon afterwards, she called to tell us that she was ill and had retired. A month later, my mother came home with Sam. Mrs. Monroe had passed away and left Sam to me. The note on the cage read, "Dear Martha, next to me, you are Mrs. Monroe's favorite student."

Parrots mate for life but somehow Sam accepted me. The South American tribes believe parrots have human souls, and I'd have to agree. He'd sidle up my arm to my shoulder after school and kiss me all over my mouth and ears. Sometimes he'd say, "Love you. Miss you. Did you pass?" Okay, so he was repeating my mother, but still, he meant it. Other times he'd repeat my depressing downers.

"I'm just a dumbfuck," I'd shout.

And he's shout out gleefully, "Dumbfuck! Dumbfuck! Dumbfuck!"

"Shut up," I'd yell.

"No!" He'd squawk back, flapping his wings and bobbing his head. Sam loved to get me all riled up. It was just a game to him, my deficiencies.

Nowadays, there's a name for what plagued me all those years. And it just so happens, it's another D word. Dyslexia.

When Sam and I first moved in with Frank, they took an immediate dislike to each other. When we'd argue, Sam would fasten his small beady eyes on Frank, morph into his aggressive pose, crouch low on his perch with his wings outspread, and peck furiously at Frank's face and hands. Maybe it was Frank's tone of voice.

"Close the fucking door!" Frank would yell at me as he retreated from Sam's sharp-hooked beak.

"Close the fucking door! Close the fucking door!" Sam would shriek back in Frank's exact same voice, as if he were mocking him. Parrots do not grow meek in the face of anger.

The two of them never did make peace even though I tried to reason with Sam. He continued to bedevil Frank in sly little ways. He could imitate the telephone and the doorbell so perfectly that at least once a night Frank would go running to the door and Sam would cackle and scream "Dumbfuck!"

More than once, Frank told me to give Sam away or he was going to "kill that fucking bird." It got so bad that at one point I told my mother she'd have to take him for a while till things cooled down. Sam's not mourning either.

•   •   •

I get back in my car and head to a small employment agency across from the university that came highly recommended . . . from the Yellow Pages. As I walk in the door, I overhear the agent tell a woman, "Sorry. That's all I have. You know, these days a BA is no better than high school. You really need an advanced degree to get yourself out of the assistant pool."

So what pool am I swimming in? Maybe the cesspool. I watch the woman leave. Sleek is the word I'd use to describe her. I pull on the elastic waist of my khaki pants. I'll never look like that. What does it take, anyway, to look put together like that?

No, I'm not sleek, I'm plain—sort of like a generic brand of human being. I don't naturally stand out like some women I know. Although my mother would disagree—whose mother wouldn't? She tells me I have "good bones," like one of those characters in her classic myths. But I certainly don't feel that way. Maybe it's my hair. I wear it pulled back in a long ponytail with Peter Pan bangs in the front. I don't know, I've always done it that way. Frank liked it that way too. Every time I wore it down, he'd ask me why.

"You look better with it off your face," he'd say. But he never did say I looked good. Come to think of it, whenever I got dressed up he'd tell me I looked like I tried too hard.

I take the application form and slowly start to fill it out. Name: Martha Shaw.

Education: There it is. I remember watching the Rose Bowl one year with Frank. Who played? Wasn't it one of those big schools in the Midwest? Michigan or Wisconsin. An arena filled with thousands of cheering students. Who'd ever know? A place where when asked what it was like I could just laugh and say, "Cold as hell." Okay, I'm doing it. Michigan. I know about Michigan. They make cars there. Shit. Major: Now what? My hands are shaking. Well, I'm turning into a psychopath, so how about psychology? Sounds good. Everyone knows about psychology.

I fill out the rest—driver's license, Social Security, address (my mother's post office box, we haven't had mail delivered in two years), medical, etc. When you really think about it, most of the application is true. Anyway, doesn't everyone lie on these things? I hand in the application.

"So how'd you like Michigan?" the agent asks. I focus on a hairy plant in a too small plastic pot on the windowsill with roots trailing out the bottom like worms.

"Cold as hell," I reply. She laughs.

"Well, I see why you're here. Psychology. What can you do with that?"

"Right." I laugh conspiratorially.

"It says here, after the wildlife center, you worked at your husband's towing business."

"Yes, I did. He recently died." Okay. So I played the widow card. So sue me.

She immediately softens. I hate that look. Pity. Surprise. I can hear her thinking. "And so young too."

"Well, we don't have much right now but we do have an entry level job at the university. And it is in behavioral sciences, so you have some background."

I am oddly pleased by the compliment—even though it's based on a total lie.

"Look, I'm not going to kid you. Basically, it's answering phones, typing, delivering mail, filing, you know, front office stuff." Better than the back office stuff I haven't been offered. I casually agree to go on an interview. I'm elated. That is, until I hit the street, at which point I start to get nervous about my lies. But this wasn't just a lie. It was a Category 2, maybe Category 3 lie. Oh, come on. Frank was a lying piece of shit and God didn't strike him down. Well . . . I carefully look both ways before crossing the street.

• • •

My mother likes to say that the universe, as we know it, has many secrets, but in my opinion nothing is quite as dark and enigmatic as the titanic tug of the Black Hole. The stuff that gets sucked into it is gone forever, as if it were whirling around in a massive toilet bowl, and nothing, not even light itself, can escape.

I think about black holes every so often when events in my life get so warped that time stops and the gravitational pull of the world turns me into another one of those burned-out souls with no place to go—like a star in the galaxy that explodes and then disappears into the darkness. But this time I'm doing something about it.

Maybe I'm delusional. But I've lost count of the number of people who've looked at my résumé with pity and said, we've nothing for the likes of you. Well, now things have changed. I'm on my way to one of the country's most prestigious universities for a job interview—and I feel guilty about it, I do. But my best friend Tiff would probably say, "Good one, Martha!" She thinks I'm in my own world, wasting my life away. So finally I've done something worthy. Lied.

Tiff and I are as close as can be, but oddly enough, we couldn't be more different than a moss-covered boulder and a pet rock. It goes all the way back to when we were kids and we'd read those stories in animal picture books. She always identified with City Mouse and I with Country Mouse. For her, the flow of life is not outdoors—it's in places that have roofs and walls and music and people. Whenever I've tried to pull her over to the Green Side, it's been a disaster.

There was the time, for example, several years ago, when we went down to the Malibu Lagoon, and I reveled in the sight of a rare white egret while she ogled a group of ripped surfers at a nearby beach. Sometimes I can still get her to go on weekend hikes, but usually by the end of the day I'm thinking it's not worth it. The sunlight hurts her eyes. The forest is "teeming" with mosquitoes and ticks. The sand scratches and irritates her skin. And the boggy meadows are wet and dirty, filled with poison ivy, snakes, and Lyme disease.

Tiff looks at our dilemma in a different way. I am basically alone, she reasons, because I'm over the top about nature, and men, as a rule, do not find this at all attractive. In fact, in Tiff's mind, men view women like me as "weird and unappealing, even threatening."

"The next time I fix you up," she'll preach, "do *not* go on and on about the Wildlife Center. For one thing, Martha, no one wants to hear about all that road kill you call your 'patients.' Especially when you describe how you chop up frozen rats for food. For another, your long, detailed Animal Kingdom stories are a total yawn. You're just kicking yourself right out of the market."

Or, "You know, Martha, when you do that thing with the food in your mouth and your parrot sticks his beak in between your teeth and pulls it out—you know what I'm talking about? I know you think it's sweet, but trust me, it's not. It's gross."

"You're wrong, Tiff. It's cute. Everyone who has a parrot does it," I argued.

"Well, don't do that with a guy around, okay?" she added, not letting up. "Promise me, Martha. Let them find out later, after they like you, that you're not normal."

Okay, so maybe she's right. But here's the thing: I find comfort in the color green—the glossy heart-shaped leaves of the philodendron, abundant and generous; a handful of mint; the lobed leaves of the oak shining like taffeta; and the tiers of maidenhead ferns that lift and dive, capturing the light. I rarely talk about my feelings in this area, especially to Tiff, who prefers to keep her emotional world sunny and uncomplicated and has no love for the great outdoors. Her heart doesn't throb when she's in the woods and she doesn't get that urge to break away, climb a mountain, lose consciousness, and blend right into the landscape, like a caterpillar on a piece of bark.

"I'm sorry, Martha," she'll say sympathetically, "but have you ever noticed that you and your mom have absolutely no sense of humor about anything natural? There's always this undercurrent of doom and gloom—like global warming will eventually cause mass extinction. Really, I can't take it. Even if you're right. Why can't you just hang out with me and ignore it like everyone else?"

It's a disappointment to me, really it is. I do love her, however. The same way I love Sam—even though both of them are pretty much hopeless in the green department. It's ironic, when you think about it, that I love a bird who has absolutely zero talent for living in the wild. Sam, like most domestic parrots, has a fixed, profound sense of home and if I were to let him fly free, even in the backyard, he'd get lost and never come back. Sad but true.

The fact is, I can never remember a time when I wasn't drawn to the outdoors—all that life bubbling under the surface, forming ring after ring around those massive tree trunks. When I was a child, I used to venture out just before dark, when I could just make out the forms of trees, leafless and silent, and the soft, transparent crescent moon. I'd imagine the trees bending over me, like black skeletons, whispering secrets of the creatures who dwell there—witches and deer-men, elves and fauns. Werewolves, vampires, and ancient hermits. They dine on honey and acorns, drink from fairy goblets of sea-green moss, sleep in bristlecone pines. You can just make them out in the stubble of roots, leaves, thorns, and buds. Like seeing faces in the clouds.

Green is still the most important part of my nature, as much a part of me as my skin. When I feel hollow inside, I swear to God, I go outside, inhale the fresh earth smells, and feel a part of something holy. Not like I feel most of the time. Like someone who's missed the boat.

All that goes away when I'm in the woods, enveloped in the violet afternoons or watching the show of day heroically bursting forth. I feel boundless and eternal, as if I could stop at any point and perform miracles.